LONG DISTANCE SLEEPWALKER

ANDREW SYERS

ANTI-GRAVITY BOOKS

PUBLISHED BY ANTI-GRAVITY BOOKS
47 Warwick Gardens, Haringey, London N4 1JD United Kingdom

All rights reserved

Copyright © Andrew Syers

The right of Andrew Syers to be identified as the author of this work has been asserted by him in accordance with Section 77 of the Copyright, Designs and Patents Act 1988.

This book is in copyright. Subject to statutory exception and to provisions of relevant collective licensing agreements, no reproduction of any part may take place without the written permission of Anti-gravity Books.

First published 2010

This book is sold subject to the conditions that it shall not, by way of trade or otherwise, be lent, re-sold, hired out, or otherwise circulated without the publisher's prior consent in any form of binding or cover other than that in which it is published and without a similar condition including this condition being imposed on the subsequent purchaser.

ISBN 978-0-9566867-2-5

longdistancesleepwalker.blogspot.com

Antigravitybooks@rocketmail.com

www.myspace.com/553899727

*To my partner, Claudia, my parents, Themi & Sam
and my sisters, Stacey & Joanna*

ACKNOWLEDGEMENTS

A big thanks to Nic Raoux without whose editorial advice this book would not have been anywhere near so good. Other persons or organisations that provided me with helpful feedback include: Steve Poulacheris, The New River Writers, Julian Duffus, Raymond Blake, Jay Merrill, Norma Pollak, Brigette Bennett, Ben Golomstock, Rob Williams, Julian Upton, Jason Wood, Dave Cheepen, David Stacey, WriteOn.Com, Fiction Workhouse and Authonomy.com. Also thanks for technical assistance from Catherine Tosco, Beth Hazel and Brynn Binnell.

FAST FORWARD

Too loud. Whatever infernal, manufactured pop music was playing in the shop off Oxford Street; it was too loud - too loud for thought, too loud for insight and too loud for sanity. People were shopping fairly modestly - apart from one man - a man in his early thirties - adding more and more to the pile in his basket.

Scowling intensely in his hoodie, he made his way to the tracksuit rack. More clothes... More clothes... More clothes... He needed more clothes... If he got more clothes... then he would be all right. A shop assistant approached, but he snarled and scared her away.

He hated everyone and assumed everyone hated him. And how right he was. There wasn't a single friend he hadn't alienated - a single relative he hadn't disgusted. Shaking their heads despairingly, they had all washed their hands of him and showed him the door.

'What a bastard!' they said of him, 'What a git!' 'Why, he doesn't even have the compassion of a banker!' A kind of venom seemed to flow through his veins - a type of poison that allowed him to live, but with hardly any of his original personality.

More clothes... More clothes... Yes, he needed more clothes all right! More clothes to disguise his failure - more clothes to cover his self-hatred - more clothes - despite having credit card bills up to his eyes - more clothes - perhaps those jeans on the rack opposite.

As he picked up a pair, a sophisticated gentleman in his early forties - sporting a gigantic multi-coloured Afro and an eye patch, grabbed the shopping from him and said: 'Stop! Don't buy them! You're the victim of a terrible experiment!'

REWIND

'Did you see the game we played against the Cincinnati Tigers last night? Huh? Huh? Did you see it? Did you see the game?'

'Yeah... I watched it...'

Twenty-one years ago, these walls were white. Now it was the same paint, but it wasn't white. Bill had been working there since the paint had dried and now felt almost as flaky.

He opened the patient's mouth and looked inside. The sedative had not been swallowed.

He handed the patient another plastic cup of water; checked again and then passed some pills and water to the next patient.

'What a game, huh?' said Mark - opening a patient's mouth on the other side of the ward. 'We showed them a thing or two! We *pulverised* them!'

Bill took a donut from a bag of donuts parked on top of the medication trolley and bit into it. 'Big deal... My *grandma* could beat the *Cincinnati Tigers*..'

'There's no way your grandma could beat the Cincinnati Tigers...'

'Okay, maybe with *your* grandma's help she could.'

Six beds back, a shaven-headed naked patient started screaming.

'Got it.' said Mark. Bill nodded - finishing the donut and licking the sugar off his lips. Without a further word, Mark trotted to the patient; checked the rope he was tied to his bed with; gave him another tranquilliser and returned.

'Thanks.' said Bill and bit into another donut.

Mark watched him eat it... 'Aren't you going to offer me one?'

Bill sighed. 'If you were an ounce lighter, I would. Sadly, that is not the case.'

'Son of a bitch.'

They carried on down the ward - a well-trodden route - one they could easily have done in their sleep - their footprints almost matching the footprints of the previous evening.

Bill gave water and pills to the patient who lay with his arms stretched out - thinking he was Jesus Christ. He took them with a forlorn dignity. 'Why has everyone forsaken me?' he whispered.

Next to him, lay a patient who thought he was Judas. He, Bill liked - less hoity toity than the other guy.

'Shit!' said Mark.

'What?' said Bill.

'I've stepped into some shit.'

'You better wipe your shoes on his bed. Don't want to spread it everywhere.'

'...There's still some left.'

Bill stuffed another donut into his mouth. 'It'll have to do. Come on...'

They approached their longest residing patient. He spoke in a strange language that no one could understand. Bill had this theory that he wouldn't have had to stay if an interpreter had been found. Every time they saw him they tried to guess what language he was speaking.

'Albanian?'

'Bulgarian?'

'Californian?'

Bill sat down, took a library phrase book from his back pocket and listened to the patient.

'We haven't got time...' said Mark.

'Five minutes.' Bill flicked a few pages as the plainly frustrated patient spoke.

'Bill, we're running late.'

Bill slammed the book shut. 'It's not Latvian either.'

***

The last pills and water dispensed and the last mouth opened and closed; they took the trolley to the storeroom and made their way to the seclusion chamber. 'This, I'm going to enjoy...'

'They should have done this months ago...'

'You don't have to tell me that...'

They opened the door. The stench was abysmal. Bill threw up on his shoes.

'You shouldn't have eaten all those donuts.' said Mark.

'At least I haven't got shit on my shoes.'

'Well, at least I haven't got vomit on mine.'

'Shit's worse than vomit.'

'Oh yeah?!'

And there lying on the floor with his eyes shut was the biggest pain in the butt in the world - the most unreasonable madman in the whole damn asylum.

'Glad I don't have to see your sorry face again.' said Bill, 'You're being transferred.'

The patient just continued to lie on the ground with his eyes shut as if they weren't there.

'Hey!' said Bill, 'Hey! Open your eyes! Open your eyes - I'm talking to you!'

But he didn't open his eyes. He kept them shut. He kept them shut as he had for the past three days.

'You're not asleep! Come on! Get up!'

They needed reassurance of their existence, so they kicked him a little and dragged him to his feet. He flopped down again - refusing to stand.

'Right!' said Bill.

Grabbing hold of his straitjacket, the pair pulled him out of the room. Through corridor after corridor, they dragged the patient while he clenched his eyelids ever tighter.

***

Waiting outside in the ambulance, the driver moaned to himself. 'They expect me to wait *here* all day? Huh! I don't know... I do have better things to do with my time... I don't know... Tsk!'

He drummed his fingers on the dashboard and glanced at the mirror. There they were. He sighed. 'What's taking you so long?'

Bill pointed at the patient he and Mark were dragging. 'Can't you *tell*?!'

'It's open.'

They dumped the patient in the back of the ambulance.

An orderly was sat there - chewing gum. 'Hi...' he said to them.

'Hi...' said Bill.

'Is he trouble?'

'Yeah...'

He got out a hypodermic needle and injected him. 'He won't be now.'

***

Two hours later, Bill and Mark heard a frantic buzzing at the gates. It was the driver. He was all red faced and panting and didn't have his ambulance with him.

'What's going on?' said Bill.

'I wanted to call you,' the driver puffed, 'but he took my cell phone and there's no call boxes for miles.' He caught his breath. '...I ran all the way here.'

Bill looked at the driver's beer-gut; three miles in two hours was probably the best he could do. '...What happened to the ambulance?'

'He stole it! The patient stole it!'

'How?'

'I don't know - it was quick! He knocked out Ted and sprang on me, kicked me out and took over the wheel. The worst thing was, I think he still had his eyes shut!'

'How?'

'I could only hazard a guess that you didn't check that his straitjacket was securely fastened enough...'

In all honesty, Bill couldn't recall if they had checked the straitjacket. The patient had been so much trouble, it was possible they didn't get round to it. Some of those buckles may have been undone for days. All it would've taken was for the patient to have dislocated his shoulder... And perhaps they should have told the orderly to give him a larger shot of tranquilliser since he had built up a fair amount of immunity to it... Still... they weren't going to carry the can.

'Hey!' said Bill, 'Hey! We checked those buckles! It must have been your fault!'

'Bullshit! I'm a driver. I *drive*. It was *your* responsibility..'

'Shut up!' said Bill, 'Shut up! We don't have to listen to you! We're not going to be your scapegoats!'

'It was your negligence!'

'Our responsibility ended the moment he was in your vehicle.'

'I reckon the director's gonna have a different opinion!'

'Call him!' said Bill, 'Call him! It's not going to make me cry...'

ONE

Peter Papapanos stood in Leicester Square station by the shop that sold the dodgy looking hotdogs and checked his watch for the forty-third time... His blind date was meant to have turned up at 6.30. It was now 7.20...

He was tempted to leave, but they had got on so well on the phone - well, better than the other ones he'd tried to call!

'What's wrong with women?' he wondered, 'If I was a girl, I'd jump at the chance of going out with me! I've got a lot going for me... Well potentially I do...'

Another ten minutes and that would be it. He pretended to read his Observer again.

Tick... Tock... Tick... Tock... It wasn't his watch that he could hear. Tick... Tock... Tick... Tock... It was the ticking of his internal clock. Tick... Tock... Loneliness... Tick... Tock... Misery... Tick... Tock... Unfulfilled ambitions... Tick... Tock...

The alarm was set at thirty and that was only a month away. What an awful sound it would make - a sound that would pierce his eardrums and his heart.

Tick... Tock... Badly paid, insecure employment... Tic... Tock... Tick... Tock... Try as he might he couldn't switch the alarm off or set it for a later age. Tick... Tock... Going bald... Tick... Tock... Going really bald! Tick... Tock... Big nose... Tick... Tock... Even bigger nose - growing bigger by the second... Tick... Tock... Rubbish watch...

Ten minutes had already gone by... Maybe he should give Susan another ten...

It was getting cold. He buttoned up his coat - a second-hand herringbone coat that had seen better decades. A button came off in his hand. He put the button in his pocket and adjusted his scarf accordingly.

There hadn't been many women in Peter's life. The number could be counted on one finger. It was in a life drawing class at Art school, that he had first caught sight of Helen with her long golden dreadlocks shimmering in the sunlight. Slimy and matted, they were often mistaken for road kill.

'Oh please, God...' wished Peter, 'Let there be a day when I can run my fingers through her lovely hair... But I suppose that would be too much to hope for. There's no way anyone as beautiful as *her* would want to go out with *me*...'

While Peter snapped a piece of charcoal and scrounged a piece from the person next to him, Helen shyly gazed at him. She saw someone with huge, curly bouffant hair - the kind you could lose your door keys in and thought to herself: 'Oh please God... Let him become my boyfriend... But no, I suppose that's too much to hope for. There's no way anyone as handsome as *him* would want to go out with *me*...'

The lesson over, the pair went their separate ways: Peter to the painting department and Helen to the sculpture department.

Several lessons went by without either exchanging a word - merely gazing at each while the other wasn't aware. Peter gradually advanced to sitting next to Helen, but nothing braver than that. So behind their easels they remained - non-communicative and completely frustrated.

They were in the process of drawing a skinny, naked, sixty-five-year-old man - posed on an old charcoal stained sheet covered bundle of cushions and beanbags and were making a complete bodge of it.

'Mmmm...' said the tutor dismissively as he peered over their shoulders. None of the students' work that day seemed to please him - not even the girl he was having it away with.

'Just popping out.' he said - unable to bear for a minute longer being surrounded by such mediocrity. 'I'll be five minutes.'

Peter watched Helen as she tried to salvage her picture. 'Come on!' he thought, 'Say something to her! Don't be such a shy prat! Say something! But what? 'What fine weather we're having today?' That's a stupid thing to say... It's raining! Maybe I could say it in an *ironic* way. Oh fuck irony! Er... what about if I said: 'I wish it was *you* we were drawing?' Brilliant! Fucking brilliant! I might as well say: 'Hello! Can I rape you?' It's just my luck the only people I get to see naked are hideously ugly! Maybe I could ask her if I could borrow her pencil... No! She'll just get the impression that I'm just after her for her pencils! She'd think: 'Hello, *Mr Freeloader*! I know your game! Buy your *own* pencils! *Stingy*!!'

'Though asking for one of her pencils would be a kind of test. She wouldn't lend me one of pencils unless she really liked me... No... No... It's too much of a risk. I'd rather cling onto whatever hope I still have than have it immediately shattered... Mmm... maybe I should offer her one of my pencils? Maybe... Wait a minute! I've only got one pencil! If I give her a pencil, I won't be able to draw! Anyway, who goes round offering people their pencils? I suppose generous people and nutters... Why can't she talk to me? If she really liked me, she would have made the first move. She can't be much of a feminist! Oh, I give up... We probably wouldn't have that much in common anyway. For a start I do painting and she only does sculpture...'

At that precise moment, something rather wonderful happened. The model fell asleep. And when the model fell asleep; something happened to his penis. It got bigger... And bobbed up... And bobbed down... And bobbed up... And bobbed down...

Apart from Peter and Helen, the class saw no humour to the situation. They regarded the pulsating member in stony, po-faced silence and adjusted their drawings accordingly. Peter and Helen could not contain their mirth even when the tutor returned.

He chucked the pair out and told them to grow up. 'Tsk... So immature!'

They sat down in the canteen and had a coffee and a chat, the skinny sleeping sixty-five-year-old model's bobbing erection having broken the ice. Their tongues were no longer tied. And as the days went by, their tongues became quite active in each other's mouths and other parts of their bodies.

Lunch breaks were spent on the hill opposite the college where they admired the view and saw the future. Such hopes they had - such dreams. They could almost hear the roars of applause and accolades for their future Turner Prize winning artworks. They could almost feel themselves being mobbed by adoring crowds and being ushered by bodyguards into stretch limos.

But when they graduated all they could hear and feel was the cold breeze of indifference. The harsh realities presented by the first year post Art School, persuaded Helen to put down her chisel and go get a job. So she had her dreadlocks cut off and got one. She would come back late from work shattered, a shadow of her former self - practically covered in the digestive juices of the company machine.

It was a Saturday morning - a few months after Helen started the job. Peter was sat in the kitchen - quite innocently eating his cornflakes when she slammed a job application form onto the table. 'Fill it in.'

'Er... Yeah...' said Peter, 'I will after I finish the painting I'm working on.'

'Fill it in - *now*.'

'Er... Yeah... I'll just finish my cornflakes first - okay?'

'You better!' said Helen.

'I will!'

'I'm not going to carry on paying the bills all by myself - you know!'

'Okay!'

'Well, I'm not!'

'Okay!!'

Wolfing down the final spoonfuls, he flicked through the form. It was almost the size of a novel. And there were bound to be loads of people competing for that position what with the state of the economy and all that... 'There must be quicker ways of getting a little work...' he thought. 'Oh fuck it; I'll join an agency. They'll get me something...'

And the agency did get him something - some low level admin work at a university for a few months. The pay was derisory, but it demanded less from him than Susan's job. And when he returned from work he was still able to summon up the energy to paint.

Initially Peter's actions had eased the strains on their relationship, but Helen took exception to the fact that he spent all his evenings and weekends painting. 'Don't you *like* spending time with me? Don't you *like* me anymore?'

'But I'm working during the week. When am I going to get my paintings done?'

'Right! I can see where your priorities lie!'

'No, it's not like that!'

'If it isn't like that - then make time for me!'

'I will!'

'When?'

'Tomorrow. I've got this painting I need to finish...'

However, over the ensuing months, there were always some painting that desperately needed to be completed and the couple saw each other rarely.

After an exceptionally terrible day at work, Helen found Peter painting in the bedroom. 'Peter,' she said, 'have you ever considered getting a job that doesn't pay fuck all and was less *temporary*?'

Peter carried on painting. 'Mmmm... the thought hasn't really crossed my mind...'

'Don't you ever want us to go to restaurants and on holidays abroad?'

'That stuff isn't that important... Could you pass the turps?'

'I *work* ten hours a day and *commute* three hours a day and I could do with going to restaurants and on holidays abroad!'

'Do you know what I think? I reckon if you got a less demanding job that was less far away you wouldn't need to go to restaurants and on holidays abroad.'

'What about us?' she said, 'Don't you ever us want to buy a home together?'

'Good God no! Homeownership increases unemployment.'

'Are you always going to be like this?'

'Like what?'

'Like *this*! You've really got to wake up!'

'No I don't. I'm not even asleep.'

'Yes you are! You're *fucking* asleep! You're living in a *fucking* dream world! Wake up - Peter! Wake up! You'll never get anywhere with your art!'

Without considering the consequences, Helen pushed the easel to the floor.

For a while, Peter just stood there and surveyed the damage... The painted side of the canvas had fallen onto the carpet just like a piece of toast always falls onto the floor on the buttered side...

He showed no anger. He merely put the canvas back on the easel and started painting again. 'I know I haven't got my art right yet, but it's like scientists with their experiments. They don't give up when their tests go wrong.'

Helen wiped a tear from her eye. 'You really love art - don't you?'

'Don't you?'

'Look, I'm sorry for...'

'I could try to find one of those career jobs. But my mates have tried and they haven't had much luck...'

'No! No!' she said, 'You must carry on with your painting... I'm going to Belgo's this Saturday with some friends. Would you like to come? It'll be my treat.'

'No, it's okay. I was planning on doing some painting that night...'

The tension between them totally dissipated. Helen went with her friends to restaurants while Peter stayed in and painted. Then Helen became busy. She had to stay even later at work, have drinks with the boss and then spend weekends away at conferences.

One evening, Peter was overcome with a sense of romance and decided for a change that he would make time for Helen. He swapped shifts with a colleague and booked a table at her favourite restaurant.

The past few weeks he had been putting some money aside, so he reckoned he could afford it.

Catching the flower kiosk by the station, a minute before it was about to close, he managed to buy some carnations and rushed homewards.

From now on he would get his life/work balance sorted. Yes, from now on he would see far more of Helen. She would be the priority in his life; he promised to himself before arriving home to find her in bed with a colleague from her office.

'Peter,' said Helen, 'I don't think it's working... I think we should call it a day.'

Peter sneered at Jeremy in his thong. He had met him several times in the pub. When they had spoken, Jeremy appeared to have donated his sense of humour to 'Comic Relief'. Using 'irony' wouldn't get you very far with that guy.

'Why him? You haven't got anything in common with him.'

'At least he's got *time* for me...'

There was no room for Peter at any of his friends' places. There had been a cluster of mutual friends splitting up, so the sofas were already occupied. Perhaps it was the season for it - like leaves falling off trees. So, with no viable alternative, he moved back to his parents. Then his hair started falling out.

That had been several years ago. He couldn't believe that so much time had passed so swiftly without him having fun. What had he been doing?! In all those temp jobs, he must have met somebody that he liked? But no, he kept on comparing potential partners to Helen as if she was the ideal - as if that was going to help. There must have been some wonderful women that he missed out on. How he wanted to kick himself and knee himself in the groin.

It was only now - after all those times the Earth had gone round the Sun and all those lunar cycles that he felt ready to move on. But he was still a temp that painted at night. (Something inside him continued to stop him from diverting his energy into applying for a permanent position.) And he was still undiscovered. Surprisingly, he found that there weren't droves of women clamouring for such a man of that age and at that stage in his life, so despite ten minutes having gone by, he still found himself waiting in a tube station with an Observer in his hands - looking at his watch for the forty-fifth time.

***

People streamed out from the barriers. Another train had emptied out. Perhaps his date, his potential 'Significant Other' was amongst this crowd.

A rather attractive woman appeared to be walking in his direction. His gratitude towards God was short lived. Her six-foot muscular, pony tailed boyfriend scooped her up in his arms.

Then a podgier woman appeared to be walking towards Peter, still attractive but *heavier*. This was more realistic - far more likely to be his date. And why not? He'd be happy to get to know her. Then another six-foot muscular, pony tailed man scooped her up in his arms.

Peter looked at the hunk. Couldn't he do better than that?!

To pass the time, he watched others waiting for their partners and saw their faces light up as their wait finally ended. He found it strangely consoling that he was still able to feel happy for them.

The ebb and flow petered out. Was his Observer visible? Then he noticed something. There was another man waiting a yard away - holding the *same* newspaper.

With a determined frown on his brow, Peter stepped directly in front of the stranger and opened out his paper.

With a stern glint in his eye, the stranger stared at Peter; stood in front of him and opened out his.

Peter considered standing in front of the stranger again, but decided that such a move would only yield temporary benefits, so he stood to the side of him and eyed him closely.

His competition was better dressed than him... That much was true... And more handsome, but apart from that Peter wasn't overly worried.

Crowds of passengers from the Northern line converged with those from the Piccadilly line. Then the tide went out.

Peter's competitor looked at his watch, folded up his newspaper and left.

Peter considered it a sort of victory, though it was debatable. He had been waiting for one and a half hours. If he waited for another hour and she didn't turn up, then the other guy would have won.

***

It was after finishing the lifestyle section of the Observer that he realised he was not alone. He folded up the newspaper to find two policemen standing before him - staring at him intensely.

Without saying a word, they looked at him as if they could see straight into his inner core - back into his childhood - back to the time he said his first swear word - back to the first cigarette he tried to smoke - back to when he tried to say his first swear word, but couldn't let himself do it and back into the snug, dark comfort of his mother's womb.

Having quenched their thirst for gaping, the oldest of the pair said: 'Can we ask what you are doing here?'

'I'm, er... I'm waiting for someone.'

'For two hours?!'

'Er... Yes.'

'Hold out your arms.' The officers patted his arms and his legs and his torso. They emptied out his pockets, but only a chewing gum encrusted two-pence piece and a mummified tissue could be found.

The senior policeman sighed, 'Okay, I'd move along if I was you.'

'But she hasn't turned up yet.'

'Move along or we'll have you done for loitering.'

'Can I make a phone call?'

'Two minutes.'

He rushed to the phone and dialed and waited. The evening needn't be totally written off, he thought. There would be no point calling her cell phone since she was most probably on the tube, but what he could do was leave a message with one of her flatmates.

Perhaps he could arrange to meet at a different rendezvous. Possibly the evening could be retrieved - assuming she would call home to see if he had left a message at her home after waiting for *him* half an hour fruitlessly. 'Hello?' said a nervous voice. It was she.

'Oh... hello, it's Peter. Weren't we meant to meet at Leicester Square at six?' She put the phone down. He tried to phone again, but she didn't pick up.

'Come on,' said the policemen and escorted him out.

It wouldn't have been so bad if she gave a reason for her non-appearance, but as it was, the whole situation was shrouded in mystery. As it was, he could only speculate.

Maybe she had turned up, saw him and decided not to go through with it and went home again. Maybe there was something about his looks that had changed her mind. But maybe she hadn't turned up - couldn't be bothered.

He stroked his chin. Neither theory pleased him. Maybe she had turned up when there were two of them with an Observer and she found it too embarrassing a situation for her to cope with? Forget it! he thought. Forget it!! Why bother dwelling on it? It didn't happen and that's it!

It was only when he stepped outside the station that a fact became apparent. He turned to the police officers and said: 'Actually, I need to get back in so that I can get a tube home.'

'Well, you're not coming back in this one. Try Piccadilly.'

TWO

Too slow. The traffic in Charing Cross Road, no matter which way you looked at it, was too slow - too slow for movement and too slow to get anywhere. If you wanted to go nowhere then this was the perfect route.

The consensus among the drivers was that they wanted the jam to cease. But sat inside a Porsche was a driver who couldn't care either way. Sharply dressed and wearing shades, he watched the people go by. For the first time in years, they had become interesting to him. A cigarette poked out of his lips - conjuring up gigantic plumes of smoke.

The traffic lights pointlessly changed to amber and a young man caught his eye - coming out of the station - accompanied by two policemen.

'Didn't that use to be a Herringbone coat?' thought the driver in a transatlantic accent. 'Good grief... Its glory years must have been long ago...'

The policemen released the man. He got caught in the people jam on the pavement as he tried to edge towards the cinemas.

The driver continued to stare. Not much to go on... But he reckoned he could guess his whole life story. He reckoned he was good at reading people. In fact he reckoned he could *speed read* people - especially since they were so *predictable*... No... He wasn't a vagrant... Too clean-shaven for that... And his shoes were polished... Maybe he was some sort of activist... Anyway... Sweeping his long, thick, raven-black hair away from his eyes, he put out his cigarette and smiled to himself... He would be the one... He would be the one...

THREE

Multitudes poured into the tube compartment and then some more multitudes. Neither the heat, nor the rancid meaty smell of sweaty armpits deterred them. Peter hung on to the rail near the doors as the passengers flooded in. There was no way that any more people could cram themselves here, he thought. But he was wrong. Seconds before the tube doors shut; an amorous couple pushed in.

They squeezed themselves between him and a hundred others. Then, half a centimetre away from his face, the couple proceeded to snog and snog - so close that his face was being flicked with their saliva. He shut his eyes. He wasn't there. He was back in Art School. Life was joyous. Half his face wasn't being drenched with spit.

He opened his eyes. The male of the couple had an annoying habit of leaning on him. This habit was also painful for Peter's back. Perhaps they would get off at the next stop, he thought. He would tolerate it until then. They didn't get off at the next stop. Perhaps they would get off at the stop after that, he thought. He would tolerate it until then. They didn't get off at the stop after that.

It felt like his back was going to snap.

Right, he decided; if he was going to save his backbone he was going to have to show it. As the couple pressed against him, he pressed back to cancel it out.

This continued for three stops until the boyfriend turned slightly towards him and said: 'Will you stop pushing me?'

'I'm sorry?'

'You heard. Stop pushing. My girlfriend needs some space.'

'It's funny you should say that because..'

'No, *nothing's* funny about it. Stop pushing.'

'I was going to say it's funny you should say that because you were pushing *me*!'

'No I wasn't!' grunted the boyfriend. 'You're talking shit, mate!'

'No I'm not!' said Peter.

'Are you going to stop pushing or am I going to have do something about it?'

'Oh I see; you're trying to impress your girlfriend. Let me spare you the trouble...' Peter addressed the girlfriend. 'I just like to tell you; your boyfriend's *really* tough - he's a *real* man - okay?'

'Shut up you *stupid* wanker!' said the boyfriend.

'Yeah, shut up wanker!' said his girlfriend.

The boyfriend's nostrils flared aggressively. His eyes resembled those of a rabid dog. A violent event looked inevitable.

'For your information,' said Peter; 'if I moved anymore towards the left I'd crush this pregnant woman behind me.'

It was a good point. Even alpha male over there couldn't argue with that.

'Yeah, whatever!' he said and turned back to his girlfriend.

'So that's that then. I can't move any further.'

'Whatever!'

'Good.'

'Whatever!' The couple continued to lean on Peter for another three stops.

***

Peter got off at Manor House station and caught a 141.

There was only one seat available. It was next to a young man in a Hoodie - sitting with his legs wide apart as if he had elephantiasis of the testicles.

Peter knew that the youth's body language meant that he didn't want anyone to sit next to him, but he thought fuck it, he paid his fare like everyone else and he was entitled to a seat. He sat down. The youth did not move a millimetre and Peter could only properly park one of his buttocks down. He turned to the Hoodie: 'Excuse me, but could you please give me some more room so that I can sit down properly? I've got a bad back.'

'Not my problem.'

Peter felt like saying: 'Well, I'm going to make it your problem! I'm going to kick you in the balls so that you really do have elephantiasis of the testicles! Fucking idiot! You're making my back worse! Have a punch in the face as well!' but he didn't say that. Instead he opted for saying something mildly sarcastic: 'Thanks for your consideration, then?!'

The youth shrugged his shoulders; put on his iPod earphones and turned it on full blast. Peter saw little point in asking him to turn it down. It was the latest number one hit by that pop star that had topped the charts for the past five years... The name was on the tip of his tongue... You know!! What'shisface!!

He looked out of the window. Little progress had been made. He rang the bell.

'Excuse me... Excuse me, please...' said Peter as he scrambled through the crowd clustered around the exit even though it wasn't their stop for ages. '...Excuse me... Excuse me... Excuse me...' Had somebody stuck a 'Kick Me' note on his back?! What the Hell was going on?! 'Excuse me!! PLEASE!! Let me get off the bus!'

'What is it with people?' thought Peter. So many dickheads! God hope he never turned into one. Thoroughly dishevelled, he got out of the vehicle.

The heavenly aroma of charcoal grilled kebabs hit his nostrils... Turkish and Greek music blared out of thoughtfully double-parked vehicles as fleets of police cars screeched by... He weaved around a trail of dog shit and an abandoned fridge and an abandoned washing machine with abandoned washing inside it...

The Internet cafes were doing a roaring trade - as they did every day. Even late at night he would see people there - tapping away at the keyboards - keeping in touch with their loved-ones on the other side of the globe...

He continued past the Kurdish Men's Social Club and the Turkish Men's Social Club and the social clubs for other ethnic male types...

He paused at a barbershop. There were at least seven along that stretch of road before Turnpike Lane. Why so many in such a small area, he wondered? Did people's hair grow quicker there? Did people just spend their time having their hair cut? Or was it the ethnic thing again - a barbershop for every ethnic group? Well, it wasn't a place he needed to go.

It wasn't much to look at; Green Lanes, but he loved it. To him, its beauty was deep down - under its carpet of cigarette ends and rubbish - in its aura. He loved the twenty-four hour grocers and their twenty-four hour reasonable prices; the pound shops; the bakeries; the music shops; the pubs; the takeaways; the restaurants; the night-clubs; the wedding photo studios; even the exhaust fumes and the traffic jams and the Greek Orthodox Priest pompously parading down the street in full regalia. It made him feel like he was abroad - which was just as well since it wasn't as if he could afford to go anywhere.

Builders had set up scaffolding on one of the restaurants along the street. Shit, thought Peter, shit! Please don't renovate the area, he thought; it'll make his rent go up! But he had needn't had worried; Haringey Bridge had been freshly graffiti'd again.

He walked down Kimberley Gardens. Broken TVs, broken cookers and broken stereos were generously left in front gardens for anyone to take. A car stopped by. A youth poked his head out of the window. 'Wanna buy a laptop?'

'No - you're all right...'

Finally, he arrived home. He could hear his flatmates in the living room watching TV. He entered and for want of something better to do, he sat down next to Stuart.

The Zack Contemporary Show was on. Five wardens led a gigantic handcuffed man on stage. His tattoos, crew cut and ponytail suggested he came from the poorer side of town.

The studio audience booed at him as he sat down next to his brother. Below him, the subtitle appeared: 'I murdered my brother's wife and had sex with her corpse while wearing her underwear.'

Zack made his stand: 'First of all, I'd like to say you're way out of line killing your brother's wife and having sex with her while wearing her panties - you don't do that! It's not the sort of thing you do!'

The audience cheered and ranted: 'Go Zack! Go! Go do him Zack! Go Zack! Go!'

Zack continued, 'I can't *begin* to sufficiently *condemn* what you did... So, what *else* did you do?'

'Well... I also killed my brother's pet dog and had sex with it while wearing its collar.'

'That's *terrible*! No way do you kill your brother's pet and have sex with it while wearing its collar! I wouldn't treat a *dog* like that! You make me sick... So, what *else* did you do?'

'Well... I... I..'

'Come on!'

'I... I..'

'The public has a right to know!'

'I... masturbated on my brother's wallpaper.'

'Oh... Is that all?' Zack turned to the cameras. 'We'll be back after the break... Is that all you can come up with?'

The commercials started. Peter turned to Ricky. 'Do you think these people would give the most intimate details of their lives if they weren't poor and uneducated?'

Ricky slowly turned to him. 'You having a go at me for watching the programme?'

'No, I was only saying..'

'The adverts are over - okay?!'

Peter left the room. It was hard for him to like them. It had been easier before he moved in with them. It had been easier still before he had met them. He could never have called them 'friends'. They were 'friends of friends' - or enemies. He couldn't remember which.

Basically, he had moved in with them because there wasn't anyone else to move in with and he couldn't live with his parents a minute longer (maybe a minute, but not much longer than that). He was determined to move out before he was thirty. He had heard that males these days were known to live with their folks well past their forties, but not him - there was only so much self-loathing he could tolerate before throwing himself off a cliff.

His housemates were 'all right' when he had first moved in with them, but in the space of three months; their indifference towards him deteriorated into downright disrespect.

Peter entered the bedroom and lay on the bed. In some ways he was glad that his housemates hated him. Only *bland* people were universally liked.

His back still ached from the train journey. Maybe he should get a massage, he thought. Though, what would be the point? After a while, the masseur's hands would get achy and the masseur would have to get someone to massage her hands and then that masseur would have to get someone to massage her hands. All that happened was that the pain was transferred. It never disappeared.

Maybe he should have continued looking at other flatshares. He had looked at the ones listed in Loot and the Guardian Weekend Guide, but when he visited them it was obvious that the occupants wanted a female flatmate really and only agreed to let him see the place out of politeness. Maybe it was an issue of tidiness or sexiness. Any woman was better than a man in their book and he had to concede they had a point.

A bug crawled up his leg. He gazed at the wallpaper. It was only partially attached to the walls. God, he lived in such a dump, he thought. He gave the bug a swipe. The place was infested. If cockroaches were gold, he'd be a wealthy man.

He got up. No... Getting depressed wasn't the way. Getting depressed would be counter-productive. His meagre lifestyle would pay off some day. As long as he had energy to paint in his spare time there was still a chance. He went to his basin; splashed some water on his face and prepared a canvas.

FOUR

Popcorn and hotdog smells wafted in the air as one hundred thousand people waited eagerly in the Hollywood Bowl.

Chuck didn't do that many concerts these days so it was a special event. Tickets sold out quicker than it took to say tickets sold out quicker.

'We want Chuck! We want Chuck!' they cried. Only an empty stage lay before them. The show was meant to have started an hour and a half ago and he still wasn't there.

***

In the dressing room, Chuck was sat - reading a book with his feet rested on the table. A monitor showing the expectant audience emitted a soothing hum. P.A. Gavin Priestly entered and handed Chuck a bottle of mineral water.

'Thanks.'

As Chuck sipped the drink, Gavin studied the screen. 'They're looking pretty eager...'

'This water's too warm.' said Chuck, 'Could you get me a *cooler* bottle?'

***

Foot stamping commenced. 'WE WANT CHUCK!! WE WANT CHUCK!! WE WANT CHUCK!!' CHUCK!!!!!!!!!!!!!!!!!!!!!!!!!!!!!!!

***

Gavin entered the dressing room to find Chuck filing his fingernails and handed him a bottle of colder water. 'Chuck, I think you should seriously consider going on stage.'

Chuck took a sip. 'This bottle's *too* cold. Could you get me a bottle that's *slightly* warmer but *not* as warm as the previous bottle you got me?'

'Yes, but what about the audience?'

'...Show them the documentary.'

***

In the stadium, several huge video screens came to life. A film proceeded about how Chuck overcame poverty and childhood leukemia to become what he was today.

'Chuck Harlem: pop sensation and movie phenomenon... a man who likes to take risks... Seven years ago at the tender age of eighteen, Chuck won a major TV talent show... The world was never the same again... But if one thing hasn't changed, it's Chuck. He's remained the same down-to-earth guy. We interviewed one of his best friends - Leroy, Leroy Jones.'

A close-up of a 'street-wise' Homeboy appeared. 'He's still the same down-to-earth guy...'

'CHUCK!! WHERE ARE YOU?' roared the crowd.

***

Gavin returned to the dressing room and handed Chuck the water. Not much had changed except he had given up on that book and started another. 'Chuck, the documentary isn't doing it for them. You've got to start the concert.'

Chuck opened the bottle and sipped from it. '...Let me think about it...'

He put his hands together and pondered in front of the mirror. Now had he let the audience wait long enough? It was a question he always asked himself... You see; he understood human psychology... He knew the audience would appreciate him more if he made them wait... But at the same time... he didn't want to make them wait *too* long... Mmmmmmmmm... Now if only he could find that happy median...

***

The anticipation was becoming unbearable - almost bringing the audience to the brink of death. Hadn't they displayed enough devotion?! They bought his CDs, wore his clothes, watched his films and ate his food! What else did they have to do?!

At the moment it looked certain that violence would erupt and the stadium end up a burnt-out crater; a plane soared by, and from the cheapest, remotest seats, a spectator spotted something falling from the sky.

It flickered in the hazy twilight - a large fluorescent Harlem logo floating gently downwards.

The spectator alerted the others. 'What is it? What is it?' The video screens were still showing the documentary, so most of the audience were mystified. 'CAN'T SEE!!! CAN'T SEE!!!!' Finally, the screens showed a parachute with a figure in a gold jumpsuit and a gold skydiving helmet, drifting down towards the stadium.

'And now, descending out of the heavens,' said the announcer, 'it's none other than CHUCK HARLEM!'

Several hundred spectators fainted with excitement and had to be carried away in stretchers. Several thousand took slow and steady calming breaths so that they could remain.

The figure in the gold jumpsuit and skydiving helmet landed. A motorcycle was wheeled on. After extricating himself from the parachute, he got onto the bike - waving to the audience as he drove around the stage.

From a trap door, came a ramp. And from another trap door, came a ring of fire. The jumpsuit-clad person revved the engine and drove up the ramp. 'He goes through the ring unscathed.' said the announcer.

Several more spectators had to be carried away. It was just too much.

Lethargically, Chuck's band members went on stage to plug in their instruments. A roadie came on stage dragging handcuffs, padlocks and chains behind him. Four members of the audience were beckoned on stage.

'I believe Chuck is asking them to chain him up.' said the announcer, 'For what purposes, I'm not sure.'

From a trap door, an immersion tank rose.

'...Oh, I *see*.'

Chained up, the performer demonstrated that it was impossible for him to move his arms. Then he was lowered into the container and a curtain was drawn around it. 'I've just heard that Chuck plans to do some singing after he escapes from the immersion tank - *if* he escapes.'

The drummer sighed and started a drum roll. All the audience had to look at was an immersion tank - for ages and ages. Tidal waves of enthusiasm grew. 'We want Chuck! We want Chuck! WE WANT CHUCK!'

Ten minutes passed; the chants died down and the drum roll petered out. The audience all stared at the immersion tank in silence.

'...Wow, he's been there an extraordinarily long time.' whispered the announcer, 'The amount of time Chuck's been deprived of oxygen would have brain-damaged a *normal* guy.'

The band members unplugged their instruments and walked off stage. '...The question is if Chuck does get out; will he have the ability to even string a simple sentence together? Don't try this at home, folks.'

As the emergency services rushed to the stage, the lid of the immersion tank popped out into the air like a champagne cork. A shiny wet figure struggled out of the tank. He crouched on the floor, gasping. Then he took small, slow gulps of air and tore off his sky diving helmet to reveal his gorgeous face.

His eyes were beautiful - so blue. They made other people's blue eyes look like *brown* eyes. His hair was beautiful - so blond. It made gold look tarnished. It made gold look like worthless shit.

He winked to the audience. Using the microphone stand to prop himself up, he drew in some deeper breaths. Then he unzipped his gold jumpsuit to reveal his fluorescent multi-coloured robe and waved benevolently to the cheering masses.

'There will be a concert! There will be music!' said the announcer.

Listlessly, the band returned to the stage and plugged in their instruments. Nobody noticed that Chuck's guitar wasn't plugged in.

Chuck addressed the audience. 'Are you having a good time?'

'YEAH!!' screamed the audience.

'I can't hear you! Are you having a good time?'

'YEAAAHH!!!!' screamed the audience.

'I still can't hear you! Are you having a good time?'

'YEAAAAAAAAHH!!!!!!!!!' screamed the audience until their tonsils almost bled.

Satisfied, Chuck continued, 'Tonight's going to be a crazy night, dudes - like all the nights in my life, but it's also a special night - my Birthday. Glad you could make it, so let's rock!' He strummed his guitar - magically producing a beautiful riff and began slowly:

They may say
That our way
Is the wrong way...

Gradually, the song built up speed:

But we know they are wrong
And we know we are right
Like day is day

And night is night...

'Come everybody! You all know the words to the chorus!' Chuck yelled. The audience obliged him:

We don't care what you say
Our way
Is the right way!

'Again!'

We don't care what you say
Our way
Is the right way!

'That's more like it' he yelled and the song accelerated:

Now they have to listen to what we say
They can't block their ears
They have to obey!
We'll live our lives how we like
If they don't like it
They can take a hike!

For the final part of the song he slowed down to a crawl:

Perhaps one day we will hear
Everyone cheer
And say
Our way
Is the right way!

The audience lapped it up with the urgency of a thirsty dog. 'YOU ARE GOD!!!!!! YOU ARE GOD!!!!!!!!!!!!!!'

***

Outside the venue, a stuntman in a soaked gold jump suit and helmet was being carried into an ambulance. Gavin stood by the entrance - absentmindedly unfolding his monthly wage slip and turned to the paramedic. 'Do you think he'll live?'

'Maybe...'

***

Eventually, the ovation died down. Chuck smiled, modestly shook his head and gazed at the audience. There they were: his disciples waiting with baited breath for every word he spoke. '...For my final number, I'm going to sing..'

The audience protested.

'Hey, I've got to go! I've got a hot date waiting - know what I'm saying?'

The band started and Chuck looked above to see his monitor - strategically positioned near the lights. He often forgot the words to the songs and he found that this quite helped. Strumming again tunefully on the turned off guitar, he started to sing a song about being in love with a girl in his high school class who was moving with her family to Australia and how he didn't want her to move there.

...Don't move to Australia!
Don't move to Australia
Don't move to Australia!
Stay here
And don't move to Australia!

Chuck found it curious that none of the audience were waving their cigarette lighters in the air. They had perturbed expressions on their faces and so did the members of the band. Then it dawned on him: these were the words to a different song. Some how the wrong lyrics had appeared on the monitor.

***

Chuck slammed the dressing room door shut. He opened the door then slammed it louder.

Ten minutes later, Gavin happened to be walking down the corridor when he heard some strange noises emanating from the room.

He entered to find the place completely wrecked. The TV was smashed and in flames. The wardrobe was smashed and burning brightly. The chairs were smashed and had been set alight. The costumes were ripped to shreds and on fire. The mirror was shattered and was somehow burning brightly too.

Chuck was sat on the only intact piece of furniture in the room - staring vacantly at the wall.

'Are you alright, Chuck?' said Gavin.

For a while, Chuck slowly breathed in and out. Then he gradually turned to Gavin and said: 'How - how could you let this happen to me?' and broke into a fit of coughing.

***

Gavin finished putting out the fire and put the extinguisher down. 'I don't think it's that big a deal, Chuck. It was still a great show. You started the song again and it was fine.' He opened a window.

For some time, Chuck gazed at his shattered reflection. He said: 'I looked *bad*... It looked like I didn't even know the words to my own song. I looked *bad*... I don't feel *good* when I'm made to look *bad*... This has done me a lot of psychological harm... I have no idea how long it will take me to recover... It does not make me happy... I *hate* it when I'm not happy - I *hate* it!!'

Chuck hurled pots of make-up and mascara everywhere. '...I'm so *angry* that I'm not happy! So *angry*!!'

Gavin wiped the mascara off his face. 'Do you want me to get you something?'

Chuck said nothing.

'I'll get you some water and get someone to clean up the mess.'

Chuck still said nothing.

'I'll get you some water - okay? I'll be back soon.'

The door shut. With trembling hands, Chuck applied cleanser onto a cotton pad and began to wipe off his makeup.

He knew it! He knew it was too good to last! The papers will have a field day. All you have to do is show a little vulnerability and everybody's ready to pounce on you and tear you to shreds - stripping the flesh from your bones and sucking the marrow from your skeleton - until even dogs would have no use for you.

Getting to where he was today hadn't been easy - no it hadn't. It had been a slow and painful journey. It had taken a lifetime of trauma and now it was all slipping away from him. Once his dependence on monitors gets revealed, all the other things would come out - all the *truth* about him - all the sordid facts. Then he would know true humiliation - humiliation on an unprecedented scale...

Gavin returned with the janitor and handed Chuck a bottle of water.

'It's your fault it happened.' said Chuck, 'You realise that? It was your responsibility the running order of the songs on the monitor. It was your fault.'

'I'm sorry Chuck. I don't know how it happened.'

'You should have checked the monitor.'

'I did.'

'Then that could only mean one thing: *sabotage...*'

Somewhere deep in the recesses of his subconscious, he knew that someone; someday was going to try to ruin his life - somebody - some nutter with nothing to lose. The only thing was that he didn't know who...

'Chuck, sometimes machines go wrong.'

'What would you know about it - you sad talentless fuck?! A machine manufactured by my company doesn't go wrong!'

'Oh... I suppose it must have been sabotage then.'

The room became smoky again. Before Gavin could check if any of the furniture had re-ignited, a man swaggered into the shadows and said in a transatlantic accent: 'Great show, Chuck.'

'Shut up!!' said Chuck. The last person that he wanted to see in the entire universe and all the other neighbouring universes had entered the room: Bryan Fahrenheit.

Bryan drew his cigarette away from his lips. 'That's... not nice... It took me a long time... to get here... Getting a parking space was... almost... *impossible*.'

'Well, you can go back to your parking space; get in your car and go fuck yourself!'

'That's... not nice... either... Especially since I reckon you need me more than I need you..'

'I don't need you! That's why I kicked you out..'

'Oh yeah? I've heard there's a recession on it's way..'

'Haven't we just recovered from one?'

'These recessions... come as regular as buses.'

'So?! We'll be okay!'

'Now I was hacking into your database and what did I find? The figures for this quarter... Not good, Chuck... not good... A dip in sales - not a substantial one... but as you know... dips have a funny habit of getting bigger... and that *incident* on stage... might not have *helped* matters...'

When was Bryan going to get to the point? wondered Chuck. Did he think he had time to burn? Did he think he had months and years to put into an incinerator? '*What* do you want?'

'Read this.' said Bryan and threw Chuck a report. 'A proposal for a project - a *special* project.'

Chuck poured through the pages. 'This is crazy!'

'No, it isn't.'

'It'll never work.'

'It will.'

'You're no scientist. You can't do this.'

'No, but the scientist I smuggled out of North Korea *can*... Oh yeah, you better take a look at this.' said Bryan and passed Chuck a photo.

'Why you showing me a picture of a bald guy with a big nose? Do I show you pictures of bald guys with big noses?'

'There's more to this guy than being bald and having a big nose...' said Bryan, 'He's the guinea pig... I've kept this man under surveillance for several weeks... And in all that time he hasn't spent a dime on your goods.'

'Not a dime?'

'Not a dime.'

Chuck shook his head in disbelief. '...What's he got against me?'

'I wouldn't take it personally... You see he prefers to waste his disposable income on art supplies... He's one of those arty, non-materialist types who buy their clothes from charity shops - etcetera, etcetera. If the device works on *him*, it'll work on *anyone*...

'Yeah?'

So... are you going to welcome me back into the bosom of the company?'

Chuck grimaced. The ethics of the enterprise seemed dubious... But on the other hand, if it worked all his worries would be over... 'No, Bryan we can't do this... It'll be... *wrong*.'

Bryan smiled. 'If we don't do it... *someone else* will.'

FIVE

The rain poured down so hard you could have sworn that it was a Monday. But it wasn't a Monday. It was a Friday - a Friday evening to be slightly less vague.

Peter stood outside the house with his broken and ineffectual umbrella and wondered if he should ring the doorbell... He was getting soaked... And the journey had taken a lot of effort what with Greenford station being closed and most of the tube lines requiring emergency surgical intervention...

He psyched himself up, 'Okay, let's do it! Let's ring the doorbell!!' He jabbed the buzzer and waited.

A short, olive-skinned man in his early sixties; opened the door and said: 'When are you going to get a proper job?'

'Hi, Dad...' said Peter.

***

They sat around the dining table in the living room - eating soup. Peter's mother passed some sesame seed bread rolls around and said: 'Don't you want to make money?'

'Could you pass the salt?' said Peter.

His mother passed the salt. 'Don't you ever want to buy a flat?'

'No, homeownership increases unemploym..'

'You won't be able to get a wife if you don't get a proper job and a flat.'

'If she's only after me for my money, and food, and shelter then I don't want to know.'

'She might be a good girl! She might be decent.'

'Who?'

'The girl who's after you for your money, and food, and shelter.'

'Mum, I'm talking about a hypothetical woman!'

'Oh...' said his mother disappointed. She sighed. 'Helen would have stayed with you if you had a proper job and a flat..'

'It wasn't as simple as that.'

'It's a shame you drove her away. She was a lovely girl.'

'What're you talking about? You hated her!'

'I did not!'

'You used to say her hair stank!'

'Not after she had her hair done - not after she had those things cut off. Her hair smelt fine after that - though it was a bit short..'

'It's been *three* years since I've seen her! She's married now! What's the point about talking about her?'

'...It could have been you that married her - if you weren't so silly. It could have been you, isn't that right, George?'

It was now his father's turn. His mother started eating her soup. 'Your mother's right, Peter. It could have been you who married her, but no, you decided to carry on painting. Now you're unmarried and *alone* - *alone* and *unmarried*..'

'Yes, I think we've established my single status..'

'All because of painting!'

'Give me a break!'

'No! You must give it up! You will never be a success at it!'

'In ten years time, you will eat those words!' said Peter struggling to spit out these words with his mouth full.

'You said that ten years ago.' said his mother, 'How old are you - thirty?'

Peter almost choked. 'Twenty-nine!'

He poured himself a glass of water and gulped it down.

'Most people have proper jobs and are settled down at your age.' said his mother, 'You're not getting any younger.'

'No,' said his father, 'you are getting *older*!'

Peter anxiously stroked the few beleaguered strands remaining on top of his head and said: 'The jobs market isn't particularly great at the moment. I'm probably doing quite well considering.'

'No you're not!' said his father.

'It's never too late, Peter.' said his mother; 'You could still become a lawyer if you got a further qualification.'

'You mean a *degree* in law?'

'No, it's not like that. You could do a conversion course - converting your art degree into a law degree and then you'd do a placement..'

'That would still take quite a bit of time.'

'Your cousin Maroulla's a lawyer..'

Peter dipped the other half of the bread roll into the soup.

'...Androulla's a lawyer, Mario's a lawyer, Themi's a lawyer too, why not you?'

'It would take years of studying for me to become a lawyer and I'd have to support myself so how would I do it?' Peter said as he swayed the soggy bread in the air.

'You'd study in the evening.'

'But how would I have time to study law in the evening?'

'Well, you'd give up painting.'

'I don't want to give it up!' Peter shook his bread in anger and sprayed half the tablecloth in soup.

'Don't shout at your mother, Peter.' said his father, 'A man does not shout at his mother.'

'I'm sorry, Mum.'

'It's all right, Peter... Have you finished your soup?'

Peter looked at his bowl. He had barely started his meal while his parents' bowls were completely empty. 'Er... yeah... I've finished.'

'You've hardly touched it...'

'Yeah, it's cold... I'm not going to eat anymore...'

His mother collected the bowls.

'I'll take them to the kitchen.' offered Peter.

'No, it's okay.'

***

They started the main course. His mother continued with her words of wisdom. '...It's all very well with your ideals and all, but people don't like those types of paintings. They want something that makes their living room look nicer. They don't want to be disturbed and have nightmares. Why don't you do paintings of flowers, Peter? People like paintings of flowers.'

'Because I'm an artist - not a prostitute.'

'Who's talking about prostitution?' asked his mother, 'That would be a terrible line of business to get into.'

His father interjected: 'If your paintings were any good, people would have bought them.'

'That's not necessarily so. Look at Van Gogh, he hardly sold any of his work in his lifetime.'

Peter's mother put her knife and fork down. 'Is that the life you want - full of misery and despair?'

'Don't worry; I won't come here so often.'

'Ha?! Ha?! You are a funny man - a funny man who throws his life down the drain!' bellowed his father.

Peter put down his knife and fork. 'Even if I never sell a painting - not a single second would have been wasted.'

'Have you lost your senses?'

'If you can't see that your son is a genius, then I feel sorry for you.'

His mother interjected: 'Maybe there aren't any other geniuses around to like your work and buy it!'

'If people are too thick to appreciate my work it's not my problem.'

'But it is!' said his dad, 'It's *your* problem - not *their* problem! They're fine not appreciating your work - you're not! You're hitting your head against a brick wall! A man cannot feed himself on air and snow alone!'

'Then I'll have a tomato with it.'

Peter's mother said: 'Are you able to feed yourself properly?'

'Yes.'

'You look like you've lost weight - are you sure?'

'Yes! I get by!'

'Is getting by - good enough?' said his mother, 'We love you, Peter. We worry about you.'

'Don't worry about me. Worry about yourselves.'

After an uncomfortable silence, his father sighed. 'Ahhh... Let's change the subject...'

'Fine...'

They returned to their meals. His father cut his chicken into smaller and smaller pieces. 'I've been thinking Peter, isn't it about time you got yourself a car - a car with a lot of luggage space?'

Peter slammed his knife and fork down on the table. 'I don't believe it! I can't even drive and you want me to get a car!!'

His mother helped herself to some more potatoes. 'Why don't you want to drive? Most people are driving at your age.'

'Because it's bad for the environment.'

'Tsk!' said his father.

'It's true!'

'Last time I gave you a driving lesson - you were shaking like a leaf in the wind. You were scared out of your wits.'

'Okay, I was scared. I am far from perfect - I admit it.'

'You're going to have to learn to drive at some point, Peter.'

'Why? Why do I need to learn?'

'To carry the children.'

'What children?!'

'The children you'll have after getting a decent job and getting married. You'll need to drive them to school.' said his mother.

'Why can't they walk there?'

'Do you want our grandchildren to get run over - do you want our grandchildren to die?'

'Mum... There are no grandchildren... Not even hypothetical grandchildren.'

'Even without children you're still going to need a car.' said his father.

'Why?! I live in London. There are no parking spaces in London.'

His mother held up a piece of chicken impaled on her fork. 'Why don't you want to drive and get a decent job, and a wife, and flat, and have children? Most people do.'

'What can I say?! You were Hitler and Stalin in previous lives and God has sent me here to punish you! It's a conspiracy that I as an individual don't want to do the things that you want me to do!'

Peter's mother sadly looked down at her plate. 'That's very hurtful, Peter. You don't have to talk that way to your mother.'

'Apologise to your mother, Peter!' roared his father, 'A man always apologises to his mother!'

Peter looked down at his food and played with it with his fork. 'Sorry...' He shook his head. 'It's a shame you didn't have other children, because I've obviously failed you...'

SIX

A Cadillac went round the car park of the Washington Head Office of Harlem Enterprises. It was coming up to nine. As like the previous time, the vehicle completed the circuit only to have to do it all over again. 'One parking space...' groaned the man in the car, 'One parking space; that's *all* I'm asking for... Not two - not three, but *one*...'

He took his glasses off and wiped them.

Adrian Gluckman had already known that it wasn't going to be his day before he had set off. For a start, it was Monday and Monday was nobody's day. But he had no inkling of how 'not his day' this day would be.

At 7.15, that morning, he had spilled coffee on the crotch of his trousers. 'Arrrrgh!!!' At 7.25, he had cut himself shaving. 'Owww!!!'

He hadn't realised the significance of his scalded genitals. He hadn't appreciated the significance of his bleeding cheek. He hadn't realised that these were *bad* signs - signs that portended the terrible events to come.

Up to this day, his life had been fortuitous. Mainly good things had happened to him. He had a good job, a beautiful wife with a gorgeous butt (which she let him spank on his Birthday as she lay on his lap, 'Happy Birthday, darling!') and three beautiful kids. It wasn't even as if he had put that much effort into becoming successful. It was as if he had merely sleepwalked into happiness. But today this effortless run of good luck had ground to a halt.

'Please... One parking space... I'm not asking for a full head of hair or for wealth beyond compare, I'm asking for one parking space... Come on... One parking space; that's all I'm asking for... Not World Peace - not for the hole in the ozone layer to be repaired - not an end to World Hunger - not for universal happiness but one Goddamn parking space!'

Around again he drove only to be met by hundreds of gleeful vehicles - occupying spaces that his car could have taken.

This was not normal, thought Adrian. And it wasn't. *Normally*, he was one of those employees who didn't have to worry about finding a parking space because *normally* there was a space reserved exclusively for him. But for today, *normality* had ceased. The space wasn't available. Someone else's car was parked there... The only conclusion he could come to was that someone... possibly *male* or *female*... had *taken* it.

He made another attempt to call reception to have the car towed way... Still engaged...

***

Having forked out forty dollars to park in a private car park, Adrian swiped his entry card at the barrier in the building.

Eddie Winfrey, the security guard nodded hello.

'Hi, Eddie,' said Adrian, 'How was your weekend?'

'As good as you could expect if you've been working a weekend shift.'

'Oh... *Right*... You wouldn't happen to know who's taken my parking space?'

'Haven't you heard?' said Eddie, 'Bryan Fahrenheit's back!'

'Fuck!' said Adrian, 'Fuck!!'

It had been two months since the security guards had ejected him. Two months of unbridled bliss. Two months of unbridled ecstasy. No one ever felt relaxed when he was present. And the problem was that he always seemed to be there - even after midnight. Tick... Tock... Tick... Tock... Dong! Still there. Tick... Tock... Tick... Tock... Dong! Dong! Still there. Tick... Tock... Tick... Tock... Dong! Dong! Dong! Still there...

Even as the clock chimed six am, the security cameras frequently filmed him - roaming the corridors as the strobe lighting hummed - stopping occasionally to get a drink from the water cooler.

Yes, he was always there especially when you didn't want him to be - which was most of the time. All too often, Adrian and his colleagues would be sharing a joke about Chuck to suddenly find at the punch line; Bryan standing behind them - smiling an ambivalent smile - a smile that could be saying: 'Well done! Funny joke!' or 'Har! Har! I'm going to tell Chuck!' One found out in the days to come that it was normally the latter.

It was a mystery how they never heard Bryan walking towards them. Adrian remembered discussing the issue with his colleagues:

'Have you ever heard Bryan's footsteps?'

'No, can't say I have...'

'Neither have I...'

'What sort of shoes do you think he wears?'

'Hushpuppies?'

Oh God, Adrian thought to himself, how he was going to miss Bryan *not* being around! Everyone felt sick when he was there and that wasn't just because of his personality. No one had missed that feeling of nausea when he had gone. And that feeling was coming back.

Maybe Eddie was *joking*, thought Adrian... April Fool's day was only *yesterday*. But no, thought Adrian, that Security Guard's pretty sharp... He wouldn't get his days mixed up like that...

Adrian loosened his collar. He didn't feel good. He needed someone to talk to about all this - someone who was going to reassure him. Someone who was going to tell him that everything was going to all right. Even if everything wasn't going to be all right, he wanted someone to humour him.

He saw Monica from 'Mergers and Acquisitions and Aggressive Takeovers' rush by. She would be perfect. They were close friends. She would be perfect to confide with. 'Hi, Monica! Monica!!'

At first, she didn't seem to hear him so he ran up to her. 'Monica!! Hi! I was calling you! Couldn't you hear me?'

She stopped and turned to him. 'Oh, er, hi, Adrian... Have you heard?'

'Tell me it isn't true.'

'I saw him in your office an hour ago.'

'What's he doing in my office?'

'Taking your stuff out.'

'Why?'

'To give himself room to put his stuff in.'

'Why?'

'Haven't you heard? He's not just back, he's been promoted.'

'No!!!!!'

Everything started to spin before him.

'You'll have to take orders from *him* now.'

'Wait a minute! Wait a minute! Have I been demoted?'

'Mmmm, *sort of*... Anyway, got to go...'

'Where am I supposed to sit?'

'Oh... you'll have to 'hot desk' like the rest of *them*. Yes... Er... I'll see you around sometime.'

Adrian watched their friendship disappear into the distance... He had half a mind to resign right then and there, but the other half told him: 'No you don't! You've got a mortgage and isn't there a recession on its way? Your wife and kids depend on you! What would they do if you resigned? Jobs don't grow on trees, you know! And your wife's very good looking! Don't think for a minute that she would stay with the likes of you if you could no longer bring in the bacon! She's a ten and you're barely a five! You'd have to kiss that gorgeous butt of her's goodbye! She wouldn't let you look at it let alone spank it!'

Okay, he said to himself, okay... He would carry on in his demoted capacity with as much dignity as he could muster. Now, in his present situation, it was appropriate for him to '*hot desk*' so 'hot desking' was what he was going to do.

To the uninitiated, 'hot desking' is a way to provide surface area for people to work on and make them feel utterly insecure about their job. So another circuit was embarked upon. From one floor to another and round and round he went - seeking an unoccupied table. Sometimes he thought he spotted one only to find that a jacket had been left on the chair. It was tempting to throw the jacket out of the window, sit down and plead ignorance, but that was not hot desk etiquette. Anyway, the computer was probably locked.

He noticed his colleague, Tom, on the other side of the office - carrying his coat and briefcase - on the same quest. Adrian waved.

Tom waved back.

A cell phone went off - playing a Mambo tune. The recipient of the call was away from their desk, so the music continued. As the music progressed, a woman in the middle of the office, logged off from her PC; put away her papers; picked up her jacket and left.

Adrian and Tom realised they had the same idea. They shot towards the desk, panting and puffing for all they were worth. Tom hurled himself onto the seat as the music stopped. He wiped away the sweat pouring down his forehead. 'Sorry, Adrian, but I've been looking for over an hour!'

Tom logged onto the computer. Adrian looked on enviously and said: 'Terrible news - isn't it about Bryan being back? Real bummer...'

'Well... it's a *surprise*.' said Tom, guardedly.

'Yeah, but don't you think it's *extraordinary*? Isn't it *amazing* that Chuck took him back? Especially if you think about what he did...'

Bryan had left under a cloud - the darkest cloud imaginable - and possibly a typhoon. It was only at the last minute that the company found out that the consignment of leather jackets Bryan had co-ordinated the production of had been made of human skin. If they hadn't been withdrawn from the high street shops one minute before they opened, a PR tsunami would have occurred. Until the very end, Bryan kept arguing that they should still sell the coats and that perhaps they would set a new trend. 'The anti-fur lobby will lap it up!'

'It was way beyond the pale, what Bryan did. That's why it makes me wonder.' said Adrian.

'Yeah, yeah...' said Tom.

'Chuck must be *mad* to take him back!'

And there - standing behind Adrian was Bryan. He smiled ambiguously and shook Adrian's hand. 'Hi, good to see you! Don't mind about your office - do you? Got a *big* project on... and I need some *big* space.'

'Oh, right..'

'Surprised to still see Susan here - aren't you? She's brave - very brave... Don't know how she does it... Not after having that nervous breakdown... You'd think hearing all those voices would *distract* her... Anyway, better get back to my office - I mean *your* office. Don't worry; this is only a *temporary* arrangement. So... *see* you later.'

Adrian waited a while for Bryan to silently leave and said: 'Do you think he heard what I said about Chuck?'

Tom nodded solemnly. 'Yep...'

***

Now was he or wasn't he going to tell Chuck? wondered Bryan... He hadn't quite decided.

Bryan wouldn't call himself a vindictive person, but there were a number of scores he wanted to settle. He didn't take too kindly to all the cheers and jubilation when he had been booted out of Head Office.

He swiped his card and went into the washroom. Swiping his card again, he entered a cubicle. He pulled the lid down and sat down.

From his jacket pocket, he pulled out a thermometer, shook it and put it in his mouth. His temperature was up. He thought as much. For the past hour, he had been feeling nauseous and giddy.

From his jacket pocket, he took out a jar. He opened it and swallowed some green pills. A minute later, the symptoms subsided. He took his temperature again. It was closer to normal. He looked at the jar. Only a few pills left. He would have to email the Doctor in Thailand and order more.

During Doctor Fuk's initial examination, Bryan had been warned that the pills could only supply a short-term solution and would not cure his maladies. '...This will only make you feel better for the time being - okay? In the long-term you will have to..'

'Can I just stop you there?' said Bryan, 'There is no *long-term*... There is only the *short-term*... I *live* in the short-term... It's *results* I'm concerned with... Let me tell you something: I have never taken a day off sick in my life... and it's going to *stay* that way. If I'm still able to do a fourteen-hour day then that's good enough for me... *Don't* tell me about long-term... I *don't* do long-term...'

***

At eleven o'clock, a temp had her contract discontinued and Adrian of course offered her his condolences - agreeing how hard it is to be a temp and then pounced upon her desk. He logged onto the PC. Logged onto the phone. Summoned all his powers of recall and typed in the multitudes of security passwords that allowed him into the database and was ready to work when the phone rang.

It was Gavin. 'Chuck wants to see you in his office: five minutes.'

'Oh... right. I'll be there straight away...'

Adrian knocked on the door. 'Come in.'

He entered the room and found that he could not see anything. All the blinds had been drawn and the lights switched off. 'Hi, Chuck, how're you doing?'

'Sit down, dude...'

'Er... it's not so easy to find a chair...' said Adrian - groping the air.

'Sit *down*.'

After he found himself a seat, a blinding spotlight fell upon him and Chuck began to talk. 'You said I was mad. It makes me *mad* when people say I'm mad. Would you like it if I said you were mad - a loony - a *drooling* maniac who should be put in a strait jacket and *lobotomised*?'

'No Sir, I - I wouldn't..'

'That's right, dude, you *wouldn't*. So remember: be more careful about what you say. People can get upset - catch my drift?'

'Yes Sir, I - I do..'

'Okay, you can go.'

Head hung low; he left the room as Bryan strolled in to speak to Chuck. 'Wish I could be like you - so forgiving... If someone had said the same thing about me, I'm not so sure I would be able to continue paying his wages..'

'Maybe I *am* mad to have you back.' Chuck grunted.

SEVEN

Telephones rang. 'Good morning! Eager Beavers!' shrilled Nannette and Rose. Telephones rang and they were answered.

It was 11'o clock and Peter had been sitting in the office of Eager Beavers Personnel for the past hour and a half - waiting for work to crop up. Being there very slightly raised the probability of being offered employment since it gave the impression of being more 'eager'.

He put his newspaper down and gazed at the plastic plant wilting in the corner.

Telephones rang. 'Good morning! Eager Beavers!' They were always bright and breezy, Nanette and Rose - always full of enthusiasm. World War Three could have been declared but they'd still be radiating rapture. 'Super duper!' they'd remark practically every five minutes whether or not they had palmed someone off with another low paying temp job.

'...Yes, what nice weather it is for this time of year! You're *right*! Why I was saying to Rose today, Rose what nice weather it is for this time of year! And she said why *yes*, she was saying to her father only the other day, what nice weather it is for this time of year. And he said yes, it's normally much colder... Any work? Why *yes* my dear! It's funny you should ask! I think we may well have something you'd be interested in! They're lovely people. They're bailiffs and they need someone to help with the paperwork. Do you think you can do it? Super duper!' What sort of anti-depressants were they on? One day they could snap, get some guns and take out half the neighbourhood.

Gary's phone rang. Gary sighed and said: 'Good morning... Eager... Beavers...' You could see him straining to keep up with Nanette and Rose's sunny disposition.

'...Why yes, it's funny you should ask' continued Annette, 'I was only asking Rose five minutes ago whether there was any work for you, and she said there was...'

Gary put the phone down. 'Peter, I think I've got something you might be interested in.'

Peter sat by Gary's desk as he proceeded to write down the address of the job and the name of the supervisor. 'Had a good weekend?' asked Gary. 'It's was okay,' said Peter, 'How about you?'

Gary's face dropped. '...It was... *quiet*... Didn't get up to much.' Gary tore a page from his note pad and handed it to him. 'The job should last a month. If you could arrive there tomorrow, at 8.30, that would be...' Gary winced. '...that would be... super... duper...'

***

In the Incontinence Advisory Service Department of East Finchley Community Hospital, Peter sat by the phone and waited.

Basically, his job was to answer the phone and say no. People would ring up and ask for an emergency supply of incontinence pads and Peter had to say: 'No, you can't have any. You have to ask your district nurse.' The person on the other line would say: 'What're you going on about? I don't get another delivery for another week, I need them now!'

Peter had to tell them that they did not stock emergency supplies of incontinence pads at the hospital and that the caller had to contact their district nurse to arrange to get them. 'Would you like me to get the number of your district nurse?' he would offer.

'Didn't even know I had a district nurse.'

'If you give me your name and address I'll get it for you now.'

Peter jotted down the information and went to the filing cabinet.

The caller's surname started with a B so he looked in the B drawers. He looked twice and he looked a third time. It was nowhere to be seen, but Mrs Roseblum was there and so was Mr Joliffe. How did that happen? Right... their first names began with B... Perhaps there was a type of system... The caller's first name began with T... so let's look in the T drawers... No, that didn't work. He found a file there where the surname began with G and the first name began with H. Why? Did the middle name begin with T? No... it didn't.

Years of clerks rushing from the phone to the filing cabinet and then haphazardly sticking back files in drawers had yielded its inevitable harvest. If he was going to find that district nurse number he was going to have to search through the whole sixty drawers.

An easier method existed - looking at the patient's record on the computer, but it would be several days until IT would be able to have him logged into the network because they had so much on and staff cutbacks to contend with.

Stephanie Rivers, the Head of the Advisory Service Department had said: 'Oh dear... We don't seem to have a password for you yet... I don't suppose you will need to use the computer much. If you need to get the District Nurse numbers of clients you could always use the filing cabinet. It shouldn't take long... Failing that you could always get Tracy to look on her computer for you.'

'Can't I just log in using Tracy's password?' said Peter.

'Mmm...' said Stephanie dismissively because she hadn't thought of that idea herself. 'No that wouldn't do at all... We need to keep our passwords secret. That would be a breach of security. And the computer would be recording that Tracy had made notes on the client files and not you since you would be logged as Tracy - ruining our audit trail. No... For the time being I would prefer if you didn't use the computer... No... the filing cabinet should be fine for the time being...'

While Peter struggled with the file cabinet, Stephanie stormed in. 'Have you seen Tracy?'

'No.' said Peter.

Only another ten years she told herself - only another ten years and she could retire. 'If you do see her could you tell her that I'm looking for her? She's over an hour late.' She stormed out again.

Stephanie's colleague, (slightly lower in authority) Ms Patricia Sether burst in. 'Have you seen Tracy?'

'No.' said Peter.

'Are you *sure*?' said Patricia.

'*Yes*.' said Peter.

Patricia probably liked to think of herself as a formidable woman - forthright - doesn't take any crap, but the truth of the matter was that she was a cow. Only another five years she told herself - only another five years and she could retire. 'If you do see her could you tell her that I'm looking for her? She's over an hour late.' She exited - slamming the door.

Ten minutes later, Ms Tracy Jackson struggled into the office with her walking frame. She suffered from a curvature of the spine. 'Has Stephanie and Patricia been looking for me?'

'Yes.' said Peter.

'Shit.' She collected the post from her pigeonhole. Only another fifteen years, she told herself - only another fifteen years and she could retire though she had heard the government was planning to raise the retirement age yet again.

'Look, if Stephanie and Patricia come back and ask if you've seen me please say you haven't. I won't have any time to get any work done if I have spend all day talking to them.'

'Okay,' said Peter 'I've been getting a lot of callers who don't know their district nurse numbers..'

'Have you tried the filing cabinet?'

'Yes... Some of the files appear to be... misplaced. Ms Rivers said you could get some of the numbers for me from your computer.'

She wiped her brow. 'Oh... I've got a mountain of work to catch up with.' She wrote down on a piece of paper: the login and the password and guided him round the database.

'I was given the *impression* that they didn't want me to use the database.' said Peter.

'I know, I'm sorry, but I'd appreciate it if you did. I've got so much on my plate at the moment.'

***

The day slowly dissolved and during the course of it, Peter found that the callers had problems that he couldn't merely say 'no' to. He would go to Stephanie's office and seek advice. Each time he saw her; he could have sworn that she seemed slightly more fed up. 'You haven't seen Tracy - have you?' she asked. 'She went to lunch one hour and fifteen minutes ago. She's switched her cell phone off.'

'No.' said Peter.

The instant after he gave the caller her district nurse's number and logged out, Patricia poked her snout in. 'You haven't seen Tracy - have you? She went to lunch one hour and seventeen minutes ago. She's switched her cell phone off.'

'No.' said Peter.

The snout disappeared.

The next caller wanted the delivery of her incontinence pads *postponed*. It was a strain on the ears to understand what she was saying. Her voice was so creaky. She must have been ninety years old. 'I'm going to be in hospital for two days.' she said, 'Could you deliver the pads later in the week?'

'Hold on, I'll check.'

Peter entered Stephanie's office. It was becoming obvious that she didn't want him to keep seeing her. It was almost as if she would have preferred him to have fobbed them off with 'no' rather than sort out their problems. Anyway, she informed him that the delivery only happened once a month and that the old lady couldn't have her delivery rescheduled.

Peter returned to the caller. 'Would you have enough pads to last you another month?'

'No I wouldn't, dear. Could you deliver on Wednesday? I'd be back on Wednesday.'

'I'm sorry; we only deliver once a month. Can't you get a neighbour to look after the pads for you?'

'I don't know my neighbours...'

It turned out that she lived on the top floor of a block of council flats.

Peter went back to Stephanie who informed him that the delivery could be diverted to a friend or relative's house. 'You really shouldn't be spending so much time with the same caller.' she told him.

Peter returned to the caller: 'We could divert the delivery to a friend or relative of yours..'

The old woman's voice trembled. 'I don't have any friends or relatives... I don't know any one.' Immediately, Peter could visualize her horrific lonely life; her damp dismal flat - only seeing people about her medical needs and no one else. There had to be a solution.

'Look, I'll cancel the delivery for this month.' said Peter. 'What you'll have to do is call your district nurse when you've run out of pads. You haven't got her number - have you?'

'No...'

'I'll get it for you.'

Peter logged back into the computer. As he was reading out the phone number to the old woman, Ms Rivers and Ms Sether entered the room. 'What are you doing on the computer? Didn't I specifically say that you weren't to use it?'

Peter finished reading out the phone number.

'Who did you get the pass code from?'

He didn't answer. He was no Sherlock Holmes, but he had received the distinct impression that she and Stephanie hated having Tracey there. You didn't even have to be a Miss Marple, Columbo or Kojak to figure that out. Tracy probably didn't want the job anyway. Perhaps she had been forced on to it by some government scheme. But just in case Tracey wanted financial security, Peter kept his mouth shut.

'Who gave you the pass code?'

He remained silent.

***

Peter glumly walked down Rutland Gardens. At the end of the day, he had been informed that they had found someone in the hospital to replace him. A month's work thrown away. Always remember, he sighed to himself: Just say no!

He stopped and turned round... No one... Weird... He could have sworn he was being watched... It's easy to be paranoid, he thought, when the whole world's against you...

EIGHT

'The question is...' thought Bryan, 'where's Gavin?' He had been calling him and emailing him for the past half hour, but Gavin hadn't got back to him. He wasn't by his desk... And he wasn't under it...

Normally, Bryan couldn't give a shit about Gavin's location, but his own P.A. had got sick again. What to do... What to do... At some point in the day, Gavin would have to go to Chuck's office... The best thing would be to stand outside the room and wait...

This proved to be a good tactic. Gavin appeared - laden with paperwork and resigned to the fact that there was no way he could avoid Bryan - save getting out the window and climbing across to his boss's room. Bryan patted his shoulder and gave him his most realistic looking smile. 'Gavin, hi... Tried to call you... Could you do me a favour? I've run out of cigarettes. Could you run out and get me a pack?'

Again?! All day Bryan had been barraging him with calls requesting him to type up documents and bring him coffee on top of all he had to do for Chuck. 'I'm not your P.A., Bryan.'

The smile remained suspended on Bryan's face. 'I never said you were... I was asking you to do that... as a *favour*.'

'Smoking isn't even permitted on the premises. Getting you cigarettes does not constitute work relating to the activities of Harlem Enterprises..'

'But I need cigarettes...'

'In that case, the only suggestion I can make is that you get them yourself.'

'Thanks...' said Bryan, 'I'll *remember* that.'

Gavin knocked on Chuck's door and entered. What had he done? he thought. He had made himself an enemy for life! Bryan of all people! Why couldn't he have got him the cigarettes? Hopefully they would have helped him die of cancer sooner, but *no*, he had to make a stand. He had to make a stand when there wasn't only him to worry about - when he had a wife and kids...

Maybe he should run after Bryan and offer to get him a *hundred* packets and pay for them himself. But it was too late, Chuck was now talking and he needed to take notes... Anyway... if he really thought about it: it was ridiculous. Why had he got himself so worked up? You have to draw the line somewhere. He had stated his case reasonably. He wasn't rude. It wasn't as if he hadn't done any favours for him that day. What sort of person could hold a grudge against him just because he refused to buy him a packet of cigarettes?

NINE

'...He was the most charming psychopath you could ever meet...' said an Irish voice. A pint of ale was picked up from the bar with a beer mat instantly attached to it to accompany the drink in its short but merry life.

'The Green Man' was no ordinary pub. It was an establishment that time forgot. More specifically, a Free House that time couldn't be bothered with.

Hidden on a deserted stretch of Holloway Road bordering on Archway with a sign hanging outside of a Green Man from a pedestrian crossing, its owner/manager referred to the place as his business empire - his chain, even though he only owned one pub.

Many different types of people came here. People who wanted to get drunk - they were in the majority. But there were customers, who didn't have sorrows to put in a sack and drown in a pond, but there were only two of them and they weren't regulars. The majority sat round in their professional cliques: market traders; bank robbers; policemen and teachers. Nobody drank as much as the teachers.

'...Apparently,' said Chris – fingering his sticky-out trendy hairstyle, 'when a broadcast wave is broadcast it doesn't disappear. It goes on up there for all eternity in space. So what you could do is get on a spaceship and catch a wave transmitted in 1969 and then you could get one of the episodes of 'Dad's Army' that the BBC wiped from their tapes.'

Ken's bushy eyebrows sternly twitched as he considered the idea. He pulled off his horn-rimmed glasses and rubbed the bridge of his nose. '...I don't know, Chris... There's a recession coming... It would cost too much.'

'Guys, I'm talking about *'Dad's Army'*! It would be worth it!'

Joseph butted in. 'Now if you were talking about 'Doctor Who', I'd be with you there...'

Nobody agreed or disagreed with Joseph because as was often the case, no one had been listening to him in the first place.

Chris was actually a qualified scientist with a BSC in biological chemistry and a wealth of voluntary experience under his belt. He might have been just the right person to discover a cure for cancer, but such was the amazing level of opportunity in the UK; he worked for a bank in a call centre that hadn't been relocated to India yet.

Ken on the other hand, had assumed that working for a charity would be a warmer, cuddlier experience. There he sat, cooped up with a hundred other people in another call centre that hadn't been relocated to India yet. (From then on he made a point of only ever buying *free-range* eggs.) No 'World Music', beaded hair or sandals - just patrols of power-suited people who had originally come from the business sector. Maybe they had hoped that working for a charity would be a warmer, cuddlier experience and were also wondering why it wasn't.

Like Chris, Ken still had to sell. He still had to read from a script - one that was flat and unconvincing. It took all his powers of voice inflection and every ounce of his charisma to get any people to part with their direct debit details. And the targets kept rising despite it never getting easier.

As a poet and occasional playwright, he had offered to rewrite the script, but the managers were happy with it the way it was.

The other day, supervisors had issued him with a warning about his inability to achieve the new target. 'We wouldn't ask you to aim for this new target unless we thought it was achievable,' they said, 'We wouldn't want to, but we would have to consider *letting* you go.'

So that night, Ken took his favourite pen out of his pen pot and did some rewriting. Out went all the dead bullshit and in went in something more poetic... with greater... immediacy. So this morning, using this new sales pitch, he tripled his success rate.

In the afternoon, halfway through winning over another person he had cold called; Nigel, his supervisor interrupted him. 'Ken, can I have a quick word with you?' Ken followed him into his office.

'Well, at last I've been noticed', thought Ken, 'Maybe they'll promote me.'

Already in the office sat Christine - Ken's manager.

Nigel sat down.

Neither Nigel or Christine offered Ken a seat. Christine shook her head with disappointment. 'We were listening in on your phone call. You weren't using the script.'

'I tripled my..'

Nigel shook his head. 'We told you we didn't want you to change the script, but you went off and did it anyway.'

'But I tripled my..'

'It's so unprofessional, you changing the script like that. The charity paid a *professional* writer to write that script, so the least you could do is use it.'

'I did use it, but it didn't work..'

'Really, you should have *made* it work. We wouldn't have given you the script if we didn't think you could make it work.'

'But I tried..'

'We know you write as a *hobby*, but that's really *no* excuse..'

'But I tripled my success rate!'

'Please don't raise your voice to me; I'm trying to tell you something. You can have your say later.' said Christine.

'But I..'

'Yeah, that's really unprofessional. She's trying to tell you something. You can have your say later.' said Nigel.

'But I..'

'Look, I'm sorry; I've discussed it with Nigel. You're simply not showing the right attitude, so we're afraid we're going to have to let you go.'

'But I tripled my..'

The security officer entered - carrying Ken's coat and his belongings in plastic bag.

'Yes,' said the manager, 'If you can go with Tim, we'll say no hard feelings - shall we?'

'But what about my say?'

Both the manager and the supervisor earnestly scrutinised their watches. 'Ken, we are busy people. We have other things to do. You have taken up a lot of our time already.'

'But..'

'Look, if you have got anything to say to us; then it's probably best if you write to us. We always value feedback from employees - even ex-employees.'

And before Ken had a chance to tell his managers in the most offensive terms available what he thought of them, he was escorted out.

Joseph was the most fulfilled of the group, but then again his ambition was to never work. His only real unfulfilled aspiration was to grow a proper moustache. Since the age of eighteen he had been growing it. A wispy and light coloured thing it was. He grew more substantial hair on his buttocks. From eighteen to twenty-five, it was his secret moustache - which only he knew about.

On his twenty-fifth birthday, he told his girlfriend that he had been growing a moustache behind her back and she said that's a funny place to grow a moustache. Eventually he split up with her because she grew a better one than he did.

With his long droopy hair and wispy goatee, he resembled more a person who performed the odd minor miracle than one who did the nine to five.

Today had been unsettling for him. It felt as if his last six-month review for his jobseekers claim had been only yesterday, but there he was again in the Job Centre being prescribed 'Restart'.

He didn't mind really. He regarded it as a minor inconvenience, but he was sure the Restart trainer was getting sick of the sight of him. 'Oh... it's *you*.' he would say. Joseph would probably ask him how little Jimmie and Sarah were doing; do his time and then resume his daytime occupation of contemplation and reading long books.

He knew he would come out of it relatively unscathed. He had gone through countless government training schemes, job placements and courses without a single job materializing. He was adept at website design, digital editing and computerised architecture, but his fingertips had yet to earn ten pee.

His was a barren field that grew no cash crops - no matter how much fertiliser was thrown on it. He did wonder why the job centre didn't just give up on him and carry on paying his benefit. Some psychometric test would surely prove that his personality was not suited to a paid occupation.

The friends philosophised and drank. They were about to discuss the hypothetical scenario: if you weren't raised by a pack of wolves but were adopted by them at the age of ten whether your table manners would deteriorate; when Peter strolled in; pulled a stool from another table and joined them. 'I don't know, maybe we could learn something from the beasts of the forest.'

'Thought you were seeing your folks tonight?' asked Chris - rearranging his sticky-out trendy hairstyle.

'I did see them... but I decided to cut my visit short.'

'You can't win' said Joseph, 'If you defend yourself - you hurt their feelings. They're old and frail. It's okay if they hurt your feelings - you're young and strong you can take it...'

***

'...Heard the story about the guy who has an almighty row with his wife, puts on his jacket and walks out the front door?' said Chris, 'She asks him where the *Hell* he thinks he's going and he says he's off to buy some cigarettes, bitch, and then he never comes back. She can find no trace of him anywhere - vanished off the face of the universe..'

'Yes, I've heard it.' said Peter.

'Do you know why? Because it happened more than once! It happened loads of times! Some of the wives hired private detectives to investigate and in all these cases of disappearance it always turned out that the husbands always smoked the same brand!'

'I don't remember that bit.' said Ken.

'The wives tried to take the cigarette company to court, but they couldn't prove anything and they weren't exactly sure what they were trying to prove. Was the company abducting these blokes? Who knows? The company came up with the theory that in these cases it was the same man and that he happened to be a prolific bigamist.'

'That's bad, but what about the dinosaurs?' said Joseph.

'What about the dinosaurs?' said Ken.

'Why did they *really* die? I reckon it was a *conspiracy...*'

***

'Time Gentlemen, please!' said the barmen. 'Finish up your drinks please! Finish up your drinks!' they said - coaxing the most reluctant to at least drink a little quicker. One tired barman noticed a young bearded man with a practically full pint that he had served to him two hours ago. 'Finish up your drinks! Haven't you got no homes to go to?!'

'No.' said the young bearded man, 'I'm homeless.'

'Tough!' said the barman, 'Finish up your drink!'

Peter, Ken, Chris and Joseph checked their watches in disbelief. Was it really that time yet again? Chris rearranged his hair. 'Did you know that dog saliva is the *best* saliva in the world?'

'Can't say I've tried it,' said Ken.

'In the First World War dogs were used to lick the wounds of injured soldiers because of the antiseptic qualities of their spittle. If you think about it; it's a bloody miracle - the antiseptic qualities of their spit - especially if you consider what dogs do with their tongues..'

'Can you finish up your drinks?' said a barman standing at their table.

'Yeah, yeah, we're finishing up.' said Peter.

'I wish they wouldn't do that, it completely destroys the flow of conversation.' said Ken, 'So... what's cat's saliva like?'

'Overrated..'

'Really, I'm surprised - especially since cats also lick their..'

'Can you finish up your drinks?'

'Yeah, yeah, we're finishing up.' said Peter.

***

'...If... If I had a cutlery shop, I'd refuse to let Uri Geller in. I'd... I'd have a sign outside banning him.' slurred Chris.

'Th-that's, th-that's not nice - that is - that's prejudiced – that is...' said Joseph.

'I don't want all my spoons going floppy! If, if if all my spoons went floppy - I could go bust - unless I sold the spoons to a Salvador Dali Museum!'

The same barman approached but now with a redder face. 'Finish up your drinks and get out!!!'

'Oh, you want us to *leave* - why didn't you say?' said Peter.

The lights were switched off.

***

With their heads hunched forward, Peter and his friends marched through the heavy rain, their destination: the chippie. They looked forward to its shelter and its greasy warmth. And there it was - its yellow sign and bright interior cheerfully lighting up the darkness - an oasis in the gloom.

They shot a glance through the window. They had come at a good time. The chips had been freshly fried - chunky chips - proper chips - not French fries. And the curry sauce had been freshly microwaved, always hard to resist - despite the consequences on the toilet the next day.

***

They entered. The aroma was heavenly. Surely Heaven would smell of vinegar and grease. They joined the end of the queue. Only ten people - it wouldn't be long... All your problems dissolved away when you bit into those chips.

And as they contemplated this culinary Nirvana, a large, drunken, muscular twenty-five year-old who had been playing on the video game machine, barged in front of them. He was the type of guy who only had one eyebrow, which stretched maliciously from one side of his face to the other, but Peter chose not to be deterred by this fact.

'Excuse me...'

'Peter, forget about it!' whispered Ken.

'No, it's the principle!'

'I wouldn't mess with him if I was you,' said Joseph, 'Have you looked at his score on the video game?'

The mono eye-browed youth ignored Peter, so Peter tapped him on the shoulder and spoke louder. 'Excuse me!'

The young man turned to him. 'What?! *What*?! What you touching me for?'

'You've pushed in front of us.'

'No I didn't.'

'Yes you did!'

'So? What *you* going to do about it?'

'Why do *I* have do anything about it? Why can't you wait your place in the queue?'

The one eye-browed guy shrugged his shoulders as it was now his undeserved turn to be served.

'I'm not going to tolerate this!' said Peter.

'It'll hardly make any difference!' said Chris.

'Cod and chips..' said the one eye-browed guy to the chip man.

'Excuse me! It should be us you're serving!' said Peter, 'He pushed in front!'

'Oh yeah?' said the chip man - disinterested.

'Yeah! And if you serve him ahead of us then you'll lose the custom of four people forever!'

'What'd you say that for!' whispered Ken.

'Is that right?' said the chip man.

'Yes!' said Peter.

Taking his time, the chip man served the one eye-browed guy his cod and chips.

'Right!' said Peter, 'We're going!'

The man turned to them and said: 'He's a mate, so I couldn't give a shit. Far as I'm concerned you lot can sling your hook. You're all banned.'

The friends left the shop without a chip or even a gherkin to their name. 'Great! Thanks Pete!' said Ken, 'That was a fantastic chip shop and now we can't go there! Couldn't you have kept your mouth shut just for once?'

'Where we going to eat?' said Chris.

'Er... Burger Express?' said Peter.

'Their chips taste like excrement!' said Ken.

'Everywhere else is shut now.' said Joseph, 'I know you were angry, but you shouldn't have made us suffer..'

'I'm sorry,' said Peter, 'I'll make you some toast and haloumi...'

TEN

It had been a long wait, but at last, after queuing two hours, it was Zizanie's turn to use the village tap. The girl positioned an old battered bucket while the man who had been in front placed the bottles he had filled into his backpack. Drip! And then no drop. No drip and then no drop. She shook the tap, but no more came.

The man in front shrugged his shoulders and slopped off. One measly drop: that was her reward for being patient. She felt like crying, but knew that would be a waste of water.

She hurled her bucket at the gigantic security wall. By it, a friendly sign proclaimed in Philippine: 'NO ENTRY! KEEP OUT! TRESPASSERS WILL BE PROSECUTED!' And in case that was too ambiguous there was another line: 'WE HAVE ARMED SECURITY GUARDS!'

The wall had been present most of her childhood. She couldn't remember a time it had not been there. As far as she knew, no one had scaled the barrier.

She went to pick up the bucket and a golf ball narrowly missed her head. It thumped to the ground a foot away - leaving a dent.

She had heard about the golf balls that flew over the walls - raising sparks from the electrified barbed wire. Frowning and squinting, she tried to look at the wall as if she had X-ray vision. But her gaze could not penetrate the bricks and mortar. What happened beyond the wall - *apart* from golf? One day, one day, she told herself, she would get onto the other side. One day, she would defy the sign...

***

'...Easy does it...' said Brendan Kelly to his new student.

Chuck holed the ball. 'Fantastic!!'

The water sprinklers hissed - nourishing the green throughout the day. A monk walked past - talking to the grass. The 'Golf Course Hermit' was employed to encourage it's growth. 'Become stronger and more plentiful... Become stronger and more plentiful... Grow internally and externally...'

The sound of the sprinklers soothed Juan Sanchez. It took him back to another time and place - thirty years ago when he was nine.

His mother had been washing their old second-hand Volkswagen Beetle with a hose and sprayed water on him. (His father would have been washing the car had he not disappeared when he was five. He said that he was only popping out to buy a packet of cigarettes.) Then he got his water pistol and sprayed her back... And they had this brilliant water fight... They got drenched...

His mother's dress had got completely translucent. She looked so radiant in that sunlight. It was as if the sun worshipped her and who could blame it? He remembered that he used to think his mother was the most beautiful woman in the world.

When he was slightly older, he used to have dreams that he and his mother were in bed together - making mad passionate love. He always had a deep sense of shame in those dreams. Okay, he was having sex with an attractive lady, but she was his mom! He couldn't show off about it with his mates. Any *fool* could have sex with their mother if you nag them long enough. 'Mom, *please*!!!! Mom, *PLEASE*!!!!!!!!!'

'Juan!!' said Brendan, 'I said a number five iron! Juan!! We don't have until Kingdom come!'

'What? What?'

'Wake up! A number five iron - if you can be so good!'

Juan fished in the bag and handed Chuck a golf club.

Brendan inspected the club and handed it back to Juan. 'I said: a number five!'

'Sorry...' The correct club was handed.

Chuck practiced his swing. A helicopter could be heard overhead. The vehicle hovered a few feet off the ground and out stepped Mr X.

Chuck waved.

Mr X yelled: 'Nice golf course!'

'Thanks, had it for five years. Thought it was about time I started using it!' shouted Chuck. He turned to his trainer and his caddie. 'Okay, you two - take five.'

'See you later, Chuck.' said Brendan, 'Juan, I'm telling you; you got to get your shit together. You can daydream in Mexico, but not over here..'

Chuck sliced the ball and turned to Mr X. 'So, lay it on the line. What have you got?'

'Not much.' said Mr X.

'Man, that's a bummer. You sure you got no names? I can't have the wrong lyrics appearing on the monitor again.'

With a manly stagger, they ventured further down the course.

'As far as our investigations have gone, it looks unlikely that anybody in Head Office deliberately sabotaged your show.'

'I don't believe that for a second. I reckon it was Gavin.'

'We've found no evidence to support that theory.'

'I bet you'll find I'm right... Now let's rock and roll!' said Chuck potting the ball.

***

Three months ago, Gavin had called Chuck's office. It was 2.15 pm. 'Chuck, my father's been rushed into hospital - I need to go.'

'Sure, sure,' said Chuck, 'Did you book the hotel and send the invites?'

'No Chuck, I haven't had time..'

'Could you do that before you go? You see, the conference's pretty soon, so it's important..'

'Yeah, I'll do that. Okay.'

An hour later, Gavin called Chuck again. 'Right, that's done, so I'll be off..'

'Sure, sure, by the way, have you typed up the dictation on 'New Roads Ahead in Corporate Strategy'?'

'No Chuck, I haven't. My father's in a pretty bad way..'

'Then don't worry, just that it needs to be put in the conference brochure pretty soon and the brochures have to be printed Monday..'

'No, no, I'll do it. It shouldn't take long.'

A few minutes later Gavin called Chuck again. 'Okay, that's finished, so I'll be off..'

'Sure, sure, send him my love, oh wait a minute, have you emailed the new draft of the contract to Silverman?'

'No, er, I've turned my computer off..'

'Don't worry about it. The only thing is that it's going to be signed tonight and I'd like the lawyers to give it a last look over, but you go..'

'No, no, it's fine, I'll do it now.' Gavin turned the computer back on and sent the email. He thought better of calling Chuck and rushed to hospital.

'Apparently,' said Bryan to Chuck the next day, 'Gavin only missed his father by five minutes. If he had got there a little sooner he would have had a chance to say goodbye.'

'Five minutes?' said Chuck.

'Yep... five minutes... That's what I *heard*...'

'Bum rap...'

Gavin returned from compassionate leave to provide the same high level of service, but something irked Chuck. After pacing up and down his office had done no good, he wandered off to Bryan's to pace on his carpet.

Bryan was sat by his desk - typing a report. 'You okay?'

'Sure... sure, dude...'

'You know, Chuck... if there's... *anything* you need to talk about... The door's always open.'

'I don't need to talk to *you!*'

Bryan stopped typing. '...*What* is it?'

Chuck slumped down on a chair. '...It's *Gavin.*'

'What's he done?'

'It's... it's nothing...'

'Chuck, you might as well spill the beans... because this is obviously... *troubling* you.'

'Gavin... he's... he's all *sad*... It's getting me down... I can't enjoy myself with his sad mug all over the place.'

Bryan pursed his lips and squinted his eyes. '*Sad*, huh? He's acting *sad* - you say?'

Chuck grimly nodded.

'I think I can see what's behind it... He's trying to make you feel guilty about being deprived of his final moments with his dying father.'

'Is that it?'

'I'm afraid so... The bastard hasn't got the guts to blame himself for being too late so he's *blaming* you.'

'I only gave him a few tasks to do before going to the hospital..'

'Of course... It wasn't as if you gave him... a *lot* of tasks to do before going to hospital... was it?'

'Mmmm... there were a few...'

'Anyway... if it was too much for him then he should have *insisted* on leaving earlier... He didn't *have* to do those tasks - did he?'

'No...'

'It wasn't as if you were holding a gun to his head and saying that he had to *do* those tasks and *miss* his final moments with his dying father.'

'No... I didn't hold a gun to his head.'

'I know... You didn't hold a gun to his head - *at all*.'

Chuck's conscience began to clear.

'It's not as if you would have sacked him if he hadn't done those tasks...' said Bryan.

'No...' said Chuck less convincingly.

'There you go... He should have been more assertive... He should have said to you: 'Chuck, I'm not doing those tasks. I'm going to hospital to see my father. I'll do those tasks *after* he's died...' What is he... a man or a mouse?'

'A mouse! A mouse, dude!'

'It's not *your* problem he's such a pussy!'

'No it isn't. It isn't my problem *at all*!'

'That's right... I bet he thought you'd sack him if you didn't do those tasks... I bet that's what he thought... What sort of *monster* does he think you are?'

'He thinks I'm a monster?'

'Probably... He probably thinks that you're scum... that you're some sort of psychopath...'

'He thinks that about me? The son of a bitch!'

'What you've got to consider, Chuck, is: whether it's safe for you to continue to employ a person who can't stand the sight of you? What's a man like that - who hates you and hates you - what's he going to do to you?'

'What's he going to do to me, Bryan?'

'Revenge can take many shapes and forms...'

'What's he going to do?'

'You have to admit... he is party to a lot of *'sensitive'* information...'

'He's going to leak my secrets to the press?'

'There's probably no point speculating about it and there's probably nothing to worry about, but get this... I understand human psychology... A human being can only contain those feelings of resentment and loathing and wanting you to die for so long... Sooner or later he's going to make you suffer for what he *thinks* you've done to him, but then again... he might not.'

'What - what should I do, dude?'

'Sack him.'

Sack him? thought Chuck. Could he sack him for being 'sad'? 'Sack him?' said Chuck, 'He's got a wife and kids..'

'He should have thought about that before hating you.'

Chuck shook his head. 'He's more likely to go the media if I do that...'

'I wouldn't risk having such a man as my personal assistant.' said Bryan, 'I wouldn't be able to trust him as much as I can throw him and I've got a bad back so I can't throw him any sizeable distance...'

'Mmm...' said Chuck, 'I'll keep him away from my more 'sensitive' projects...'

'Maybe...' said Bryan; 'Maybe he's had his revenge already. Maybe he had his revenge *before* his father died. Maybe it was him who put the wrong lyrics on the monitor. And as if that wasn't enough... He might do... something else *as well*!'

It made sense, thought Chuck; Gavin had probably always hated him and put the wrong lyrics on the monitor as revenge before his father died, but he wasn't going to do anything rash. He was going to wait for evidence first. But once Mr X had unearthed it, boy... Gavin would really have something to look sad about!

***

Chuck holed the ball. 'Did you check the concert security footage? Cause I'm sure you'd find something in that concert security footage.'

'Yes,' sighed Mr X, 'I checked the concert security footage...'

***

The concert security footage had been played backwards and forwards, forwards and backwards, sideways and upside down, but no treachery had been visible. 'Hey, zoom in on the left corner of the picture over there!' said Mr X in the screening room. The technician zoomed in. 'More, zoom in more...' The technician zoomed in more. 'More...' The technician zoomed in more.

'Do you want me to zoom in anymore?' asked the technician.

'No, no, that's fine...' said Mr X as he stared at the screen. He slowly turned and smiled back at the technician. 'Now have you ever seen a pair of titties like those?'

***

Brendan and Juan stood by a palm tree - participating in their favourite pastime of blowing cigar smoke into each other's faces.

The wind was in Brendan's favour. Juan coughed. He had had enough of Brendan's criticism and his smoke. He yanked the cigar from Brendan's mouth; stamped on it and said: 'This golf course isn't big enough for the both of us.'

'What're *you* going to do about it?'

'I propose that we play three rounds of golf. The one who loses; leaves the country. The one who wins; stays.'

'Okay, you're on...'

'Alright, I'll meet you here at nine...'

***

The floodlights went on. Brendan spotted Juan in the distance. 'Decided to show up - did we?'

'Someone called, I got delayed..'

'Sure you didn't have second thoughts?'

'Let's play.'

Juan teed off.

'Not bad, Juan, not bad... But not bad - isn't *good* enough...'

Brendan struck the ball... It went further. This was not going to be easy.

Further on, Juan found himself in the bunker. Brendan wandered over to 'encourage' him as he practised his swing. 'Quite a fix you've got yourself into... Never mind... I'm certain you'll get out of it before dawn...' Juan's next shot failed to extricate the ball from its unenviable position. 'Maybe not...' said Brendan, 'You know what; perhaps you should have used a number five iron...'

Brendan won the first round hands down. 'Sure you don't want to give up? You're only going to get *worse* as you get more tired...'

Fuck you, thought Juan, fuck you!! He had lost at a lot of things: marriage and rounds of golf. He never lived up to the promise he showed in his early teens, but this was a game he was going to win. 'I said we were going to do *three* rounds...'

The next round was far closer. Hole after hole, hour after hour, they competed equally. Only by a narrow margin was Juan victorious.

'Well...' said Brendan, 'That was lucky...'

By the third round, Juan was trouncing his adversary. Brendan seemed to be losing concentration and confidence. He had even dropped the mind games and had grown silent.

Their eyes grew red with the dawn. The green was bathed in an orange light. Both players were exhausted. Juan stood a yard away from the final hole he needed to conclude the game. He practised his swing.

By his mid-thirties, he had resigned himself to the fact that the 'Grand Open' was never going to happen for him. He was never in a position to get enough practice to get to world standard. Despite all his efforts, he couldn't overcome his fairly humble background. But he could overcome being bullied. He could overcome being treated like shit. His moment of triumph would come.

'The deal's off.' said Brendan.

'But you agreed..'

'I'm not going to leave a well-paid job just because I've lost some stupid game..'

'But you said..'

'Was anything written on paper?'

'No.'

'Did anyone witness what I said to you?'

'No.'

'There you go then.'

'But..'

'But what?!'

'But that's not *right*.'

'What?!'

'You should keep your word!'

'Oh shut up, you stupid motherfucker!'

'What did you say?'

'Motherfucker! You're a stupid motherfucker!'

Before thinking about it, Juan whacked Brendan's head with a number six iron. 'Crack!'

***

Juan's 'Pringle' jumper was splattered in blood. Brendan lay on the green - completely still. Blood poured from his head into the eighteenth hole - more copiously than the liquid that flowed from the tap beyond the wall.

Juan shook. He didn't remember striking him with the club... But he must have... And maybe he should have used a number five iron... He took out his cell phone. He knew it was pointless, but he wanted to speak to her... He *needed* to talk to her - even though she had died years ago. 'Mom... Please answer the phone... Mom, *please*!!!' Unmoved by his plight, the water sprinklers hissed on...

ELEVEN

On a path near The Mall in Central Park, a six foot seven, portly, ginger haired man in chequered shirt and faded jeans waited by a bronze of two large eagles with wings spread swooping down on a trapped goat. Their talons were sunk into the back of the half-dead goat they were about to devour.

He swept his mop of hair away from his eyes and watched the people pass by. Anxious parents making sure their children did not stray from the path and get raped and murdered. Young couples walking hand in hand before their first recriminations. Young couples after their first recriminations - wondering what they ever saw in each other in the first place. Birdsong and blossom was in the air... Yes... it was a good day for waiting...

The man's patient wait was rewarded by the woman's arrival. Dressed in red hipster trousers, a tee shirt and a fluffy white jacket, she was so beautiful that even the flowers in the park thought she was a bitch.

'Hi.' she said.
'Hi. Had trouble finding the place?'
'No, been here before.'
'Right... Nice here - isn't it?'
'Yes.'
'Yeah... I like it...'
'So... what's the next assignment?'
'Mr Merriman will tell you... Follow me...'

They walked through the park. It had been six months since she had first started working for the organisation and she had never met her boss. She imagined he was one of those busy aloof types - which suited her fine. Previous managers had been way too 'friendly'.

They reached a fountain. A weird green substance gushed out from the mermaid's mouth as if she had spent the night drinking cocktails.

Near by, a crowd, maybe twenty people, stood - watching a silver-faced performance artist doing a robot mime.

The ginger haired man stopped. His eyes searched the area. 'He should be here...' He shielded his eyes from the sunlight. 'Now this is the hard part...' He squinted and scrutinised all the faces gathered there. He looked confused. 'Mmmm...'

'What's wrong?' asked the woman.

'I might not be able to recognise him.'

'Haven't you met him before?'

'Plenty of times, but he's always in disguise.'

He went into the crowds and began to sniff them. Eyebrows were raised. People walked away. Undeterred, the man continued sniffing until he stopped sniffing and returned to the woman.

'That's him! I can tell by his aftershave!' he said as he pointed at the silver painted performance artist.

The large man waved to him and shouted: 'Hey Opus!'

An irked expression appeared on the mime artist's silver face. He bowed to some muted applause and picked up the collection hat that had been resting on the ground. The man put on his coat and walked up to the pair. 'Keep your voice down...'

He scooped up the coins that had been thrown into his hat and poured them into his pockets. 'I'd prefer it if you didn't call my name out in public.'

His was a refined, cultivated English voice - though maybe a little *too* cultivated and maybe a little *too* refined as if it may not have been his original accent.

He turned to the woman and stood transfixed. His pupils dilated. It was *her*. It didn't look like her. It didn't sound like her. But he *knew* it was her... '...I've been waiting for you for *so* long...'

How long it had been - since he had been graced by her presence. Six hundred and fifty-six years to be precise. Twelve lifetimes, he had been waiting, twelve lifetimes he had spent searching for her - twelve *lonely* lifetimes.

The last time they chanced to meet was when they were tied to a stake on top of a pile of wood and were being burnt for witchcraft. His accurate weather predictions had proved costly.

They chose a rendezvous to meet in the next life, but she somehow managed to knock her head on a window ledge in the spirit world and forget the arrangement.

In all his incarnations, he traveled thousands of miles to find her. Then once he had reached his true love's domain he encountered the small problem of not speaking the same language. And then there was the social disparity to contend with.

An Empress was she, then a Warrior-Queen, assorted members of royalty, a philosopher, scientist and political reformer.

His incarnations tended to be lower: eunuch, village idiot or village idiot's assistant, but he tried not to let the social disparity obstruct their happiness. But her bodyguards did.

It was all he could do to catch glimpses (while standing on tiptoes in crowds or jumping onto people's shoulders) of her in carriages - leading Royal processions, in galleons - sailing away or floating upwards in hot air balloons.

And now here she was... So close he could almost touch her. Better not, he thought. There was so much to say - so much. But he didn't say anything. Experience had taught him to be circumspect about his past lives.

The vision of loveliness said: 'Sorry, if I was late.'

'No need to apologise. You're here and that's what's important. If you were somewhere else then I'd be upset... Tell me, do you believe in reincarnation?'

'Maybe.' said the woman, 'How about you?'

The silver faced man pretended not to hear the question and wandered over to a rosebush and sniffed some flowers. The woman and the ginger-haired man followed. 'Whenever I get the opportunity, I sniff a rose. You should always sniff a rose - if you get the chance - even in periods of war...'

Pangs of hunger prompted the woman. 'It's been a while since you've paid me... Could you give me my wages?'

'Ahhhhh... yes...' he said. He emptied out the mass of coins in his coat pockets and handed them to her. 'Sorry, I've only got small change.'

'How am I meant to carry this?'

He took off his coat and rested it on her shoulders. 'You could carry them in this... Anyway, for your next assignment I need you to...'

TWELVE

'Happy Birthday.' said Peter listlessly to his reflection in the bathroom mirror.

It was a Saturday. He felt that it might as well had been any other Saturday than one coinciding with the date of his birth.

Overall his life had not changed that much from last month. The post had arrived an hour ago, but his expectations were low. It could wait.

Eventually he shuffled to the porch to have his low expectations confirmed. A phone bill... Whoopee... A dodgy 'You have won a prize!' letter where you had to ring a premium rate line number to find out if you won a car or *perhaps* a worthless voucher... Another dodgy 'You have won a prize!' letter from a different criminal gang, wondering why he hadn't rung its premium rate number. In large print it stated: 'YOU HAVE <u>DEFINITELY</u> WON A PRIZE!' Perhaps the letter would have appeared more convincing if the lettering was a little larger and stated: 'THIS IS <u>DEFINITELY</u> NOT A CON! HONEST GUV!'

Peter tore the letters up. What else was there? Aha! Something in a pink envelope that could possibly be a Birthday card - a solitary Birthday card - addressed to him. (Ken, Chris and Joseph would probably have a card for him at the pub, but he didn't expect blokes to post him one.) He opened it. It was from his parents. Some job-cuttings from 'The Times' fell out.

'Thanks.'

He tore up the jobs adverts.

One more thing remained to be opened: a magazine in a plastic wrapper - addressed to him... Didn't look like junk mail... The cover was beautiful. An Arts and Current Affairs magazine... He flicked through the pages... Well designed and witty... Fascinating articles... Interviews with artists who had been recluses for years... Amazing... How did they get them to talk? He had always wanted to read a magazine like this. It was almost as if the magazine had been designed with him in mind. And stapled to the cover, was a ticket to the Abstract Expressionist art exhibition that was on at the Royal Academy. He had been meaning to go to it. Those tickets cost a bomb. The only problem was that the expiry date on the ticket was for today... Right... he'd better get dressed and go there.

THIRTEEN

Peter nervously walked through the gates of North Finchley High School for Boys. Lightning crackled in the night sky. He wondered why he was going to the reunion. Try as he might he couldn't recall any happy memories linked to the place. Surely he was far too young to get sentimental. Yes, even at thirty! Bats flew out of the hole in the school roof. If anything the place seemed more forbidding than he remembered and more dilapidated.

The doors creaked as he entered. No, there was a reason - a very good reason he was going to this event. He was confronting his fears. There was a bully in his class who had persecuted him for the whole four years under the misapprehension that he was Jewish.

'But I'm not Jewish!' Peter would protest after suffering Darren Sumner's violent anti-Semitism.

'Yes you are - you lying Jew!' And he'd punch him again.

'Look, this is a photo of me being christened in a Greek Orthodox Church!'

'You're Jewish! You've got a big nose!'

'But so do you!'

'What?! You calling me a Yid?!' And he'd punch him again.

Once he had ruined a picture of Peter's that he had been working on for weeks by casually flicking paint at it. Peter needed to tell him that he had no right to treat him like that and then Darren who would probably be far more reasonable by now would explain why his behaviour had been so bad (father beating him, impoverished childhood, broken home, learning difficulties, brain damage, needing to be sent to a special school - all that) and then he would forgive him and then move on. This unresolved relationship could be the reason he wasn't succeeding in his art.

He had read an article in a magazine that said that people who had been bullied at school tend not to earn as much as people who weren't bullied. It all made sense.

He walked through a corridor sporadically lit by flickering fluorescent tube lighting. The place was deserted.

He checked his watch. He wasn't early. He checked the invite. No, it was the right day. The music was now audible. It sounded like the insipid hits of his adolescence, but not as he recalled them - far more distorted and creepy. He entered the hall. Dusty banners on the walls proclaimed the year his class finished at the school. The balloons were covered in dust and so were the plastic cups.

Where was everyone? In the corner, by the cobwebby, moldy punch bowl, he could make out the distinctive huge profile of his adversary. Peter drew in a deep breath and approached him. 'It's Darren - isn't it?' The huge hulk didn't deny it. Possibly he was too ashamed to talk.

'...Peter Papapanos. I don't know if the name means anything to you. You made life very difficult for me here.'

He didn't even move. He still only offered Peter his profile. Probably he was too embarrassed to look him in the face. '...As far as I'm concerned you had no right to treat me the way you did.'

Still the hulk said nothing.

Peter thought he could possibly detect a faint glint of contrition in his left eye. '...I've come here to tell you tonight: I forgive you.' He held out his hand. 'Let's shake and consider the whole thing forgotten.'

Darren looked at Peter's hand, grinned and grabbed it. His grip was strong. Peter already thought the handshake had gone on for far too long when Darren shifted his whole torso towards him and revealed that the other half of his face had no skin and an eye with a maggot crawling out of it. Peter screamed: 'Arrrrrrrrgh!' yanked his hand away and ran.

At first, he tried calling out for help, but as the air in his lungs decreased he couldn't run and call out. A choice had to be made. He chose running. He looked behind him.

Unoriginal as Hell, Darren had donned a pair of metallic gloves with razor sharp blades coming out from the knuckles. Laughing dementedly, he soon caught up. He grabbed hold of the remaining hair on Peter's crown as he pulled away.

'You bastard! You've made me even balder!'

Down an unlit staircase, they ran. Luckily, the fluorescent Harlem logo on Peter's trainers helped him judge the distances from one step to the next - otherwise he would have fallen down. He jumped the nine remaining steps and landed on the floor, his trainers taking the impact. From the periphery of his vision, he spotted an exit sign and gasping, ran towards it.

The doors were now in Peter's sight. With only yards to go, Darren leapt upon Peter's shoulders as if he had been conserving his energy. It was as if he had been playing with him.

Pinning him down onto the floor, Darren drew his bloody pus-covered face nearer. His filthy breath made Peter retch.

With grotesque relish, Darren smiled at him and ripped his own eyeball from its socket. It was obvious that an organ donation from close at hand was going to be sought.

Peter kneed him in the testicles. And with the full force of his trainers, Peter kicked him there and then again for luck and ran to the exit.

The doors wouldn't budge. Darren was catching up. Peter pounded the doors with his fists. Darren was nearer. He gave the doors a kick and then another. With Darren's blades barely an inch away from Peter's throat, he kicked once more and the doors opened and daylight streaked in.

***

Daylight streaked in through the curtains as Peter woke. He got up and opened a window. Fresh autumn air cleansed the room of his trauma.

For a second he thought he could smell burnt toast. Strange... No one who lived in this place got up early enough to have breakfast before going to work. The carcinogenic odour faded quickly.

What a nightmare, he thought. What a nightmare. He rubbed his sleep-crusted eyes and looked at his watch. 7.14 am. It had only been an hour since he had gone to bed. Due to a lack of viable alternatives, he had been working the midnight 'til five am shift at a West End 'All-Day' restaurant that week. The twenty-four hour society certainly messed up your sleep patterns. He lay back in bed... and listened. He could hear the Brontosaurus roar of the Silver link train to Barking and the whirr of the almost extinct milk float.

A thought struck him. He looked under the bed. He thought so. His trainers were not the Harlem make. Mystified, he went back to sleep.

FOURTEEN

An old song played on the jukebox - some Glam Rock anthem. It had been a while since anyone had heard it - the jukebox having been broken the past three years. The song transported customers back to a happier, more carefree time. They wished that the song would last forever so that they could remain in that halcyon era.

Suddenly the song stuck. '...dudes, dudes, dudes, dudes, dudes...' Their wish had been granted.

Within earshot of the song, stood Ken, Chris and Joseph by the entrance - puffing away on their cigarettes.

'...Apparently, there's this tribe who hardly have to work.' said Chris, 'They don't have to fight and struggle to survive. They take the fruit off the trees and the fish out of the lakes and then spend the rest of the day swimming, doing tribal rituals and having fun. They don't have to strive or compete. The fish and fruit replenish themselves without them lifting a finger. They enjoy life. It must be the real Garden of Eden they're living in.'

'Sounds great,' said Joseph.

Ken wasn't listening. After six pints, his sorrows still wouldn't drown. They floated to the surface like polystyrene slabs for learner swimmers. The honeymoon period in his new job had been short - in fact, there hadn't been one. 'I'm going to kill her! I'm going to kill my manager!' he snarled.

'No you're not.' said Chris.

'No, I will. I will. I was that close to putting something in her coffee today.'

'What were you going to put into her coffee?'

'Tipp-Ex! I was going to pour Tipp-Ex into her coffee!'

'Don't you think it would have been obvious that you poured it into her drink?'

'I would have stirred it.'

'I think it might have floated to the top.'

'I would have stirred it.'

'It's a different consistency. I've tried.'

'Then, then I'll gradually get her addicted to drugs! I'll pour heroin and Crack and ganja and mushrooms - all of that stuff into her coffee instead!'

'Isn't it possible she might not drink it with all those things in it?' said Chris.

'Why don't you resign?' said Joseph.

'And give her the satisfaction?'

'Do you think she'd really care?' said Chris.

'It'd probably be quicker if I put a bomb in her coffee..'

'But you'd end up in prison and then you'd be fucked.'

'Not necessarily, I'd work really hard sewing mail bags and become a trustee and then work very hard until they promoted me to warden and then work very hard until they promoted me to governor and then I'd walk out.'

'You should let your success be your revenge.' said Joseph.

'Okay, I'll work very hard until I'm promoted to Managing Director of the Call Centre and then I'll sack her..'

'Perhaps you'll win a poetry competition and she'd be jealous of that.'

'I'm far too *good* to win a poetry competition. Only the wankiest, most boring, most pretentious shit has a cat in Hell's chance. No, what I need to do is shag my manager's husband. That would rattle her. He sometimes comes to the office at lunch. Quite handsome - looks younger than her. That's right, I'll shag him. Have it filmed and project the film of it on the office wall during the office Christmas party... Though it's going to be hard... because I'm not gay and I don't think he is either..'

Peter joined them; stuck his hands deep into his coat pockets and pulled out a packet of Zoo cigarettes. He took one out. 'Got a light?' Ken handed him his lighter. 'You've joined the fold. Congratulations.'

'It's not congratulations.' said Chris, 'You were the only guy at uni who didn't smoke. How come you're smoking now?'

Peter flicked the lighter. 'Because I've seen the light... Girls smoke. They don't want to go out with some whinging self-righteous fucker who talks to her about Cancer. They want someone they can smoke with. The way I see it - you have a choice. You either die from cancer or you die from loneliness. I know what I'd choose.' He lit his cigarette and took a drag.

'I don't know how you can smoke that brand.' said Ken, 'They taste horrible.'

'It's because of the marketing.' said Chris.

'I heard a rumour that it's a subsidiary company of that Chuck Harlem that makes them.' said Joseph.

'Really?' said Peter - not bothering to feign interest.

Ken took out his wallet. 'I'll get the drinks. What'll you have?'

'A Harlem Humdinger.'

'Right, why not ask for the most expensive drink in the place?!'

'You did ask what I want and that's what I want.'

'You don't normally ask for that!'

'Don't get me a drink then if you don't want to.'

'No, no, that's fine. A Humdinger it is then..'

FIFTEEN

After handing Gavin an audiotape, Chuck noticed that his P.A. hadn't gone and was still standing in his office - wistfully sighing to himself. 'What?! Is there something you need to tell me, dude?'

'Sometimes I wonder why we bother, Chuck.' said Gavin, 'All this fighting and struggling and competing in life - what's it all for? Apparently, there's this tribe that don't fight or struggle at all. They hardly have to work. They take the fruit off the bushes and trees and the fish out of the lakes and then spend the rest of the day swimming, doing tribal rituals and having fun. There's no stress - there's no turmoil. The fish and fruit replenish themselves without them lifting a finger. They enjoy living. I wouldn't be surprised if the place they're living in was the real Garden of Eden.'

Chuck stood up. '...They don't work?' He slowly shook his head with incredulity. '...They've *got* to work.'

'They don't need to, it's like I said..'

'People work... That's what they do.' He rotated the globe parked on his desk. 'Show me where this tribe is. I'll do something about it... If we sold their fish to England and their fruit to Tasmania, I could sell them hamburgers and cigarettes.'

'Do you think that's such a good idea?' said Gavin.

'If I don't someone else will...'

SIXTEEN

Bill opened the patient's mouth, checked that the sedative had been swallowed and then passed some pills and water to the next patient.

'That game we played last night against the Pandas - that was some game...' said Mark - opening a patient's mouth on the other side of the ward. 'I think the way it looked like we going to lose in the first half, and then caught up with them in the second and then won; I think it added something to the drama...'

Bill pushed the trolley and continued down the ward.

'You see,' said Mark, 'I don't think I would have enjoyed the match so much if we led from the beginning. No, when our side were the underdog, I really *felt* for them. I was *gunning* for them to win... Bill, are you listening to me?'

Bill stopped pushing the trolley. 'Sorry?'

'I wonder why I bother talking.'

'I wonder too...'

Bill had been preoccupied with the events of last night. He had been at home, in the process of doing the washing-up when something weird happened.

Doing the washing up was a strange occurrence in the first place. Living alone, he was fairly relaxed about the amount of washing-up he would allow to accumulate before entertaining the idea of tackling it.

That evening he had been reduced to using an oily spanner to spread peanut jelly so there was no more putting it off. Anyway, the weird thing was this: he picked up a glass that he was about to wash and found some lipstick smears on it. A woman hadn't been at his place for years.

In the good old days, Bill was quite the ladies man. Ladies used to fall for his cheeky charm, but the good old days were long gone. He would still smile at a young pretty woman at a bar, but the smile would not be reciprocated.

These lipstick smears had to date back from at least four years ago. Could he have been such a shoddy washer-upper? He guessed he was. This lipstick smear had to have been left by the last woman to have ever kissed him. He held the glass up to the light and wondered what he should do with it. Should he clean it or keep it as a memento?

Bill and Mark continued down the ward. Today there had been a new arrival... An Adrian Gluckman... A catatonic husk of a man if there ever was one. Compassion fatigue had settled in for the pair years ago, but he was in such a state, even they felt sorry for him. 'Wow... what do you reckon happened to him?'

***

Chuck sat by his desk and waited. This was the day he was going to sack Bryan, he told himself - project or no project. Nothing was going to persuade him to do otherwise. Not with so many of the staff at Head Office handing in their resignations.

Chuck checked his watch... He was late... So, okay, his scheme was amazing, but... No! He had to go! His gut feeling said: kick him out! Boot his ass before you change your mind!

He looked at his watch again... How long was he going to keep him waiting? He wondered if Bryan even respected him. Every so often there was a slightly insolent edge to his voice. You just had to keep your ears open and you could find it.

There was an insolent knock at the door. It had to be Bryan. 'Come in!'

'You wanted to... *see* me, Chuck?'

'Sit down...'

'You okay, Chuck? You seem quite tense..'

'Shut up!'

'It's Gavin - isn't it? He's pissed you off again. You don't have to tell me. Actually, I can't guarantee this, but I think I overheard him tell a colleague that he thinks that you're a wanker..'

'I said shut up! I reckon I'll be doing fine once you're out of here...'

'Chuck, I'm sure you would... once I'm working for Nike...'

How Chuck loathed and detested him. His sliminess. His odiousness. His cocksureness. Sometimes he resembled a vulture ready to pounce and sink his talons into him. Entrails hanging from his beak, he would carry on gnawing away at Chuck's bones until there was nothing left.

'Nike wouldn't want to know you. Not even Reebok would give you the time of day..'

'The results coming in from my project would suggest *otherwise*... Adjustments to the device are being made as we speak... It won't be long until we can use it on *more* people... *Millions* of more people... Possibly *billions* of more people... The recession... is edging *nearer*... ready to turn any fertile business into a dust bowl... This device would make your company *recession-proof.*'

At that precise moment, Bryan's resemblance to a vulture ceased... Maybe, thought Chuck, he should ignore his gut feeling... Maybe he should use his head... Maybe this guy was right to be so self-confident. Maybe he had a lot to be arrogant about. Maybe he was going to be his saviour.

'Okay, Bryan... I'm going to give you one last chance, but..'

'But what?'

'But you can't go round destroying staff morale..'

'*Who* said I was destroying staff morale?'

'Loads of people..'

'Oh I wouldn't rely on what *loads of people* say, Chuck. At one point the *majority* of people said the world was flat. Only the *minority* said that it was round..'

'Yeah, but..'

'What you've got to decide is who you're going to believe. Are you going to believe the words of loads of low down, worthless underlings or someone much higher up? My success is far more tied in with your success. If you fail: I fail. Your failure wouldn't mean much to Gavin, in fact he might enjoy it.'

'Look..'

'And while we're on the subject of termination of contracts etc; I think it's best to let you know that I've taken precautions in case you wish to carry on the project without me. Copies of research materials have been left in trusted hands... I need not elaborate... Anything else?'

'No...'

Bryan got up. 'Good... I'm glad we've had this conversation... It's good to clear the air... See you later, Chuck.'

The door closed. Chuck was mystified. How did Bryan do it? He was so sure he was going to fire him.

SEVENTEEN

The barman handed Chris and Ken the beers. Chris paid and stared at the jar sitting majestically on the bar. 'And I think I'll have that.'

The barman picked it. The expiry date had faded to illegibility. The company who produced the jar had long since ceased trading. He held it out to the light and could make out in the orangey brown murky waters one last pickled egg.

It was a solemn occasion. He opened the jar. A sulphurous, vinegary aroma was released into the atmosphere. It was a smell from the past - a smell that spoke of tramlines and music hall entertainers. He fished out the egg with some tongs and placed it on a Charles and Diana commemorative wedding plate.

'How much for the egg?'

'It's on the house.'

Chris and Ken made their way to the table. Joseph had saved their seats. 'You're not going to eat that - are you?'

Chris picked up the pickled egg and stared at it. The last pickled egg. There weren't going to be any other pickled eggs here anymore. Maybe he should also buy a bag of pork scratchings - there were only a few bags left. He paused - realising he was going to eat a little history and then bit into the egg.

'How is it?' asked Ken.

Chris grimaced and spat out the egg. 'Foul!'

Peter walked in. He was wearing a Harlem baseball cap, Harlem shades, Harlem coat, Harlem tracksuit and Harlem trainers and he was finishing off a Chuck burger.

Ken waved to him. 'How's it going?'

Peter wiped the grease off his mouth and burped. 'Not as good as anticipated. I won't be able to get a round in.'

'I'll get you a drink.' said Joseph, 'What're you having?'

'A Harlem Ballbuster.'

Chris went to the bar and Peter sat down.

'Nice tracksuit, how much?' asked Ken.

'Oh, three or four hundred - not sure.'

'You're earning fuck all an hour. Is it that clever to be buying all this expensive gear?'

'Yeah, what's wrong with you?' said Joseph, 'You're buying designer clothes like they were going out of fashion.'

'It's up to me how I use my credit card limit.'

'Couldn't you wait until you've got a better earning job?'

'You know how quickly these lines of tracksuit sell out. If I waited, they'd be gone.'

'Yeah, but they'd be replaced by something pretty similar.'

'I know you're thinking I'm some spendthrift shopperholic, but it's not like that... I'm buying these clothes as an incentive to become more successful. I won't be temping forever. I'm going to keep on knocking on those doors until I get a gallery to sell my work. It forces me to make sure my paintings get sold to make up for spending so much money.'

Chris returned and brought Peter his drink.

'Thanks.'

'I see,' said Ken, 'So, have any galleries shown any interest yet?'

'No, not yet. But I'm not going to give up. I'm going to keep on knocking on those doors.'

'How many galleries have you got left to try?'

'I've done the whole circuit - three times. But I'm not going to give up. I'll keep on knocking... and knocking... and knocking...'

EIGHTEEN

Peter scooped together all his unspent tubes of oil paint, all his unopened bottles of white spirit; his unused brushes and placed them in a large bin liner on his bed.

Where were the receipts? Possibly, the art shop would give him a refund without them. After all, he had been a rather good customer.

On the Richter scale of bitterness, he was a 10. What a waste of time - all those years struggling - for nothing. He didn't have a chance in Hell. He wasn't famous. He didn't have any contacts - any influential friends. None of his old art school friends had made it either. And he hadn't won any prizes.

He felt like he had been restlessly going round the block searching for a parking space - going round and round - fruitlessly - and that nobody was going to drive away from their's. He had knocked on all those doors. He had knocked on them until his knuckles bled, but the doors remained resolutely shut.

Three galleries agreed to see his work. One said he showed potential, but thought he wasn't ready to exhibit yet. Potential? At the age of thirty?

He wanted more than potential. He wanted many things. Potential was a seed. He wanted to reap the harvest. He wanted to wear flash clothes and to live in a flash playboy suite.

How was he going to impress any women with mere 'potential'? Women wanted to be wined and dined and taken to exotic places. They wanted to be driven in large expensive sports cars. Who would make do with potential?

He could picture them dismissing him totally when talking about his 'potential'. He would be halfway through his sentence and they would walk away. How long - how many more years would it take? Posthumous glory wouldn't be much of a consolation.

Van Gogh. God... Van Gogh... It would be depressing if he had to pay prostitutes to relieve his lonely nights - like Van Gogh - so not sexy.

He probably wouldn't be able to get a hard on. He'd have forked out all that money and he'd be so consumed in self-hatred and despair that he wouldn't be able to get it up. His poor defeated penis - a squeezed out tube of oil paint.

And the prostitute would think to herself: 'Sad fuck. Sad fucking fuck.' She'd have even more contempt for him than before he gave her the money. Even more contempt... Van Gogh... a cautionary tale.

Peter opened his wardrobe and took out his paintings. It could be worse. What if no one was interested in his work even after he was dead? Even then? There wasn't much else he could do to make his artwork popular than be dead. Was it possible for ghosts to promote their artwork? Had there been poltergeists that disturbed art gallery managers' crockery until they agreed to an exhibition of their work? 'Wooooo... Wooooo... Promote my installation... Wooooo... Promote my unmade bed...'

He placed his paintings on the bed. What had he been thinking of? Exactly what had he been thinking of? All those years thrown away - thrown into the garbage disposal of life. Years down the u-bend of life. Years down the sewer of life. Years buried in the graveyard of life. Years that had rotted. Years eaten away by maggots. Years that could never be retrieved - even by a well-trained dog.

What had he to show for all those years? Materially, what did he have to show for it all? No girlfriend and he lived in a poxy dump of a place - which he didn't even own.

He sifted through his artwork. This was what he used to regard as his treasure. Now he realised that the only things of value in his damp squalid little room were his Harlem clothes. They were the only things that would warrant a second look from a passing female. Those were the only things that made him feel special.

Without those clothes he felt as desirable as those hotdogs sold in Leicester Square Station - covered in congealed tomato ketchup before being put in a microwave.

He stared at the mirror. Why did he have to be Peter Papapanos? Why couldn't he have been someone else? Someone more successful - someone better looking?

He picked up a painting. What had he been thinking of? What had he been thinking of? Helen would still be with him if it weren't for his stupidity. 'Oh my God! I can't even drive a car!! Fuck!!!' Peter screamed, 'What sort of prat can't even drive a car - what sort of prat?!!!!'

His parents were frail. They wouldn't live to see him succeed. He had made them worry about him. He had made them worry themselves into ill health. They'll probably die sooner because of him! Because of his selfishness! They'll probably die sooner! He should have got himself a proper job! A career!

It was as if a spell had been broken or he had woken up from a long pipe dream.

No one was willing to give him money for his art, so logically it had to be worthless.

He punched his painting. Worthless! He slung his paintings on the floor and started stamping on them. Worthless! Worthless! Worthless! He got out a pair of scissors. Vengeance would be his. He stabbed, ripped and killed his paintings. Worthless! Worthless! Worthless!

All that work was meant to be a means to an end - a means to wealth and happiness. But all it had been was a means to poverty and loneliness.

Worthless! Worthless! Worthless! He tore into his work. Then he hurled the sculptures on his shelf against the wall.

He lost track of the time. He stopped when his fingers got sore.

Shreds of paintings were scattered around the room. Oil paint oozed from the severed parts of the canvases - like congealed tomato ketchup - like blood. Broken sculptures lay crumbled on the floor in pieces too small to glue back together. Nothing left to destroy.

There was a pain in his chest. Too much exertion - that must be it. He lay there on the bed and shut his eyes.

NINETEEN

Sleigh bells ring, are you listening... I'm dreaming of a white Christmas... Rudolf the Red-nosed Reindeer had a very shiny nose... Have yourself a very merry Christmas... Jingle bells, jingle bells, jingle all the way... I'm dreaming of a white Christmas... We wish you a Merry Christmas, we wish you a merry Christmas... Good King Wenceslas last looked out on the feast of Steven... Walking in a winter wonderland...

The shop music swirled round Peter's head. At the moment, Rudolf was dreaming of a white Christmas like the ones he used to know and his nose was deep and crisp and even. Peter stood before the DVD counter and sighed. Only a few days to go before Christmas and he still hadn't bought anything for his parents yet. It had only felt like a week since last Christmas. And it had only felt like a fortnight since the one before that.

Any second, he felt that all the tinsel, baubles and coloured lights were going to wrap themselves around him and choke him to death.

He wasn't big on Christmas. In fact he was minute on Christmas. Bigger on Easter. It had better weather for a start.

Surveying the DVDs, he was aware of a tense and aggressive feeling steadily growing inside of him. It was probably because he was in Wood Green.

Wood Green always did that to him. There was something about the area. Everyone there looked tense and aggressive. For the fifth time that hour, he checked that his wallet was still in his pocket. Something there was poisoning everyone's souls. If someone dug deep down into the road - they'd probably find some nuclear waste or discover that it had once been a Native American burial site.

The 'proper' job Peter had been looking for the past few months had proved elusive. He must have left it too late. That was what he must have done. Employers must have laughed when they looked at his CV - until tears ran down their cheeks and their trousers got wet. The one-year contract was surely not for the likes of him.

Peter continued browsing through the titles. Christmas Day should really be called 'Reassurance of Love Day' he thought, because that was what it was. You financially cripple yourself buying loads of useless gifts solely to let your family know that you still love them.

Why couldn't you just say it instead? It would be much cheaper if everyone counted: one, two three and said: 'I still love you.' to their nearest and their dearest...

It wasn't really the money that bothered him. It was the amount of time he invested - searching for the Holy Grail of gifts - trying to find something that his nearest and dearest would actually like. How often did he get it right? How many times did he receive polite thanks for his gifts - instead of thanks of the sincere variety?

And how many times did they get it right for him? The amount of jumpers he received that he actually liked was negligible. It would save a great deal of time if everyone just gave each other a twenty quid note. 'Here, have a twenty...'

'Here, have a twenty... And by the way, I still love you...'

After perusing through the titles, he picked up a DVD. His parents would like that, he thought. He looked at the price and put it back on the shelf. Might be cheaper in the shop further down the road, he decided and left the store.

He passed the shop that reactivated stolen cell phones and then stopped. A pair of Harlem trainers caught his eye. It was hard not to drool.

Needless to say they were expensive - super expensive. He had used up all his overdraft facilities and all his credit card limits.

He only had enough money for his parent's presents. They deserved nice presents. They had always been generous to him.

Tried as he might to move on, the trainers kept him there. They seemed to beckon him. They seemed to say: 'Peter... Peter... Buy me... Buy me...'

He gazed down at his own trainers. Well, they were almost *three* weeks old. He could do with a new pair... His parents weren't only generous, they were also understanding. He walked into the shop. Maybe he could find something for his parents at the Pound Store.

TWENTY

'Are you a cannibal if you eat a mermaid?' said Joseph - putting down his drink.

'Depends which end you eat.' said Ken.

'Yeah, but if you only ate the scaly end wouldn't she still die?'

'I really wouldn't worry about it...'

After several overtures to the barmen's compassion, Peter and the others were led out of 'The Green Man'.

Yet again, rain had come in a big ferocious way. Only Peter's head was protected from the deluge - his baseball cap taking the full brunt of the baptism. His friends pulled their jacket collars up for as much good it did.

Since Joseph's place was nearest, it was decided to adjourn there despite it being Joseph's place. Miraculously, it was worse than Peter's flat. The only thing in its favour being that Peter's flatmates didn't live there.

It was a lower ground floor sort of dive - a dungeon in all but name. To these walls, wallpaper might as well have come from another planet - another cosmos, but attempts at decoration had been made. A deflated balloon and a string of tinsel remained cello taped to the ceiling and sat in pride of place on the TV; were framed photos of David Niven, Errol Flynn and Ronald Colman.

'Did you know that Sean Connery wore a toupee in *all* the James Bond movies?' said Joseph as they entered.

'Wow. I'll never trust him again.' said Peter.

They sat on a sofa full of many treasures. Slip your hand down the crack and you'd find at least one half-eaten Chinese takeaway.

The TV was put on.

Their stomachs rumbled for toast. As was the usual procedure, Chris stood up and Peter sat on his shoulders - ready to catch the slices as it shot out of the toaster. A piece of toast was propelled beyond Peter's reach. Stretching out, he fell off Chris's shoulders and landed on the couch - his baseball cap landing on the floor.

'You all right?' said Chris before he; Ken and Joseph saw what lay beneath the hat. They gasped. Tattooed on Peter's balding scalp was a Harlem logo.

'Is that real?' asked Joseph, 'Or is it one of those transfer tattoos?'

'No, it's real.' said Peter.

'Why not have a Swastika put on while you're about it or 'I love Myra Hindley'?' said Ken - turning up the TV volume.

A newsreader was interviewing the Foreign Secretary. Peter grabbed the remote control and switched to another channel.

'What did you do that for?'

'Politics is boring.'

'I haven't seen the news all day. It was about the war..'

Peter shrugged his shoulders.

'Don't you want to find out about what's happening in the world?'

'Not especially...'

So they sat and watched 'One Hundred Best Lap Dancers'. It was no ordeal, that was for sure, but after a while, Ken and Chris started chatting. '...Which dog steals the most toilet rolls - Labrador, Golden Retriever?'

'Chiwawa - it's got more to prove..'

'I'm trying to watch the telly, could you please shut up?' said Peter.

'Why? I was only talking to Ken..'

'Shut up - okay?!'

'No, I don't think I will..'

'Shut up! I don't want to hear any of you - I'm trying to hear the programme!'

'What's wrong with a little talking?' said Joseph.

'Because there's no point to it.'

'What do you mean?'

'Spouting shit might distract you from having no lives, but it doesn't do it for me.'

After that, the group was more subdued. Chris tried to start a new conversation, but stopped mid sentence. Joseph also tried to initiate one, but his heart wasn't in it. Ken sat silently and kept his opinions to himself.

TWENTY-ONE

It was such a foggy night; you didn't know where you were or even who you were. A real peasouper. Like the fogs in the good old days when fog was probably the most nutritious thing you could get to eat.

Despite the adverse conditions, 'The Green Man' was doing a roaring trade. Not a single regular was missing. One suspected that even after a nuclear holocaust, they'd still be able to get there. 'Better make it a *double* whisky!' they'd say as they sweep the rubble off their shoulders.

Like the regulars, Peter's friends had made the journey and were now sat by a table.

'I was at the supermarket' said Joseph, 'and I saw all these shoppers with their trolleys piled up with food and washing powder and I wondered how much would you have to buy to impress the cashier? How much would you have to buy to make the cashier think: 'Wow! That's a lot of food you've bought! Wow!! Would you have to buy two trolleys full of shopping or five?'

'Four.' said Ken.

'...When did H. G. Wells die?'

'1940.'

'Poor guy.'

'Why?!'

'He never got to find out who won the Second World War.'

'He's dead, why should he care?'

'I'd rather die secure in the knowledge that the Third Reich had been defeated than die and be left in suspense...'

Peter walked in the pub wearing a new Harlem baseball cap, and a totally new Harlem outfit. With aggressive urgency, he scanned the place for recognisable faces.

'There's Peter,' said Joseph.

'Pretend you haven't seen him.' said Ken.

'Don't you like him anymore?' said Joseph.

'He owes me four hundred quid. I'm not going to give him any more.'

'You too?! He told me that you were tight and wouldn't lend him any money so I lent him five hundred quid.' said Chris.

'He told me that his landlord was chucking him out and that he needed a deposit on a new flat share.'

'That's complete bollocks, because I saw him coming out of the same place last Tuesday.'

'...He didn't ask me for any money.' said Joseph.

'That's because you never have any!' said Ken.

'He's obviously got problems.'

'We all have problems, Joseph, but we don't go on stupid spending sprees. I've had enough. I don't want anything more to do with him.'

***

Enterprise had never been Peter's strongest point. It was his second weakest point, which was obvious to anyone who had seen him on the dance floor. Met with the increasingly insatiable desire for Harlem goods, he found his earnings from legitimate jobs inadequate so he decided to supplement them with loans.

Having alienated the most obvious sources of loans he had been reduced to asking those less positively inclined towards him. His housemates said no. The Jehovah Witness said no. The traffic warden said no.

That morning, Peter had been strolling down the street when he bumped into Darren Sumner. *The* Darren Sumner. The Darren Sumner who had made his life a misery at comprehensive school. What were the chances of this? He knew this opportunity would not come twice in a lifetime... 'Excuse me,' he asked, 'but aren't you Darren Sumner?'

There wasn't the barest hint of recognition in Darren's impassive eyes. He sneered. 'What's it to you?'

'It's Peter, Peter Papapanos... You used to bully me.'

He scrutinized Peter's physique. '...Did I? Yeah, suppose I did...'

'You couldn't lend me four hundred pounds - could you?'

'What?!'

'I'm a bit short this time of the month and I would appreciate it if you could help me out.'

'Taking the piss?'

'I would accept it as a peace offering..'

'You're not going to get any money from me!'

'But it would make up for all you've done to me. Don't you think some sort of recompense is in order?'

'No!'

'It would ease your conscience.'

'What?!'

'Don't lie to yourself; you need to help me.

'Trust you to ask for money - fucking Yid!'

'I'm not Jewish. Look, I'm only asking for a few hundred pounds.'

'No! Fuck off!'

'Go on!'

'No!'

'Please!'

Darren backed away. When was this guy going to get out of his face? He was trying to go straight, but he was still addicted to the violence.

Prison hadn't helped. In fact, it had made him worse. His probation officer was talking shite. If he didn't act the hard man he'd be nothing. It wasn't as if he had anything else going for him. It wasn't as if anybody had done anything about his dyslexia. He wasn't going to become an artist or a scientist or even a security guard. He wasn't going to get a job ever.

It made him feel good when he beat someone up. It made him feel good. How the fuck was he to survive where he was living if he didn't act like that? He came from a broken home so there wasn't anyone else looking out for him. He didn't live in some posh place like his probation officer. Did he want the crap smashed out of him? Did he? It wasn't as if the people on the housing estate were all posh and soft like his probation officer.

Didn't have a clue, this one. Neither did all the others. Through out his life, well-meaning middle class people had failed to help him. It seemed to him that a Social Worker's job was to remain a Social Worker. Now there was this prick asking for money from *him* of all people.

'Okay,' said Peter, 'a hundred pounds, could you lend me that?'

Darren thought over Peter's proposal for a moment; head butted him and then walked away. The nurses at the hospital were not forthcoming with loans either.

***

Potential lenders had been curiously thin on the ground the rest of the day. The fog hadn't helped. Try getting a loan from a statue and see how far that will get you.

The pub had been Peter's last port of call. As he was about to leave, he spotted Ken, Chris and Joseph seated in the distance. Now, they *were* friends. *Good* friends. *True* friends. *Generous* friends. *Old* friends. They wouldn't let him down. They wouldn't betray him like so many had done during these past troubled months.

It had been a while since he had last met up with them. Ken had changed his phone number... Probably forgot to tell him...

Yes, so many friends had fallen by the wayside. Why couldn't people understand that a friend in need was a friend indeed and not a liability? Why didn't they believe him the last five times when he said they would pay them back if they gave him that last loan?

He approached the group and anticipated some sort of salutation. But they looked away.

For a while, Peter stared at them. They carried on talking among themselves. How could they do that? How could they do that to *him* - with all the financial trouble he was in? How could they do that? They weren't the friends he remembered. No, they weren't. They'd changed. They had *fucking* changed. Peter gobbed on the floor. 'Fuck you then!' he said, 'Fuck you then!' and stormed out.

***

A homeless person was sat cross-legged on the pavement outside the pub. 'Got any spare change?' he slurred.

Peter turned to him. 'I must have given you at least ten quid over the years.'

'Maybe..' he said.

'I want it back...'

TWENTY-TWO

Ken, Chris and Joseph nursed their drinks and gazed at the dance floor. It was a place of profound boredom combined with sexual frustration.

Joseph looked at his watch. It was only 10:22.

Their eyes fought to dilate quickly enough with the flashing lights. Everyone's ears fought to hear anyone under the pounding music.

It was still only 10:22.

'Is there a scientific reason why repetition is boring?' asked Joseph brushing the abundant fluorescent dandruff off his shoulders.

'What?!' said Chris, 'What's that you're saying?'

It was still 10:22. Joseph looked at Chris's watch. It said 10:30. His watch had stopped. Phew! he thought.

***

It was now 10:47. After surveying the dance floor from various viewpoints, Ken saw a girl that he halfway fancied. It was worth a try he thought and approached her. 'Hi, I'm Ken.' he shouted.

'Rowena.' shouted the girl.

'It's awful here - isn't it?'

'What'dya mean?!' yelled Rowena.

'It's so loud and noisy! It's hard to have a conversation.'

'What'dya want to have a conversation for?'

'And the music is terrible - all crappy cover versions! I'd hate to come here every Saturday!'

'What'd mean? I come here every Saturday!'

'Oh, well, I mean..'

'If you don't like it here, why don't you fuck off?'

'Look, there's no need..'

'No fuck off! Been standing behind a counter all day! I want to have a good time! Last thing I need is to see your miserable face!'

'I can see there's no sense in trying to talk to you...'

'Go on - fuck off!'

Typical, he thought, bloody typical, and shunted off to the other side of the club.

He sipped from his glass and watched the dance floor and all the people he was never going to know.

How were people meant to 'pull' here? It was always too dark to see what anyone looked like. And if suddenly the glitter ball benevolently bestowed more light and you saw someone desirable, suddenly she would disappear in a puff of dry ice. You would spend the evening trying to find her and go to the club again and again futilely searching for that woman you fleetingly saw.

And even if you found that woman within your sights and you wanted to introduce yourself to her and inquire about her name, she wouldn't be able to hear you.

That must have been what nightclub owners banked on: the sexually frustrated never finding the salvation they caught a glimpse of and the darkness and the music making it ever so.

Who has ever pulled a stranger in a club? Clairvoyants? Lip readers? People carrying infrared visual aids?

He felt lonely. And looking at the price of the drinks - it was a very expensive loneliness. He finished his drink and went home - where the loneliness was cheaper.

***

Chris entered the toilets. The first three cubicles offered little in the way of comfort, or hygiene or toilet seats or toilet paper or doors.

He tried the last cubicle. The door wasn't bolted, but two men were inside. One handed over a tenner and took a couple of pills from a guy with a baseball cap.

You had to be really green to sell drugs in toilets, thought Chris.

The pusher turned to him and sneered. It was Peter.

'...Why are you looking at me like that?'

'I'm not..'

'You are..'
'I'm not. It's, er, it's good to see you, Peter.'
'What do you want?'
'Er, to use the loo, thank you. The others are broken.'
'This is my work base.'
'You do realise you're going to get caught if you sell drugs here.'
'What're you talking about?'
'The bouncers check these areas, they'll get you.'
'No they won't.'
'You're better off selling them in crowded parts of the dance floor. They won't be able to see you.'
'I don't need *your* advice.'
'Must be your first day.'
'You couldn't be more *wrong*. It's my *second*.'
'Can I use the loo?'
'No.'
'I need to go.'
'Tell you what, buy a pill and I'll go and get myself a drink - have a break for a few minutes.'
'What?!'
'That's my final offer.'
Chris handed him a tenner. 'That's all you're getting from me.'
'Here you are.' Peter handed him two pills.
'No, you can keep them.'
'Don't pretend you never do drugs! Take them!'
'Don't want them.'
'Please yourself...'

TWENTY-THREE

Ten men sat in the room and played cards while the other two stood. The amenities were Spartan: a couple of bunk beds, a few nude posters on the wall and a bucket to shit in.

A large man tried the door.
'You know it's locked.' said the man dealing.
'How long do you think they'll keep us here?'
'How should I know?'
'Got a cigarette?'
'Yeah, have one of mine.'
'Thanks... Oh, they're the ones I smoke.'

TWENTY-FOUR

'Cut!' said the director, 'Let's break for lunch. Great work guys.'

Chuck put down the 'electro-ray' sword, took off his white robe, sat down and was handed a mineral water.

A fifty-six year-old alien film extra with a beard, long forelock and skullcap approached Chuck. 'Bernie! It's you! My God! It must be forty years!'

'I think you've mistaken me for someone else...' said Chuck.

'You're kidding! I never forget a face! You've lost so much weight! You look great!'

'Excuse me..'

'It's Johnny! We were at school together!'

'No way!' said Chuck rushing away. 'You're far too old for me to know you!'

***

Chuck stared into the mirror in his trailer. Fuck! It had worn off. He should have checked earlier... Fine lines on his forehead... Skin starting to sag under his chin... How could he have not noticed? Maybe his eyesight was failing... He searched the drawers and then pulled them out. 'It's go to be there! It's got to be there!' How could he do the scene - looking like this?

He found the syringe and the Botox. He injected it into his forehead. 'Work! Work!' He breathed a sigh of relief as the fine lines disappeared.

He picked up the cell phone. 'Hi, it's me... I've got a problem... An extra harassing me... He thinks I'm a friend of his. The guy's totally delusional. I'm afraid you're going to have to get rid of him... Thanks... Bye...'

TWENTY-FIVE

At 11.30pm, a gale force wind was building up in East Hampton. It whistled an ancient, wistful melody - sweeping a mass of autumn leaves into the moonlit sky. Needless to say, it was not a night to go out - wearing your favourite hat.

A limo parked outside a large, secluded mansion. Chuck got out - clutching a bunch of flowers.

The wind grew harsher - wanting to snatch the bouquet away - claiming it as its own. Like a jealous woman, the wind tugged at the stems, but he held on tighter and forced his way to the front door.

Chuck rang the bell and gazed upwards at the Neo-Gothic monstrosity. The gargoyles on the balcony sneered at him. Somehow they had grown more grotesque with time.

'Everything is going to be all right... Everything is going to be all right...' he whispered to himself. '...I am in control of my destiny and everything is going to be all right...'

Situations like these had arisen before and he had survived.

Slow, methodical footsteps could be heard. The door creaked open to reveal a stooped, poorly lit, solemn faced butler.

'Jenkins?' said Chuck.

'Yes, Master... Harlem...' said Jenkins.

'How is she?'

'As well as could be expected, Sir... Please come in...'

He was led through the hallway. Old, creepy portraits of long forgotten ancestors in gaudy frames peered out of the darkness.

It didn't seem to matter how many lights were on; the place was always dark. It was almost as if the walls were porous - absorbing everything electric bulbs could conjure up. He had asked her to move from this place plenty of times, but she had always refused. It was almost as if the walls had absorbed her soul and she was dependent on the place to exist.

The nurse escorted Chuck to the room. Before him, stood the four-poster bed. He froze. The nurse took the flowers. 'I'll find a vase.' she said, 'Can I get you anything?'

'No that's fine, I'd like a few minutes *alone* with her.' said Chuck.

The door shut. He pulled up a chair and sat next to the bed.

He pulled the duvet down slightly so that he could see her face. Most people would say that she was in her mid-fifties.

Her eyes opened. 'Bernard...'

'You know the name's Chuck, mom.'

'Sorry Bernard...'

'Remember you're Mrs Harlem now, not Mrs Hendrickson.'

'Sorry...'

'That's okay... What do the doctors say?'

'It's not good.'

'I'll get some other doctors. Maybe they can..'

'No Bernard, my time is up.'

'Don't say that!'

'But it is. I'm going to die.'

'You've got plenty of years left!'

'Darling, I'm ninety-three!'

'I'm not going to let it happen! If there's some vital organ you need I'll get a transplant..'

'No darling, no more transplants... no more plastic surgery.'

'You can't do this to me!' said Chuck, 'You can't die! If you die you'll make me look old!'

'I'm sorry, Bernard...' she said and slumped her head upon the pillow.

The doctor entered and examined the body. 'My condolences, Mr Harlem.'

'What for?' said Chuck, 'There's no need for condolences! She's still alive!'

'I'm sorry to tell you but your mother is dead.'

'Put her on a life support - she might recover!'

'I'm sorry, Mr Harlem. There would be no point.'

'Let me be the judge of that, dude! Put her on a life support...'

TWENTY-SIX

Ten years earlier, a fat fifty-one year-old stood by his father's grave.

The priest said the final words. Soil was thrown at the coffin. His mother was led away - weeping into a handkerchief. A relative patted his shoulder and said: 'He was a good man.' The mourners went and he was left alone.

The tombstone towered over him and overshadowed him as his father had done throughout his life. His father had built a huge business empire from a slightly smaller one from *his* father.

He didn't deserve a huge gravestone thought the son. He deserved something small - something minuscule - something minute to be remembered with. In fact something so small his father could be forgotten instantly.

His father wasn't there for him. Only bought him one limousine instead of two limousines. Only bought him one yacht instead of two yachts. Only bought him one swimming pool instead of two swimming pools. And only gave him one year for his band to become successful on his father's record label.

It was possible that his obesity had got in his way. When success failed to materialize he had been given the option of managing one of his father's subsidiaries or leaving the mansion and making his own way in life.

He'd taken the safe option. Guaranteed money. Guaranteed luxury. The safe option. Gutless spineless man that he was, he took the safe option. The other members of the group were less interested in him being their lead singer once the record deal was over and conveniently forgot to return the guitars he had lent them.

He went through a series of marriages that were short-lived and expensive. They somehow sensed his gutlessness and decided not to treat him like a pop star and got acquainted with the gardener and once he'd retired, the gardener's son.

But now his father was dead, he was no longer going to be nothing. No, he wasn't. He had inherited most of the estate, so he was going to be something - someone big - someone who was going to get an even bigger tombstone when he died.

***

The fat man sat in the cosmetic surgeon's surgery. The face was old, so he sacked it. 'I want you to make me look eighteen years old.'

The surgeon looked sternly at the man and said: 'Sir, I can make you look younger, but not eighteen.'

'I want to look eighteen.'

'I want Scarlett Johansson, but we can't all have what we want.'

'I can.'

'...Okay, I will try.'

'You *will* make me look eighteen.'

'You realise you're going to have to sacrifice a year of your life having operations and recovering from them.'

'Yes.'

'You're going to have to do your bit. You're over-weight. You need to lose at least five stone. I suggest that you do this before we proceed.'

'I'm going to have the fat sucked out of me. It won't take long.'

The surgeon took out a clipboard and a pen. 'Do you suffer from high blood pressure?'

'No.'

The information was jotted down.

'Any blood clotting problems?'

'No.'

'A tendency to form excessive scars?'

'Not that I'm aware of.'

'Do you smoke?'

'No. By the way, I want you to do the same for my mother.'

'Make *her* look eighteen?'

'Mid-forties will do.'

He could not feel much. He was still aware he was in the operation theatre. He had only been given a local anaesthetic and a mild sedative.

He could feel the tugging of his skin as it was pulled down his forehead.

There was no pain as the surgeon trimmed the fat off around his neck. No pain as more of him was sliced off - more excess flesh stripped away from him. He was detached from the surgeon's actions as he tightened the underlying muscle and membrane and pulled his skin back.

Weeks were swallowed up taking painkillers as the pain he had been made numb to during the procedure echoed back repeatedly.

The surgeon examined his handiwork. 'The bruising's gone down. Good. How're you finding it?'

His patient rubbed the stubble under his ears. 'I have to shave under here now..'

'That's to be expected. That's where areas of your beard growing skin have been repositioned.'

'Right.'

'How are your facial movements? Can you smile? Sometimes the facial nerves take a while to work again. Could you try to smile?'

'No I'd rather not. But my skin - it's not the skin of an eighteen year-old. The texture's not right.'

'Judging by what seem to be your requirements, I would recommend a Phenol Chemical Peel in a few month's time.'

'It needs to be sooner.'

'Your face needs to recover.'

'I haven't the time.'

'You've had a facelift. There are milder treatments using glycolic, lactic or fruit acids that you could have sooner, but for what you're after, you'll have to wait. Phenol will do the job - it provides a deep peel.'

His face was thoroughly cleansed. Then the solution was applied to his face. It briefly stung.

His youth had not been lost. It had merely been buried for the past thirty years. Under the layer of oldness, a layer of youth was retrievable.

Two hours passed, then the surgeon started to peel his skin off. As his old skin was shed his youth was excavated. He was reborn into the world - his face bright red like that of a crying baby waiting for the umbilical cord to be cut.

The surgeon started to coat his face with petroleum jelly. He couldn't open his eyes. He tried to open his mouth.

'Don't talk...' the surgeon continued, 'Your eyes are swollen shut. It's only temporary... It'll be best to keep conversation to a minimum for the next few days... Stick to a liquid diet... And please, keep out of the sun.'

Before leaving his estate, he smothered his new face in sun block. Although a month had passed, it was still pink. No more sun tans for him. As he had been warned, his skin had lost the ability to make pigment. It was only going to be really safe for him to venture out at night.

'Is this as good as you can get it?!' he asked his surgeon.

'You look a lot younger.'

'I don't look eighteen.'

The surgeon took out some more paperwork. '...We could try some dermabrasion and dermaplaning. Could possibly smooth your appearance more.'

The facelift did not end there. The rest of his company had to have one too. Renamed and rebranded - a 'youth orientated' image. To pay for all the advertising to kick-start his popularity, he ran a much tighter outfit. Tougher deals were made, smaller wages paid and more and more of the work subcontracted and many workers made redundant. Tighter and tighter - the business grew. Tighter and tighter - more taunt than the skin on his face.

TWENTY-SEVEN

Peter stood topless in front of the mirror on his wardrobe. His belly flopped over his tracksuit bottoms. Maybe he had eaten a few too many Chuck burgers the past few months.

He winced as he slowly pulled his arm out of the sling. It had almost recovered. The incident in the nightclub had been discouraging for him. Anyway, these days he was spending his money too fast to be able to buy the gear he was selling in the first place.

Tonight, he was going to knock the drug pushing on the head and try out something new. He pulled out a flick knife and studied his reflection. 'Hand over the wallet if you values your life! Har! Har! Har!' he said in his most menacing voice. Mmmm, bit Long John Silver... He was trying to be a mugger not a pirate.

Did he look threatening enough - threatening enough for victims to hand him their money without too many arguments? Obviously, he wanted to avoid violence if he could at all help it.

He looked at his stomach and then held it in. That bouncer who did his arm... That bouncer... He had better watch out... Yeah, he better had... That's all that he would say. One night he'll track that bouncer down... Yeah, one night he'll track down that bouncer when he was by himself... And then... and then he won't feel so tough. Yeah! He wouldn't feel so tough then..

It was no good he had to breathe out. His belly flopped over his tracksuit bottoms again. Well, it was going to be dark anyway. How difficult could it be to scare a little dosh off a stranger?

***

For hours, Peter waited in an alley in Finsbury Park. He found that not that many people walked by themselves into blind alleys. It was almost as if everybody had heard of the dangers of walking into those places.

If no one came soon, he was going to go home. He moved to the edge of the unlit alleyway ready to spring into the high street. Everybody seemed to have gone home. It was around two in the morning.

Thirty minutes went by. An old woman in her eighties came up the street with her dog. 'Jasper! No! You will not do poo poos on that lamppost! I forbid it! Wait until I take you to the garden, Jasper... Jasper! Move! You naughty dog!'

She seemed to be having quite an involved conversation with her pet.

This was it: his first victim. He waited for her to walk by the alleyway. He jumped in front of her.

'Hello?' she said straining to see him through her milk bottle glasses. 'How can I help you?'

She smiled angelically. She didn't appear to see the knife.

'Er, good e-evening,' said Peter.

'Good evening to *you*.' said the elderly lady.

'Yes, er, sorry to disturb you... I was w-wondering...'

'Yes?'

'...I was wondering if... if you could be so kind to...'

'Could you speak a little louder? I'm a little deaf.'

'Of... of course... Could you... tell me the time...'

'I'm sorry, young man, since I retired, I banished clocks and watches from my life. One hour is much like another to me, but I would hazard a guess that it's very *late*.' And with that she walked away, smiling softly to herself, dragging her dog from another soiled lamppost.

He couldn't do it. Not with that sweet old face, even though he knew that meant nothing. All old people could do that look. She could have been a Nazi war criminal for all he knew - she would have been old enough. But, no, he couldn't mug her. He had to draw the line somewhere. He had to wait for someone more his size with better eyesight. That would be fairer.

Forty minutes went by. Peter could see in the distance, someone who looked his build, so he psyched himself up. He sprang in front of him and them instantly changed his mind.

He was Asian. Well, he couldn't have people thinking he was racist - could he! He would hate his actions to be misconstrued.

As he backed into the alleyway, the Asian man gave him an odd look. After some consideration, he narrowed down his criterion for mugging customers once again: a) they should not be too old; b) they should be white; c) they should basically be just like him.

Peter waited again. He really didn't enjoy this waiting around. It wasn't as if he could read a book to pass the time.

At around three in the morning, a pasty pale-faced, non-muscular male in his late twenties wandered down the street as if he was in love.

This was more like it. This would be fairer. They both looked like artistic and philosophical people. In different circumstances they could have been friends.

Peter jumped out and grabbed the victim by the arm and brandished his weapon. 'Hand over the wallet!'

'No! Please!'

Peter held the flick knife nearer to him.

'Shut your mouth and hand it over!'

The young man's protests ceased and he gave it to him.

Peter let go of him, ran down the street, arrived home and opened the wallet. It was true that guy was very similar to him because inside his wallet was an expired British Film Institute membership card and fifty-six pence in loose change - practically the contents of his own wallet.

TWENTY-EIGHT

'Cut!' said the director, 'That's all for today. Great work guys.'

Chuck put down his electro rod and sighed.

A bottle of mineral water was handed to him.

Sometimes he wondered why he bothered. The critics were bound to pan the remake of 'Star Wars'. They always had their knives out. Didn't matter how good his films were. There was no pleasing them.

They somehow thought Humphrey Bogart was better than him in 'Casablanca'. What they seemed to forget was that Bogie had a quite *limited* acting range. And Chuck's dialogue was far more decipherable than Marlon Brando's in 'On the Waterfront'. Mumble, mumble - who wants that?

Did the critics ever make these observations? No they did not - apart from the ones who worked on the newspapers he owned. Sometimes he thought of jacking in the whole thing. He tossed the empty bottle away and made his way back to his trailer.

Even walking seemed an effort for him... The future... What future? Apart from Bryan's project, he didn't feel he had much to look forward to.

Upon arriving, however, the dark clouds above his head totally dispersed, for waiting outside was a film extra in a silver micro-skirt, silver kinky boots and pointy ears. Seventeen years old and stunningly attractive.

Could it be her? he wondered. She reminded him of Lorraine Fairweather - a girl he used to be obsessed with at high school. She could never be bothered with him since she thought he was a needy nerdy fat guy because he was a needy nerdy fat guy.

Could it be her? Unless she was a multi-millionaire with access to cutting edge plastic surgery, Chuck guessed not. Perhaps it was Lorraine's granddaughter. If he managed to get to bed with her it would be almost as good. He certainly wouldn't want Lorraine Fairweather now - no, she would be a wizened old thing.

But would he take the risk? he wondered. For the past five years he had avoided groupies and women in general. He didn't want them to find out his real age and then blabber about it in the press.

The vision of loveliness shook his hand. 'Hi, Mimi Johnson..' She smiled brightly.

'Err... Hi...'

'I want to tell you - I love your work.'

'...Thanks... I'm sure I'd like your work... if I'd ever seen any of it.'

'I doubt it. Haven't had much luck. Film-extra work mainly...' She shot him a mischievous look. 'You'll probably lose some respect for me, but I did do a few porno flicks...' Mimi covered her mouth in embarrassment.

Chuck had to admit it; she was enchanting. It was as if she carried a psychological umbrella that protected her from all the casting couch abuse that rained upon her.

'Had to pay the rent.'

'No, porn's good. What were you in?'

'Do you remember 'Open-Wide' - that hard-core porn film set in a dentists? I was the patient.'

'Man, you were sensational in that. Was that you in 'Sex in an Open grave'?

'No, but I was in the sequel.'
'What part did you have in that?'
'I was one of the half-buried vaginas.'
'Were you half-buried vagina number three?'
'Yes! Yes! That was *me*! How could you tell?'
'Half-buried vagina number three was my favourite!'
'My Gawd! Hardly anyone saw that film! I'm amazed you saw it. It got banned!'
'It's a shame! I wish they made more films like that!'
'How did you get to see it?'
'I have my ways... Look, there's a little restaurant I know...'

TWENTY-NINE

They were too small - the portions they were serving at 'La Bouche' - no matter which way you looked at it - even if you used a magnifying glass or a microscope.

After five bites the meal was over for Mimi. She put her fork down and surreptitiously licked her knife...

Since Chuck was still somehow finishing his meal, Mimi's eyes wandered round the restaurant: the waiters with their platters - pretending that the food they were carrying was heavy and the customers collaborating in the facade - saying they *simply* couldn't eat *another* thing.

A man in his sixties was seated in the corner of the restaurant. It was *him*, thought Mimi. It was - wasn't it? It was the star of at least nine of her top twenty favourite films. Though it couldn't be - could it? Surely they would have given him more to eat?

Chuck finished his meal; patted his stomach and said: 'Anything wrong?'

Mimi pointed at the man and said: 'Isn't that..'

'Yeah, it's exactly who you think it is.'

Mimi looked around the place and then noticed something. 'Hey, everyone's famous here!'

'A man's got to have a place to go to where he can eat and not get stared at.'

'Sorry, was I staring?'

'Slightly.'

'What's he like to work with?'

'Fine, if you don't stare.'

'What if you *wink* at him or *squint* at him?'

'Oh... better.'

It was raining. Outside, an actor stood forlornly pressing his nose and hands onto the window. '...I'm sure I know that face.' said Mimi.

'Yeah, shame he's not so famous anymore. No way they'll let *him* in.'

'La Bouche' had a strict policy of only allowing entry to A listed actors with their guests. They wanted to spare their customers the embarrassment of rubbing shoulders with B listed actors that they may have encountered on their ascent to stardom. Horror of horrors, they may talk to the A listed actors: 'Remember me? We were in 'The Ghost of the Poseidon Adventure'. We should do another film together...' It would be distasteful to have friends that you had conveniently forgotten - making such undignified overtures for help. They had to be spared that level of harassment.

Mimi fiddled with her knife and fork and said: 'What's your favourite animal?'

'Well, a human - 'cause you can fuck it. You could fuck other animals but it wouldn't be much fun unless you're weird.'

'Apart from a human what's your favourite animal?'

'Alligator. You could make good shoes out of alligators..'

'What's your second favourite?'

'Cow. You can make good leather jackets out of cows.'

'What about 'live' animals?'

'...Think I said human already... You wouldn't want to fuck a dead human unless you were desperate... What about you? What's your favourite animal?'

'Dog.'

'Don't think you can make good jackets out of dogs... Heard they taste alright..'

'No silly! I like dogs to play with - getting them to fetch sticks. I don't want to make money out of them.'

'Alright... though if they're a rare breed you can take them to dog shows and perhaps win a lot of money..'

'Chuck, you're something else.'

'Thanks. You're the bees' knees.'

'The *what*?'

'I heard an English man say that once. I suppose there's something special about bees' knees - maybe they're worth a lot of money.'

'Could we stop talking about money for a *second*?'

'Okay...' said Chuck, 'So... how much you getting paid for the picture we're doing?'

Mimi rolled her eyes.

'So...' said Chuck, 'Do you own a dog?'

'Used to... but not anymore...'

'That's the thing with dogs, they don't live long enough. Ten, twelve years? By the time you've got to know them, they've kicked the bucket. Now if you could genetically engineer a dog that could live up to fifty, it would be worth having..'

Mimi looked down at her plate. 'Teddy's not dead.'

'Who's Teddy?'

'My dog.'

'Oh... Why don't you see your dog anymore?'

'It's a long story...'

A waiter collected the dishes, but then stood - fixed to the spot and stared at Chuck with a solemn intensity.

At first it was flattering for Chuck... But after a while it vexed him. 'Yeah, er... is there a problem?'

'I was - I was wondering,' said the waiter, 'I was wondering if you remember me. Matt Jordan... We were in 'Delta Force Eight' together - your first film. I was second lead...'

'Er... yeah... sure...'

'I've written this script and I reckon with your help we could get this project on the road. Of course you'd be first lead and I'd be second lead..'

Chuck nodded and pressed the red button under the table. 'Yeah... yeah... send it to Head Office. I'll give it a look...'

The headwaiter appeared and grabbed the waiter's arm. 'Matt, there's other tables waiting for you - come on!'

'Nice talking to you Chuck..'

'Yeah... likewise, dude.'

'I'm so sorry about this. It won't happen again.' said the headwaiter. Chuck smiled. 'Don't sweat it, dude.'

'It's a shame that so many people want the same thing.' said Mimi.

'What's that? Oh... Right... Yeah... Suppose it is...'

'That guy's never gonna be happy just being a waiter..'

'Who?'

'That waiter who was pitching a film to you.'

'Oh... *him*.'

'Yeah - even if he takes up Buddhism or Yoga - he'll still want to become a movie star..'

'Yeah... you're probably right..'

'Take me for example, I'd be fooling myself if I said I wanted anything else - fooling myself if I said I enjoyed doing the porn stuff. Do you know how itchy it is having your pubes shaved?'

'No... tell me about it.'

'I'm glad you gave that guy some hope. If you were rude to him, I think I would have walked out...'

***

Off went their shoes, but unfortunately for Chuck no knickers followed. A prelude to hanky panky this was not. Pairs of ice skates were put on. Date number three. Apart from a goodnight kiss, nothing had happened between them. However, Chuck was hoping to soon remedy this situation.

The ice-skating had been his idea. Apparently, Mimi hadn't skated before. This was a good way to get close to her. How else can you teach someone skating without - holding their hands and their waist? 'Now keep hold until you feel more confident..'

'Don't worry, I won't be doing somersaults.' She gazed at the other skaters and noticed something. 'Hey, all the people who skate here are famous!'

'People need a place to skate without being stared at.'

She continued to watch. 'I never have thought that *he* would be good at skating.' A short stout man gracefully skated past and did a figure of eight.

'You'd be surprised at the amount of actors you'd think would be good at ice skating and aren't and the amount of actors who you'd think were crap at ice-skating and are great... You know that guy from 'Dirty Ice-Skating'? He can't skate to save his life.'

'No!!'

'His ice-skating: CGI - digitally animated... He only came here once.'

***

'I'm going to try to skate alone.' said Mimi, 'Let go of my hand.'

Off she skated - faster and faster and then fell.

Chuck rushed to her. 'You alright?'

'Yeah, don't worry...' Mimi tried to stand up. 'Ow!'

Chuck put her arm over his shoulder and walked her out of the ice rink. 'You may have twisted your ankle. I better have a look at that.'

Mimi rubbed her buttocks and the bone above it and grimaced.

'You've landed pretty hard on the lower of your back... I better have a look at that also...'

'What? Are you a chiropractor as well as a singer and actor?'

'No, I just like looking at women's bottoms.'

'You scumbag...' she laughed.

'No... I'm always injuring myself doing stunts in my movies - learned a few massage techniques that might help...'

THIRTY

Too beautiful. The beach, the Mauritius Kestrel song, the sunset, the surrounding inert, majestic volcanoes, the red flowered trees swaying in the breeze and the ocean spray - caressing their bodies as they lay on the golden sand - it was all too beautiful for Mimi.

She hadn't gone abroad before - the only travelling she ever did was in her sleep. She had dreamed about a place like this and about being with a man much like the one she was with.

Now she was awake and she was here. Something about the intensity of the sunset, the intensity of the location - it was all too much for her. Too perfect. A hot salty tear ran down her cheek.

Chuck sat cross-legged - staring at the sea - hypnotised by the waves.

'We are really here - aren't we?' said Mimi, 'Your submarine didn't get bombed - did it? Like this could be Heaven...'

Chuck continued his gaze. '...No one bombed the submarine... We didn't die.'

He grabbed the sun tan lotion bottle and rubbed more cream onto his face.

'Chuck, it's sunset, you don't need anymore.'

They had arrived too soon, thought Chuck. The sunlight was far too bright for his skin. And his bodyguards were pissing him off.

His fifty bodyguards were supposed to be hidden from sight to give the couple the illusion of privacy. Despite the camouflage, he could spot at least one of them halfway up a mango tree.

'Pinch me.' said Mimi, 'I can't believe I'm with the most fabulous guy in the whole world..'

The foam reached their feet. Chuck wrapped his body around Mimi and started kissing her. He stopped. Something was missing.

'Mimi,' he said, 'Those pointy ears - do you still have them?'

THIRTY-ONE

A homesick elephant carried a man and woman in a howdah on its back. She was a long way from India but a short way from Virginia.

'See those mountains over there?' said Chuck, 'They're known as the Blue Ridge Mountains of Virginia... Laurel and Hardy sung a song about them...'

'They're beautiful...'

'Yep, they're beautiful and they're mine... See that forest? Mine... See that pyramid?'

'Is it yours?'

'You guessed it! Cool - isn't it?' That's my designated final resting place. My staff have signed a contract agreeing that when they die they will also be buried there so that they can attend to me in the spirit world.'

Were her eyes playing tricks with her, Mimi wondered or were the electric fences surrounding the estate, slowly rising in height? 'It's amazing... And what high electric fences you have.'

'One thing I've learned; it's a terrible world out there, Mimi, full of thieves and murderers. A man needs a refuge from the world. You need a place where you can feel safe. If they think they can invade my land, they have another think coming. The more they try to get in, the higher I'll raise my fences, the more security cameras I'll get, the more bodyguards I'll hire. We are always going to feel safe here. I will always protect you.'

He was about to show Mimi his estate's flood defences when his cell phone rang. '...This better be important, dude, I'm on holiday. I don't call you when you're on vacation... Okay, so I *do*. What do you want? An apology?! What do you need to tell me?'

Oh right, business, thought Mimi and put on her iPOD, closed her eyes and moved her head to the music.

'Then talk! I'm letting you talk! Talk! Right... Okay... Tell that editor if he doesn't use that story, he is through - okay? Yes it's his decision, but I expect him to make the decision that I want him to make... That report on illegal immigrant scumbags was balanced! Yeah, yeah, I've heard it before... They're escaping from dictatorships and environmental disaster zones... Well whose fault is that?! Huh?! You relay to him what I said to you. Call me tomorrow.'

He put away his cell phone and Mimi removed her headphones. 'See? Being a managing director isn't so great - you can never separate work from your social life.'

There was a knock on the side of the howdah.

Chuck looked out and found the butler stood before them on stilts - holding a tray with an array of cocktails. '...Would Sir and Madam care for a drink?'

'Yeah, okay. Mimi, what d'ya have?'

THIRTY-TWO

'Come in.' said Chuck stood behind his desk with his hands clasped behind his back.

'You wanted to see me?' said Gavin.

'Yeah, take a seat...'

Gavin sat down. What was it this time? he wondered. Was his coffee a degree too hot or cold or too milky or not milky enough? His air conditioning a degree too cold or not cold enough or too milky or not milky enough?

One day he should really tell him a few home truths and take him down a peg. It would do him some good. Frankly, he had had it up to here with his complaints and if he thought he was going to sit there and take this crap then he had another think coming!

But deep down, he knew he was going to take this crap. The wages were good. He had a family to support. Christmas was coming up. He didn't have the time or the energy to look for another job. So, thought Gavin, let's get it over with. What do you want to admonish me for? What did I do that annoyed you?

But Chuck didn't talk. He stood there with a look of reproach on his face - as if words failed him - as if he felt so betrayed that he would never speak again. What? thought Gavin. What? What was it all about?

He sieved his memory. He sieved his conscience. But he couldn't find anything. He hadn't even stolen any paper clips. He would never take that sort of risk. Chuck looked even more hurt. What was it? What? What had he done? WHAT?! WHAT HAD HE DONE?!! WHAT?!!!! WHAT WAS IT?!!!!!!!! WHAT?!!!!!!!!!!!!!!

Chuck sadly shook his head. 'You've been holding back on me, Gavin. I never knew you had Multiple Sclerosis.'

'How did you find out?'

'Never mind about that.'

'I was only diagnosed a few years ago. Anyway, it's in remission. When I have an attack I only get double vision and..'

'Hey Gavin, it doesn't make any difference to me about your condition. I just like people being up front with me.'

'I'm sorry, but I thought...'

Chuck took off his jacket. 'You thought that I would sack you... Look around you... All the rooms in Head Office have ergonomic furniture; I pay you all good wages and health care benefits... I have only the best interests of my staff at heart. I know I can be difficult at times, but be *straight* with me.'

'Okay, Sir.'

'Chuck, call me Chuck. That's all I wanted to talk to you about. You can go.'

Gavin spoke quickly as he stood up. 'Thank you Sir, I'd like to explain that an MS attack for me would be incredibly rare. It would take an immense amount of stress for it to happen and I'd be recovered by a fortnight maximum..'

'It's okay; you don't have to explain anything to me. Take it easy.'
'Okay, bye.' said Gavin and left the room.

Chuck did nothing for a while then picked up the phone. 'Hi, it's me... You still haven't anything on Gavin? What's wrong with you? Right... Right... It doesn't make any difference... Hell, I don't want to be paying months of sick pay...'

***

Gavin parked his supermarket trolley by his car, opened the boot and started to load his bags of shopping. But something stopped him - something cold at the back of his neck. The barrel of a gun. Shit, he was going to be robbed, he thought. Where were the police when you needed them?

He turned his head and saw two police officers. Oh...

'Stay where you are! Hold your hands against the vehicle!'

'Is there a problem officer?' said Gavin.

'Shut up and spread them!'

Gavin complied and the policemen searched his pockets. What were they expecting to find - wondered Gavin - drugs, a gun? This was ridiculous.

Gleefully an officer held out a photograph of a small boy with no clothes on. 'Now look what we have here?!'

'That - that wasn't in my pocket!'

'Are you aware of the laws of this land?'

'You planted it!'

They handcuffed him and read him his rights - which didn't take long and stuck him in the back of the car.

As they drove off, Gavin remembered that the shopping trolley was still left by his car and the boot was still open. 'What about my shopping?'

'What about it - paedo?!'

THIRTY-THREE

Too loud. Whatever infernal, manufactured pop-music was playing in the West End store - it was too loud - too loud for thought, too loud for insight and too loud for sanity.

Peter carried a huge pile of clothing towards a till. It threatened to topple over at any moment, but it wasn't enough for him. He wanted more. Obviously, he would have preferred to steal the clothes, but security was tight. In fact security was tight in all these types of stores.

The shops he would have preferred to shoplift from posed an impossible challenge, so it was the poor little independent store, the little corner shop that suffered.

He bent down to pick up a pair of jeans from a rack when a man with a gigantic multi-coloured Afro and an eye patch grabbed his shopping and cried: 'Stop! Don't buy them!'

Peter pulled the pile back. 'What's it to you?'

Several tracksuit bottoms fell to the floor.

The stranger grabbed the clothes again. 'You don't know what you're doing! You're the victim of a terrible experiment!'

More clothes fell.

The clothes were back in Peter's possession, but the man continued to block him. 'Get out of the way!'

'Peter - listen to me!'

'How d'ya know my name?'

'How do *you* know your name? Please... Trust me..' The stranger put his hand on Peter's shoulder.

Peter instantly shoved the hand away and took out his flick knife. 'That's it! If you don't get out of my face...'

'Please tell me you haven't turned to a life of crime...'

'Fuck off.'

'We should go. The security guards are coming.'

'We?!' Peter kneed him in the testicles; adeptly dodged the guards and scampered out of the shop.

After a period of recuperation, the stranger spoke into his cell phone. 'Managed to fix bug. Pick me up...'

***

It was the end of the night for three fifteen year-old boys walking homewards with their chips. They had got up to a fair amount of mischief that evening - most of it innocent fun. They approached Finsbury Park Community Centre - where they were to part. 'See you tomorrow, then.'

'Yeah, later.' said Andy.

'Yeah.' said Tony.

Making his way homeward, John gazed down upon his trainers with pride. The Harlem fluorescent hologram logos on them beamed benevolently back to him and lit up his journey.

The trainers had not been easy to come to. Despite constantly nagging his mother, she refused to buy them for him so he had to save for them from the wages he got on his paper round.

Andy and Tony had had much more luck from nagging their mothers and had got those trainers over six weeks ago. Anyway, John had them now and that was the main thing. He manoeuvred round a puddle. He was going to take good care of those trainers especially since it took him such a long time to get them.

As John avoided another puddle, he was grabbed and felt the chill of a blade held against his throat.

'Give me the trainers.' said a voice emanating from a hood. Inside the hood was a brain - a brain that had once belonged to Peter. This shouldn't take long, it thought. Judging by the response of previous victims - this shouldn't take long at all. There was something egalitarian about wearing a hood. It didn't matter how weedy you were - wearing a hood in the dark made you scary.

The pickings had been good. People tended to carry more money on them these days. It may have had something to do with more cash machines charging for withdrawals.

'No!!' cried John.

Peter rubbed the knife on the youth's throat. 'Bend down and take them off.'

'No!!!'

Peter hadn't heard this word for ages. No?!

'I'm not going to tell you again!'

'Have my top instead!'

'I don't want your fucking top! I want your trainers!'

So far he hadn't had to hurt anybody. His other victims had more sense. But if it came to it he would do it. Those trainers would fit his feet. He could put himself in the other guy's shoes, but in a way he couldn't put himself in the other guy's shoes because he couldn't give a shit about anyone. That was obvious to anyone who watched him enter a bus from its exit and sit with his legs wide open to deter people from sitting next to him. That was obvious to the undeterred when he opened his legs even wider so that they had to half sit off the seat in discomfort. That was obvious to anyone who happened to glance at him, when he snarled: 'Look at me again and I'll kill you.'

Peter pulled John's arm more. 'This is your last chance.'

'No!' said John. Not after all that time it had taken to save for them - not after all those early cold rainy mornings - sticking newspapers through letterboxes with fingers numb with frost.

Peter's hand shook. Didn't the kid think he would use the knife? Did he think he was joking? Did he think he was a joker - some insignificant wanker fooling around - because he wasn't! He wasn't the wimp, the loser, the weakling he used to be. He was hard, street-wise, street-smart, street-tough - a *real* man.

'Give me the fucking trainers - now!!!'
'No!!!!!'

No?! *No*?! Fuck it! Fuck it! Peter thought. He was going to do it - he was going to hurt him - cut him and take the trainers. 'That's it!' But as he got his knife ready and psyched himself up he was aware of a siren.

An ambulance screamed down towards him, so he let go of the boy and ran. The doors burst open. Two men in balaclavas and camouflage paint ran out. Peter briefly looked back. It was him they were after.

Peter sprinted up the street; climbed over a fence and jumped into someone's back garden. The men followed. Peter forced himself over a taller fence and jumped into an alleyway and sped down a different street. He could still see one of them. He climbed up another wall. Jumped into another back garden. Climbed up another fence and jumped into another street. Ran down that and climbed into another garden.

He turned round. He must have lost them. He couldn't see any of them, but they were dressed in black... They could be waiting for him - toying with him. He couldn't take any chances, so he flung himself over another fence and jumped into another street and ran towards Wood Green.

If he were lucky, a night bus would stop on the way. But he wasn't and had to keep on running. After he reached the end of Green Lanes, he paused to catch his breath. He bent down and gobbed at the curb.

The ambulance swerved behind him. The doors opened. A huge fisherman's net was thrown over. Too shocked to resist, he found himself being dragged into the vehicle. The doors shut.

Fuck! thought Peter as he struggled with the netting. Fuck! They must be plainclothes policemen! Fuck! He had his regrets - he had his regrets all right. He could have made more money telling people on the phone they've won a prize and getting them to call a premium rate line number and he probably wouldn't have got caught. He could have made more money as a cowboy builder or a cowboy plumber or a cowboy electrician or a cowboy cowboy and the police wouldn't have been able to do anything about it. And identity fraud - could have made a mint out of that! Fuck! Why didn't he think of that before?

'It's not what it looks like!' said Peter, 'He was attacking *me*! I swear! I was defending myself!'

'We're not the police so spare us the bullshit..' said the plump darkened man - taking his balaclava off.

They weren't the police. That was good wasn't it? Or *was* it? If they weren't policemen: then who the fuck were they? Fuck! Terrorists - they could only be terrorists. Fuck!! Fuck!!!!

Peter went on his knees like a real man and sobbed: 'Don't kill me! Please!!! Please!!!! Pleeeease!!!! Pleeeeeease!!!!! I'll do whatever you want!!!!!!'

The thin darkened gentleman shook his head. 'No... you've got the wrong end of the stick.' He took off his balaclava. 'Yes, I'm sorry about all this, but you gave us no choice. You refused to meet at any of the rendezvous specified in my letters to you..'

The voice was familiar. Where had Peter heard it before? Where was his flick knife? His thoughts untangled. 'Oh... it's *you*... From the shop.'

Peter found the knife and cut the net. He remembered those letters all right: wanting to meet him outside some stupid places: BT Tower, Big Ben, Royal Festival Hall - outside in the cold to discuss some conspiratorial mumbo jumbo - but nothing religious thank God. A bunch of cranks. He could handle them.

He scrambled out of the net and held out his knife.. 'You're in *big* trouble. You cost me a pair of Harlems...'

The thin man and the fat man backed away.

'Yeah, that's right... You stay out of my way and I *might* let you live...'

The thin man closed his eyes tightly and karate kicked the knife out of Peter's hand. Grabbing Peter's arm, he threw him over his shoulder. Peter landed on the floor and the ginger haired man sat upon him. 'Arrrgh! No! He weighs a ton!'

After binding his legs and arms to a chair, the ginger haired man sat down next to him and opened a book.

The thin man wiped his brow. 'I don't know about you, but I could do with something to *cool* down.' He opened a box to the side of Peter; took out a cone and went to the ice cream dispenser to the left of him and filled it with Mr Whippy. He squirted some raspberry ripple on it and started licking it. He turned to Peter. 'Would you like one? This is the only ambulance in the world where you can get an ice cream.'

Peter shook his head. 'There's no point kidnapping me - you know! My family aren't wealthy! You won't get a big ransom out of me!'

The thin darkened man stopped licking his ice cream and looked hurt. 'We're not kidnappers... We're investigative journalists...'

'You work for the BBC?!'

'No. We've been broadcasting on the Internet for quite some while. Most of our reports have been too hot for mainstream channels, but we're now diversifying.'

'Really?' said Peter with a yawn.

'We've got a contract with a rather large TV station and we're working on a big story about Chuck Harlem.'

'For fuck's sake! Can't people shut up about him? What's he done this time? Is he having his clothes made in Concentration Camps again?'

'Yes, but that's not the story we're working on.'

Peter yawned. 'Had some more trade unionists assassinated?'

'Yes, but we're working on a big - a big story. It's going to affect everyone.'

'Since I'm here I suppose you might as well tell me..'

'He's going to turn everyone in the Western world into a cunt.'

'*What*?!'

'Don't say '*What*?!' it's true. He's turned you into a cunt already.'

'You calling me a cunt?'

'Yes, I suppose I am.'

'I'm not a cunt. You're a cunt.'

'I'm not a cunt.'

'Well you dress like one.'

'Do you believe in reincarnation?'

'No 'cause I'm not a cunt like you.'

'Ahhh,' said the darkened man, 'such a cunt... such a cunt...' He looked at his watch. 'I suppose introductions are called for..'

'Like I look like I'm interested...'

'You're right Opus, he is a cunt.' said Rex, peering over his book.

'Definitely a cunt.' said Angel steering the ambulance.

'Whether you want to know or not, my name is Opus, Opus Merriman and for over a year you've had product placements put in your dreams..'

'What?! How does anyone put product placements put in my dreams?!'

'They've got this brainwave machine that does it..'

'How?!'

'It's too complicated to explain.'

'Yeah, I know why it's too complicated to explain. Because it's bollocks!'

'Oh yeah?! What about this then?' Opus took out from a cardboard, Peter's pillow with its Mondrian pillowcase and ripped it apart - revealing a load of wires and circuitry. 'While you went out to that Abstract Expressionist exhibition, a Harlem stooge got into your bedroom and changed pillows. This helps your brain conduct the brainwaves..'

'You put that in before!'

'Why would I do that?'

'I don't know! You tell me!'

THIRTY-FOUR

 # London's burning. London's burning.
Fetch the engine. Fetch the engine...

Peter woke up - tied to his seat. Opus was humming 'London's Burning' while stirring something in a bucket with a stick... It had not been a dream... He really was being kept captive in an ambulance that sold ice cream.

'Could you hum a different tune?' said Peter.

'Yes...' said Opus and carried on humming the same song. He scooped out the pale substance and applied it to Peter's face.

'What the fuck do you think you're doing?' said Peter.

'Isn't it obvious?' said Opus.

'No!' said Peter.

'I'm making a plaster cast of your face.'

'Why?!'

'Isn't it obvious?'

'No it isn't! You fucking weirdo!'

'I need the plaster cast so that I can make a mask of your face.'

'And?'

'I'm going to wear it. Shop security cameras may be monitoring your movements. You've got to be seen to be still buying Harlem products or they will suspect something has gone wrong. Any blip and they may turn off the machine and then we won't be able to track it down.'

'Have you ever considered medication?'

Opus stared at him intensely. 'No... Have *you*?'

Peter grimaced as the cold substance covered the entirety of his face. Short straws were stuck up his nose so that he wouldn't suffocate. 'This is stupid! You're not going to look much like me with a mask on!'

'Doesn't have to be perfect. An approximation is all I'm looking for. Security cameras don't produce high definition images. I'm going to wear sunglasses. That should hide the main flaws in my disguise.'

Rex emptied out Peter's pockets and passed his loyalty cards to Opus.

'...What would you like for dinner?'

THIRTY-FIVE

A week earlier, a warden ushered Gavin into the visitor's room. It wasn't looking good. The judge had refused him bail and would have refused him food and water if he had anything to do with it. Mysteriously, his whole home computer hard drive was awash with downloaded child porn filth.

Gavin had found his lawyer wanting in the 'knowing anything about the law' department. His sister had recommended using him for no good reason except that he was her husband. 'Yes,' she said, 'He hasn't worked for ages. It would be *good* for him...' And there he was - sitting by the table before him - smiling complaisantly to himself as if he had done something that wasn't entirely stupid. He clutched his brief case - his new shimmering briefcase tightly to his chest perhaps to make sure Gavin couldn't stab him.

What a fake, Gavin thought. What a fake. Even his beard looked fake. For that matter, so did his nose. Actually, if his eyes weren't deceiving him, his nose seemed to have grown larger since the last time he saw him. It must have been the whole 'Pinocchio' effect.

'Hi, *Gavin*, how're you doing?'

'Hi, *Richard*, how do you think?!'

'That's great, I wanted to go over some things.'

'What's the point? I'm going to lose. It's all been fixed. You saw that Judge..'

'Every fact is crucial - everything you can remember. You have to tell me everything so that I can get you out of here.'

'You told me to plea guilty yesterday.'

'Er, I know... I changed my mind. I think you should fight. I think you should raise a stink.'

'But yesterday, you told me to go for the plea bargain, serve my time and keep my trap shut.'

Richard put his briefcase down. 'I've had a change of heart. It's hard not to get corrupt in this business. Sometimes I disgust myself. Today, I'm on your side. Tomorrow I may not. I'm just a human being who can be leaned on like everyone else. Tell me all you can. If I tell you to go for the plea bargain tomorrow then I want you to sack me and get yourself another lawyer - a decent lawyer - a lawyer who will let the truth come out.'

Gavin looked perturbed. 'Right..'

'*Promise* me.'

'Okay.'

'Good. Fire away.'

'It's like I told you before. Chuck Harlem found out I had MS; didn't want to pay any sickness benefit and wanted to get rid of me. He would have probably won an industrial tribunal because I've kept the illness secret, but he didn't want the bad publicity, so he framed me.'

'Are you sure that's the only reason Chuck's getting you locked up?'

'That's Chuck. He has a vindictive temperament.'

'You're doing time because you have MS? I don't buy it. There has to be something you know about his organisation that he wants you to keep quiet about.'

'I kept telling you that yesterday, but you didn't want to know.'

'Today's a different day, Mr Priestly. Today I want to know. Tomorrow, I may not.'

'You're strange... Anyway, there's this machine, okay? A brainwave machine. It's called the Message Facilitator...'

The man got out a pen and pad. 'This is good stuff - carry on.'

'Adverts for our products were everywhere; Internet, TV, newspapers, billboards, product placements in movies, schools, churches and so on, but sales were not increasing fast enough and certainly not meeting our annual targets. An economic downturn was on the horizon and it was obvious that the usual platforms for advertising were losing their potency. As with antibiotics, the general public were building up some sort of resistance.'

'The solution was to come up with a new platform for advertising and that's where the Facilitator comes in. So for the past year we've tuned sonic waves into the brain of a poor unsuspecting guinea pig as he sleeps. We bugged his pillow so that the waves could be specifically directed at him. These waves caused him to dream scenarios where only using Harlem products saved the day. If he put on a pair of trainers in his dream - then it was our product, if he ate a burger or had a fizzy drink then it was our product...'

'Amazing...' said the lawyer.

'There were a few teething problems at first: people tend to remember their dream if they wake up during it; and that was initially happening with the guinea pig. It didn't affect his shopping habits so much. However, people tend not to remember their dreams if they afterwards fall into a deeper sleep devoid of dreams and then wake up. So the machine was adapted to manipulate people so that they couldn't wake up during their dreams. And when our guinea pig stopped remembering his dreams; his shopping habits changed a lot. And this was because he had been *subconsciously conditioned* to buy the product.'

'Wow...'

'Wow, exactly. This is the most sophisticated subliminal advertising ever. You can't get any better than this - you can't. The project's been such a success, we're moving to the final part of our plan - ahead of schedule.'

'What's the final part of the plan?'

'We're going to use the machine on the general population on 4th July. Originally it was going to be November, but as I said..'

'Where's the machine?'

'I don't know..'

'Who's the guinea pig?'

'Someone from England called Peter Papapanos.'

'Have you got his address?'

'All I know is he lives in London..'

Richard rose from his seat. 'Thank you. Remember if I change my mind about the plea bargain; sack me.'

'Okay.' Gavin was escorted back to his cell.

Ten minutes later, the warden escorted him back to the visitor's room. Richard sat behind the desk - tightly clutching his briefcase - his battered old briefcase - somehow it had aged very quickly. 'I have good news about the plea bargain..'

THIRTY-SIX

On aisle thirteen, shelf stacker, Rachel Braithwaite, opened a box, took out twenty tins of baked beans and placed them on the shelf. Then she opened another box and took out twenty tins of baked beans and placed them on the shelf. Then she opened another box and took out twenty tins of baked beans and placed them on the shelf.

She grabbed another box and thought to herself if she found a severed head in it - it would really make her day. It would make that day differ from the previous one. 'Please, please let there be a severed head in this box.' she thought as she slowly pulled off the brown tape and opened the package... It was tins of baked beans again.

She counted them out. Please, at least let there be only nineteen. At least that would be some sort of adventure... No, there were twenty. There were always twenty.

Her colleague had told her that she had watched two DVDs last night as if it was some sort of victory. Two DVDs roughly equaled three hours of freedom. It was *some* kind of victory, she conceded.

She didn't have much going for herself. No qualifications. Spotty and overweight. She wasn't going to become a super model or a film star. No, the only thing that was going to change her life was if there was a million quid in the next box she was going to unpack.

As she opened one flap, she speculated on how she would keep it a secret so that the manager wouldn't get his greasy hands on it. It wouldn't be easy, but she would find a way...

It was baked beans again. Oh, if only there was someone who could take her away from all of this.

'Excuse me,' asked a man dressed head to toe in Harlem gear - wearing sunglasses, 'could you direct me to where the crisps are?'

'Middle of aisle five.' answered Rachel.

'Thank you.' he said and walked away.

THIRTY-SEVEN

There was a knock at the door.

'Come in.' said Chuck.

Bryan entered - sombrely.

'What do you want to tell me?'

Bryan grimly shook his head as if he couldn't bear to talk to him - as if the news was too devastating for him to impart.

'What is it, dude?'

Bryan grimaced and avoided his eyes. 'Chuck... There's... something... I need... to *tell* you...'

'Yes?'

'I... I...' Bryan went to the water cooler. 'Would you excuse me? My mouth's a little dry...'

'Sure...'

Bryan filled a plastic cup up with water and slowly drank it. 'Thanks... I... I have reason to believe...'

'Yeah?'

'...that...'

'Yeah?'

'...Gavin...'

'Yeah?'

'...wasn't...'

'Wasn't what?'

'That Gavin wasn't...'

'Yeah?'

'...that Gavin wasn't the only person behind... the wrong lyrics appearing on your monitor.'

'Who else?'

'It's... quite a long list... Mainly people who... work here... Essentially, it's a... conspiracy... A conspiracy... against you... I'm sorry... I'm sorry... I had to... tell you this...'

Chuck's jaw dropped. 'Thanks... Thanks for telling me... dude...'

'That's... all right, Chuck... Originally, I was going to *wait* longer before I told you... You know... *wait* for evidence... but I knew it wouldn't be right... to keep this from you...'

'No... You were right to tell me... What're we going to do about this... *lack* of evidence?'

'Arrange a substantially better plea bargain for Gavin so that he can verify the suspects I have on my list.'

'Really?'

'Yeah, because this is far bigger than we thought...'

THIRTY-EIGHT

Rex entered the ambulance - carrying a tray of food. 'Hi.' he said to Peter.

Peter did not respond.

Rex released one of Peter's hands, put the tray on his lap and gave him a plastic fork. Peter turned his head away and ignored it. 'Here you are: the Chuck Burger Meal with extra large fries..'

He briefly glanced at Rex's offering. 'Not eating it.'

'But it's what you asked for.'

'You heard me - not eating it. Take it away.'

'I don't understand..'

'I'm on hunger strike.'

'What?'

'I'm not eating anything until you release me, so if I die it'll be all because of you.'

'But we don't want you to die.'

'Tough, release me then.'

'But we can't - not yet!'

'You've got to or I'll starve to death.'

'Okay...' Rex handcuffed Peter. 'I'll have your dinner then!'

Rex bit into the hamburger. Oil trickled down his chin. The burger looked so succulent and juicy. It smelt delicious. Peter licked his lips. He licked his teeth. And he licked the inside of his cheeks - and drooled.

'So...' said Peter, 'how come you and Angel can't see that Opus is a raving maniac?'

'That's one Hell of a guy you're slagging off.' said Rex with his mouth full, 'He's done so much for me. I wouldn't be the man I am today if it wasn't for him.'

'I'd hate to have met you *before* he had sorted you out.'

Rex carried on eating the burger. Peter looked on - enviously. 'You do realise that you're in a cult and that Opus is brainwashing you - you realise that don't you?'

'You've got the guy all wrong. He isn't a cult leader - he's a journalist!'

'Never seen a journalist like that before - wearing masks all the time!'

'He has to wear masks all the time! He's a dissident investigative undercover journalist - okay? He's a wanted man.'

'I thought as much - a *common* criminal..'

'Hey, you can talk!'

'At least I don't delude myself about what I am...'

THIRTY-NINE

Rex Yates had never met his real parents, but he was shown the trashcan he was dumped in. In later life he was to use it as his very own receptacle for rubbish. It had been thirty-five years, seven months and six days since he was dumped in it outside a brothel. Good thing that he was a loud crier or 'Juicy Lucy' wouldn't have heard him when she had popped out to get more batteries for the vibrator. From the moment she pulled up that lid, she was smitten.

For several years, the prostitutes lovingly raised Rex until the Church authorities heard about it. The church argued that a brothel wasn't a decent place for a boy to be raised and arranged for him to be taken to a church orphanage where his private parts were fondled in a safe and decent environment.

One night, several weeks later, Father Luke had a heart attack while fantasising about what he was going to do to Rex next and died.

When Rex asked the Head of the orphanage if his replacement was going to do the same things as Father Luke had done to him, he was swiftly transferred to another orphanage and promised that he would be made a priority case for adoption if he kept his mouth shut. And indeed a family was found - on the eve of his sixteenth Birthday.

'Although you're a bit on the old side, the Huckleberry's are very happy to have you join their family.' said Father Thomas.

The Huckleberry's owned a farm and were only too happy to show Rex the ropes. 'There's only one rule here, Rex.' said Papa Huckleberry, 'Dinosaurs never existed.'

That night, Rex tied some bed sheets together and climbed out of the house.

For a while, the stars became his ceiling and trashcans became his bed. Though it was harder for him to fit in them now.

As he foraged for half eaten pizzas and drumsticks, he knew that something was missing from his life.

Sometimes he watched groups of students wander into museums - all carefree and happy. He would like to be like that, he thought. What would it take to become one of them? The answer was obvious, but how was he to get the money to pay the fees and the living costs?

Jobs were hard to come by and all he had to do was open his mouth and the job was pretty much ended.

Fortunately for him, he saw the light - the light that refracted on a shiny golden object that poked out of someone's waistcoat pocket - a collector's pocket watch. He saw the light and swiped it. Then the next day the light shined on a similar opportunity and he took it. Then he took other things and went where the light took him. The light never let him down and soon he had enough money for college. The plight of his victims rarely caused him sleepless nights. If anything, he slept too well and got puffy eyes and headaches.

Fraternity life gave him far more than the outside world would ever willingly offer: toga parties, genuine friendships, casual sex, drink, a plethora of drugs and last but not least: education.

So much did he enjoy the degree he went ahead and did another one. So much did he enjoy that; he did another. And so he went on to become a perpetual student who shoplifted, broke into warehouses, sold weed and picked pockets in between lectures.

An attentive student was he, but lecturers had to watch out. If they crossed him, they risked having their cars stolen.

Women came and went, but his lust for education never faltered. History, politics, geography, all of it was fascinating to him. None of his qualifications would ever land him a job, but that didn't matter to him. It was knowledge that mattered - not some tiny blinkered perception of some small subject area but a deep understanding of something vast - *knowledge*.

He was sadly disappointed with the standard of literature available in the state penitentiary when he got busted.

When Rex first came across Opus, he didn't have a mask on and his pores were open. In fact, both of them had open pores since they were sitting together in a crowded Turkish bath - sweating profusely. The toxins had reached the surface of Rex's skin but his soul still wasn't cleansed so he carefully swiped the elastic band off Opus's wrist - the elastic band that held the key to his locker.

Half an hour later, Opus went to his locker to find the door already open and his wallet and his shoes missing. A pair of moldy trainers was left on the floor. They weren't even the right size, but he put them on all the same.

FORTY

Two days later, in a diner faraway, a waitress took down a customer's order.

'You got cherry pie?' asked Rex.

'Yeah...' said the waitress.

'Have you got *more* than one cherry pie?'

'Yeah...' said the waitress - yawning.

'In that case, I'll have *two* cherry pies.'

He watched the waitress walk away - watching her was almost a dessert in itself and then he wondered that perhaps he should have ordered three cherry pies. Two might not be enough. He should've inquired about the pies' circumferences. Without knowing that, it was hard to judge.

A waiter approached - carrying a pie. That was a shame, thought Rex; he was hoping to see the waitress again. It must have been the end of her shift. Should've taken her number. He could tell that she liked him...

It all happened so fast: the pie ran down Rex's face as the waiter handcuffed him to the table. What? What? What the fuck's going on? He licked some of the desert still dripping down his face. It was custard. 'Hey! What're you doing? I ordered *cherry* pie!'

With his free hand, Rex wiped the remains of the pie from his eyes and watched the waiter pull out a cell phone and looked at his shoes... The trainers he was wearing seemed awfully familiar.

'You're not a real waiter - are you?' said Rex.

The waiter shook his head.

'You're who I think you are - aren't you?' said Rex.

The waiter nodded and turned his cell phone on.

'Please don't call the cops - please... I've done this *before* - been in prison *twice*. If I'm put away again I'll never get out. You can't make me serve life for stealing your wallet... Please don't call the cops... You can't do that to me... I've had a hard life! I've got ginger hair and I was adopted!'

'Mmmmmmmmmmmmmm...' said Opus.

'Okay, okay... Put yourself in my shoes, you'd probably do the same thing.'

'Mmmmmmmmmmmmmmmmmmmmmm...'

'Give me a break! See it from my point of view.'

'Mmmmmmmmmmmmmmmmmmmmmmm...' said Opus - standing there in a trance - possibly astral projecting himself into Rex's body so that he could see the situation from Rex's point of view. Normal consciousness resumed a few moments later. 'Okay,' he said, 'I forgive you.'

***

In the diner, the pair finished their meals. 'Tell me,' said Opus, 'Why do you steal?'

Rex rolled his eyes in disbelief that such a stupid question could be asked of him. 'Because they want me to!'

'I don't understand..'

'If the state doesn't allow me to have a vote ever again after coming out of jail then that means they don't want me to be rehabilitated and they want me to remain a criminal. If I reformed, became a successful entrepreneur and went into politics and social reform then they'd probably assassinate me. I thought if I continued stealing they'd leave me alone.'

'Don't you ever want to divorce yourself from your past?'

'You can't do it. Your past is your past...'

Opus took a sip from his tea and turned to Rex: 'Have you ever thought about investigative journalism?'

Rex shook his head thoroughly. 'No I definitely haven't!'

'I couldn't help but notice that you've spent a lot of my money... I was wondering what you intend to do about it.'

'Hey, I thought you said you forgiven me..'

Opus snapped his fingers. 'I know! You can work off the debt by working for me..'

'I *can*?'

'I'm starting my own media organisation and I happen to need someone like you to help start it up. Haven't got all the equipment yet, but I'm certain with you working for me, I soon will have.'

'Yeah, sure I'll work for you - why not...'

So with new found comradeship in the air, the pair spoke into the small hours - laughing and joking and patting each other on the shoulder as if they had known each other for years.

When the hours started getting bigger again, Rex magnanimously offered to pay.

Opus shook his head and waved his hand and told him not to worry and that he wouldn't hear of it, but Rex shook his head and waved his hand and told him that he wouldn't hear of it. 'It's time I did something for you. I insist. You get the bill and I'll go to the john.'

Reluctantly, Opus agreed. Rex went to the john and Opus asked the waitress for the bill and then he waited for Rex's return... Hmmmm... he thought as he gazed at his watch. Perhaps he was getting paranoid in his old age. The waitress came back. 'Er, did you happen to see my friend?'

'Yeah, half hour ago. Said he was popping out to get some cigarettes. He also said that you would pay.'

'Oh...' said Opus. He put his hand in his jacket pocket to find that his wallet was missing. He shrugged. 'I'll have another soda...'

FORTY-ONE

A group of Native Americans sat round a fire - smoking a peace pipe. It was passed to the new member of their community.

This was the life, thought Rex. It had been two weeks now. Opus had obviously lost track of him. Anyway he'd lie low here for a while, marry one of the women, get her pregnant and then leave. The old Rex genes had to carry on somewhere...

A lone rider dressed in a white Stetson and white cowboy suit strode towards the group, dismounted and spoke to them a while in their tongue. He returned to his horse as the group put out the fire and dispersed.

Rex followed the Chief. 'What did he say? What did he say?'

With an aloof sneer, Sitting Bull Junior stared at him; snatched the pipe from his lips and shook his head with disdain.

How often was a peace pipe wrenched from someone's mouth? wondered Rex. It meant something. It meant that he had to run. Run!!

Too late. Even before he built up a moderate momentum, the lasso went around his arms and torso and he was dragged to a tree and tied to it.

'How did you find me?' said Rex.

Opus put his hand in Rex's pocket and retrieved his wallet.

'I know it looks bad,' said Rex, 'and I know it looks ungrateful, but what can I say: sorry, I promise I won't steal from you ever again. Just please - please don't call the cops..'

'Mmmmmmmmmmmmmm...' said Opus.

'...Put yourself in my shoes...' pleaded Rex.

'Mmmmmmmmmmmmmmmmm...' said Opus more aggressively.

'A man with my past is *destined* to do a thing like this... I couldn't help it... Did I tell you I was adopted?'

'Okay,' said Opus, 'I forgive you once more, but don't take the piss.'

***

The pair sat in another diner and made their plans. 'So it's agreed,' said Opus - embarking upon a crossword puzzle, 'you'll work for me for a year. I'll pay your living costs, then after the year is over we'll negotiate a proper wage.'

'Sure,' said Rex, 'you get the bill, and I'll *definitely* pay this time.'

'Okay.'

'I'm off to the john for *real* this time.'

And so Opus waited... and waited... He wasn't altogether surprised to find his wallet gone. And he *still* hadn't got round to getting his shoes back. He shrugged and continued with his crossword... Now what was another word for betrayal?

FORTY-TWO

The plane landed. Rex breathed a sigh of relief. Throughout the flight, he had eyed everyone sitting near him suspiciously - especially the Nun. 'Why would she want to go to Paris?' he thought to himself. The place is too fun for her... What would she want with Champagne, the Moulin Rouge and Pain au Chocolat? Wasn't being on a plane a bit *luxurious* for her? Shouldn't she be making the journey on her bare bleeding knees with the sun baring down on her - turning her skin to leather or parchment - if *she* was a she...

It would be easy for a man to disguise himself as a Nun - in fact far easier than a woman... And why the fuck was she staring at him in such a strange way?

The Nun remained a Nun for the duration of the journey. Rex claimed his luggage and then made his way out. Standing by the arrivals gate was a man dressed as the grim reaper - holding a sign with Rex's name scrawled upon it in blood.

Opus didn't appear to be in the best of moods, so Rex made a run for it. Anticipating Rex's route, he soon caught up with him outside one of France's most highly prized patisseries. He grabbed Rex's legs and pinned him down. 'Money, please.'

'Don't you want your wallet?'
'Okay, I'll have my wallet back as well.'
'Sorry, I threw it away.'
'Then give me the money then.'
'How did you track me down?' asked Rex.
'I could tell you, but life wouldn't seem so mysterious after that.'
'Here.'
'Oh...' said Opus as he received a few measly notes.

'Let me lay it on the line with you.' said Rex - getting up, 'I am scum. Dog turds wouldn't want to step on me. You could not possibly hate me more than I hate myself.' He kicked his own shin. 'See? I want to beat myself up. I hate myself so much for what I did to you I want to smash my face in. So you see, there's no point calling the cops - my self-loathing is punishment in itself...'

'Mmmmmmmmmmmmmmmmmmmmmmmm...' said Opus sternly.

'Please... I know this may sound barely credible, but I promise I will never steal from you again.'

'Mmmmmmmmmmmmmmmmmmmmmmmmmmmm...' said Opus like he was going mad with rage, but suddenly he started laughing. 'Okay! I forgive you! It's hard to stay angry with you for long. It's going to be fun working together..'

'But I don't want to work for you.'

'Yes... I'm willing to overlook that... So let's get on with it - shall we?'

FORTY-THREE

In one go, Peter stuffed the whole burger into his mouth - his hunger strike having lasted precisely two hours. He looked at Angel as he wolfed down his meal. Maybe he could get through to her... He wiped the grease off his chin and put on his doggy eyes. 'Please... let me go.'

'For the millionth time, no!'

'...Look, I can see that you're not like the others..'

'You can't get round me that way.'

'If you let me go. I promise I won't call the police. As far as I'm concerned that'll be it - end of story..'

'Think I'd believe that?'

FORTY-FOUR

Life had been no picnic for Angel Jefferson. It hadn't been a banquet or a party either. The dilapidated tenement block that she and her parents lived in weren't right for those occasions.

Every morning, by their doorstep she found used needles, crack debris, spent bullets, trails of blood and pools of urine - even though she hadn't left a note in a milk bottle asking for that stuff.

Stifling her yawns, she would clear away the mess with a broom. What with the gunshots, screams and sirens in the neighbourhood, it was hard for her to get much sleep. Her parents' constant yelling and hollering didn't help either. Theirs wasn't a match made in Heaven or even Purgatory on a Saturday night.

It got on her mother's nerves that her husband worked in a bar and spent all his wages in a bar. It got on her father's nerves that it got on her mother's nerves that he worked in a bar and spent all his wages in a bar.

Dinner was eaten off paper plates because all the crockery had been broken years ago. The last china plate had left a four-inch scar on her father's forehead. They had tried hurling paper plates at each other, but it wasn't the same.

The day before Angel's twelfth Birthday, life got significantly quieter. After a comparatively mild altercation, her father popped out to get a pack of cigarettes. Some time later, he didn't come back. The police could only shrug their shoulders. His body was never found.

Later that year, rumours went round that there had been a spate of similar disappearances. They had all popped out to buy a pack of cigarettes and it was the same brand as her father's. One day, on her way home from school, Angel decided that she would investigate. She stopped at a kiosk to see what would happen to her if she bought a packet. Maybe something strange would occur so that she would be able to locate her father.

The first kiosk refused to sell her cigarettes on account of her age. She went away and returned to the kiosk when no other customers were present and succeeded in buying a packet. Nothing happened so she went to another kiosk. Nothing happened again and she went to another kiosk. She was hoping that something would happen soon since she was running out of money - money that was meant for groceries.

A man wearing sunglasses with mirror lenses and a newly laundered suit watched her as she put the packet in her pocket and walked down the street.

Her sixth sense told her she was being followed. She crossed the road. The man crossed the road. She quickened her pace. The man quickened her pace.

She realised then that she hadn't thought it through. Once she got taken and found out what happened to her father and the other smokers - then what? How would *she* escape? It wasn't as if she had any hidden microphones or bugs on her that would let the police track her down and rescue her. Where should she go? she wondered.

She couldn't go home because he would then know her address. She would have to find a public place, but this was a run down neighbourhood, so they were rare. Even the kiosks had petered out. It was then that she decided she no longer wanted to find out what happened to those smokers - not if it meant that it happened to her.

She stopped and threw the packet into a bin...

But it made no difference to her pursuer. Shit, it was too late now, she thought. She had parted with her money and now she had to take the consequences. She looked at the road. Cars whizzed by - trying to get out of that neighbourhood as quickly as possible. She darted across the road and dodged the passing vehicles.

Her pursuer fared less well and got hit by a car. In a public-spirited move, the vehicle manoeuvred away and sped down the road. Angel rushed back to ask him those essential questions: did he know what happened to her father or any of the other smokers?

His sunglasses were still intact. Unfortunately, the same could not be said about the rest of him - his once pristine suit awash with blood.

Was he a Fed or someone trying to give her back her change from the kiosk? That she would never know. At least the sunglasses spared her the dead look in his eyes.

FORTY-FIVE

Despite the odds, Angel achieved excellent exam marks at school and was offered a scholarship to study journalism.

She began her studies at the academy and met a nice young man. Kenny was one of those amazing types who could get on with your mother without repulsing you at the same time.

After a month of stimulating study and company, her bout of happiness was to suddenly cease.

In the middle of mopping a floor, Angel's mother had a stroke. When she came to in the hospital bed, she cursed herself. She knew she shouldn't have mopped that floor. She had already mopped too many floors that day. She knew she didn't feel right. If only she had stopped for the day. One floor too many... If only... But it wasn't as if she had had much choice...

There was no one else but Angel to look after her. The limits of Kenny's amazingness soon became apparent. It was almost as if all their relatives and friends had gone off to buy a pack of cigarettes. She withdrew from her studies; went back home and nursed her and helped her to speak and walk again. The first words her mother said clearly were: 'Sorry... sorry for holding you back...'

'It's okay,' said Angel.

Her mother was almost rehabilitated and Angel was ready to resume her studies when she had another stroke. She nursed her again and she was making steady progress when yet another stroke occurred. After two years of tiring painful struggle, her mother died.

A man entered her life and helped her with her grief. He was about fifteen years older than her. His name was Errol and he was a musician - a heavy metal guitarist. He told her he was going places - though she could barely remember him leaving the bedroom.

He was perpetually on the 'verge' of some big deal and always needed to be free from the confines of paid employment to realize his dream. In her own small way, she helped by paying all the rent, the food expenses, the phone bills and all the other bills.

She worked in fast food joints and then enrolled on in computer software night courses and got better-paid jobs so that he could afford to dream a little longer.

It all came to a head when her night class had been cancelled and she burst into the bedroom to find him giving cunnilingus to a big-breasted blond.

'Baby, it's not what you think.' he said, 'I've become a prostitute. I know money's tight. She said she'd pay me a hundred bucks if I slept with her.'

He nudged the companion in the bed. 'Come on. Pay up.' The blond eyed him with incredulity. Reluctantly, she fished in her handbag and handed him seven dollars and forty-three cents.

'It's all I've got.' His panic stricken eyes coaxed the blond to say some more. 'Er, I er, lied when I said I had a hundred bucks... Sorry.'

Errol placed the money in Angel's palm. She clasped it. Seven dollars and forty-three cents - that was all that her struggles had got her. Seven dollars and forty-three cents. He had never given *her* cunnilingus! She remained silent.

There was nothing for her in that room or in that flat apart from burdens and repayments of credit card debts and the seven dollars and forty-three cents in her hand. If she could walk away from it all then she would. But wait a minute, she had her monthly wage cheque in her pocket and the rent, water bills, electricity bills and phone bills were coming up - she could walk away.

Errol's 'customer' looked at her watch. 'Is that the time? I *really* ought to be going.' She started dressing. 'Yes... your boyfriend... he's very good... I'll recommend him to my friends... Bye.' She left with the back of her dress in her knickers.

'Well...' said Errol, 'Guess I better have a shower... Am I bushed! Though I might still have some *energy* for you... How about it - baby?'

'Yeah... maybe later...' said Angel.

As Errol showered and screamed out Bon Jovi songs, Angel pulled her suitcase from the top of the wardrobe; packed it and made her way to the front door.

Putting on her coat in the living room, she heard Errol coming out of the shower. She hid the suitcase behind the sofa. Dripping, and leaving a long trail of water as per usual, he came in with a towel wrapped around him. 'Where you going?'

'Oh, I'm going out to get a pack of cigarettes.'

'Oh, get me a pack while you're out.'

'Yeah, sure.'

He returned to the bedroom. She picked up the suitcase; opened the door; walked out of the block; walked down the sidewalk and then walked some more. And as she walked, her burdens shrank into the distance. She spotted a kiosk, but carried on walking.

FORTY-SIX

Standing behind the lectern, Chuck delivered the final words of his conference speech to the thousands of middle to high ranking management sitting in the hall: '...So this year we're going to try *even* harder; because nobody said it was going to be easy.'

Everyone took to their feet and applauded him. 'More!!!! More!!!!!! Give us another conference speech!' Foot stamping commenced. 'More!!!!!!!!!!!'

Chuck held out his hands for quiet. 'Dudes, I've said all that I'm going to say. It's now our Head of Development turn to talk; Susan Lamb..'

'Booooo!!!'

'Hey, I'm not going to tolerate any booing in my outfit - okay? Now treat her with respect; Susan Lamb.'

Susan shuffled over to the lectern. A bit late in the day, she discovered that she had some egg stuck on her corduroys. She tried scratching it off as she fiddled with the PowerPoint projector. She adjusted her glasses and fumbled with her papers.

'Er, I am h-happy - happy to announce that the dip in the fortunes of H-Harlem Enterprises has been reversed and we are now the tenth biggest company in the world.'

No ovation.

'But, er.. w-when it c-comes to diversity, we are the number *one* company in the world - no other company has so many workers from so many parts of the world - as these figures confirm...'

No ovation. People's attention began to wander.

'...In general, this year, the company has seen steady and sustainable growth. Th-thank you.'

She sat down to a few slow handclaps.

'Thank you for that,' said Chuck, 'now Bryan Fahrenheit has an update for us.'

A tall, thin man in shades, with a cigarette in his mouth strolled to the lectern and blew out a smoke ring. He had come quite some way.

When he had first met Chuck seven years ago, he was only a lowly 'Style Hunter'. He went to school playgrounds, poked his face through fences and called out to Black school kids 'Hey! Do you fancy a free pair of Harlem trainers?'

Bryan would hold out the boots and a few boys would come up to the fence and say: 'Yeah. A pair of Harlems would suit me fine. Give them here.'

'Cool it. Cool it. All I need in return... is you to tell me the word on the street... on the hippest styles happening.'

Occasionally a mother who had been called in to see the Principal would interrupt Bryan as he jotted down their 'cool' data. 'Excuse me, what do you think you are doing with my son?'

'Nothing, Madam. I'm only asking him a few questions. I'm interested in his... opinions.'

'So you is interested in his *opinions* - are you? Are you sure that's all you're interested in?'

'No, Madam, no! You've misunderstood me..'

'Oh, I think I understand you well enough. I've seen your type before. Yes, your type is very interested in the opinions of thirteen year-old boys!' Then she walloped Bryan with her hefty handbag. 'Get out of here - you weirdo!'

'No, Madam, please!'

'Get out before I call the police! Derrick, didn't I tell you not to talk to strangers?'

That was then. Today Bryan was here, Deputy Head of Development. There were no big Black women walloping him with handbags now.

He took another drag from his cigarette. '...Steady... and sustainable growth... Steady... and sustainable growth... Steady and sustainable growth is all well and good, but can't we do *better* than that? Being the tenth biggest company in the world is... *all right*.' He shrugged his shoulders. 'I could *live* with it... But what about being number *one* company in the world?'

Susan put her hand up.

'And not *just* for diversity? Being number *one* company in the world would be *pretty damn good*... Judging from the results of the Message Facilitator trial, I can pretty safely say that this aspiration could become... a *reality*... We estimate income could increase by five thousand percent! Now I'm happy to report that we are on track for worldwide usage. The snags have been ironed out. We don't need to change everyone's pillow... Obviously, there are people we don't want this device to affect - namely us, the police and the armed forces.'

From his pocket he drew out a neck chain. 'This piece of jewellery produces a high pitched audio signal that blocks the product placement waves from being broadcast into your head. We'll publicly award it to fore-mentioned parties for their sterling service to the country etcetera, etcetera...'

'Are you sure that they will all wear the neck chain?' said Chuck.

'Don't worry, I understand human psychology.'

'That's great.' said Chuck - thoroughly reassured, 'Could you put out the cigarette? I know it looks cool, but I don't want your cancer.'

Susan stood up. 'Chuck, do you really think we should pursue the project?'

'What do you mean?'

'We're tenth top company in the world! Do we really need to do this?'

Chuck sighed. '...If we don't do it someone else will.'

'There might be a recession happening! How are people meant to afford to buy so much more of your products?'

'If there's a recession happening then it's all the more reason we use the Facilitator.' said Bryan.

'How will they pay?'

'That's not our problem.' said Bryan.

'I'm given to understand that the guinea pig has turned to a life of crime!' said Susan.

'There's no proof that there's a correlation between the use of the brainwaves and his decline into delinquency.' said Bryan, 'And even if there is - then that means more work for our security firms. Can't you see the synergy?'

'I can see it, dude!' said Chuck.

Susan slowly shook her head. 'The - the only synergy I can see is the synergy of greed and stupidity! I quit!' She made her way out of the room.

'I'm sorry you *feel* that way.' said Chuck, 'I'd like to thank you for all your hard work and wish you the best of luck with all your other endeavours.'

'Fuck you!' said Susan and slammed the door.

There was an awkward silence.

'...You know,' said Chuck, 'I always thought she was suspect with her dowdy cardigans and overall bad taste in clothes... She was never one of us...'

He pulled out his cell phone. 'Police Sergeant Fraser please... Hi... It's a delicate situation, dude... I believe one of my employees has got a problem - a *serious* problem... Yes... Her name is Susan Lamb... She left Harlem Head Office, a minute ago... I believe you will find child pornography upon her person. Oh, no... we've done child pornography... Yeah, you're right... Er... you'll find some... er... *drugs* on her... Yeah... crack... cocaine. That'll do. Bye...'

He stared at his staff. 'Anyone else want to flush a six figure job down the water closet?'

No one said a word.

'No, didn't think so... Let's hear the rest of the report from Bryan, our new Head of Development...'

To increase his stage presence, Bryan paused even longer. Overall, it had been some year... Lost his job, got it back again, got promoted and then got promoted again. A lot of the personnel on his hate list were gone from Head Office. Many had resigned because they were tired of the constant investigations about the 'monitor' incident. Though he couldn't honestly say that he was happy with their replacements. They may have to go as well...

Never did he imagine that he would derive so much capital from changing the lyrics on the monitor and altering the sales figures. Though he knew that Chuck wouldn't have had time for his project otherwise. It made him laugh that Chuck had never suspected him. It wouldn't be that long until the old fart got senile dementia and then he would get to run the whole operation by default. Yeah, he had known Chuck's true age for years. Nothing remains hidden... certainly not from the prying eyes of Bryan Fahrenheit.

FORTY-SEVEN

The golf ball went up into the night sky - caught by the rays of the floodlights - a temporary star in the cosmos before it landed a yard away from the hole. 'Four!' yelled Chuck as he potted the ball.

Teeing off, the white rap star known as Rottweiler amused Chuck and Zack Contemporary with an anecdote: '...I'm in bed with this bitch - we're both bare-arsed naked and my main bitch starts to open the door. I say: 'You can't come in - I have a contagious disease - this place is quarantined!' but she don't believe me. She walks in and finds me with Zadie. My main bitch looks at Debbie - she has sperm in her hair and love bites everywhere. And I say to her: 'Hey, honey, don't worry. It's not what you think - she's my sister!'

Chuck and Zack roared with laughter. Tears streamed down their faces.

'...That reminds me, Chuck,' said Rottweiler, 'how's your main bitch? I heard she gives mighty good head.'

Chuck stopped laughing. He stared at Rottweiler with a combination of incredulity and rage and swung a left hook into his nose. He followed with a right to the chin, knocking the rapper down.

'Don't call Mimi a 'bitch'... You do not refer to the woman that I love in that way ever again. Got that?'

Rottweiler wiped the blood from his nose. 'Okay, man, okay! I'm sorry! I didn't mean anything... The duet single's still on - right?'

Zack was incredulous. 'You *love* her?!'

Rottweiler picked himself up.

'Sometimes... when she's sleep... I look at her. Her face changes when she's asleep. She looks like a baby, so innocent, so... I love her more than I love myself.'

'You don't *love* her more than *yourself*?!' snorted Zack.

'I'm going to marry her. She's the one.' said Chuck.

'You can't marry her! You're an A-listed film star and she's a two-bit porn actress.'

'Not anymore.' Chuck said, 'She's going to have some high profile roles in some big movies.'

'So she good at acting?'

'Is she good at acting?! Is she good at acting? She is talent! She is talent incarnate! The audience will love her! The audience will adore her! She's going to become a cinematic legend!'

Chuck's companions eyed each other.

'What's the matter with you?' said Chuck. 'Can't you tell? Can't you see how talented she is?'

'Yeah, sure...' said his friends. 'She's *brilliant*... She's very *good* at acting...'

FORTY-EIGHT

A plane soared across a crimson sky - drawing an outline of a heart. A man jumped out of the vehicle - Chuck Harlem. He free-fell as the clouds clustered together and created the image of Mimi Johnson's face.

He pulled the parachute cord and bland music played in the air as he drifted down; turned towards the cameras and sang:

 # I see your face
In my reflection
Every time I have a shave,
Mimi.
I hear your voice
In every empty room
Before I walk in
Mimi.
Your smile is
Better than a sunrise.
Meeting you was such a
Surprise.
But I never have,
I never have
Enough time
For you.
I want
More hours in a day!
More days in a week!
More weeks in a year
To be with you,
Mimi.

Mimi!
Let's turn the world off.
Let's turn time off.
Let's switch off our phones
And draw the curtains.
Let's lie in bed together
And hide

Beneath the sheets!
Mimi!
Hold me now
And don't let go!

The sky darkened and fireworks went off.

'That was Chuck Harlem's new song.' said the TV presenter, 'Although it has only been released an hour ago, 'Mimi Johnson - I Love You' has already topped the charts...'

FORTY-NINE

It was a quiet morning in Chuck's residence. Mimi had yet to rise. Sat by the dining table, in his kimono, Chuck was in the process of having breakfast. He dunked his bread soldier into his egg; flicked through the pages of his newspaper and choked.

There in type and pictures was a less than flattering report on him - revealing another scandal - a scandal that Mimi must not find out about.

Mimi walked in - her hair a dishevelled but cool mess. Chuck stuck the paper in his gown. 'Hi...'

'What would you like for breakfast?'

'A new head...'

The butler came and got her a bowl of cocoa covered rice cereal; a peanut and jelly buttered slice of toast and a glass of milk.

'What're we doing today?' she said.

'I've got a shareholders' meeting, but we can do something later..'

'Another one?'

'Yeah...'

'I hardly get to see you.'

'I'm sorry babe. There's so much to do.'

'I think you do too much.'

'You're right. I *do* do too much... It's not easy juggling it all... I just wish... I just wish the press would cut me a little slack.'

'Why?'

'They keep giving me flack. I don't do this right - I don't do that right...'

'Oh, I don't read the papers.'

'What about the ones I own?'

'No.'

'Do you ever watch the news?'

'No.'

'...Anyway, it's hurtful - criticism. I've only been used to praise.'

'Chuck, the people who criticize you are just mean miserable dorks. They're obviously jealous of you.'

'Hadn't looked at it in that way...'

'I know you're good. I know you're kind. Don't let them worry you. Criticism's just jealousy - okay?'

'It isn't just the criticism, Mimi; some real nasty rumours are being spread about me. I want you to know if you hear them that they're not true.'

'I'm sure they're not..'

'Those rumours about those villagers in Pakistan being forced out of their homes to make way for a dam built by my construction firm - not true..'

'Okay..'

'Those rumours about a boy having his head decapitated at one of my dockyards by a crane due to poor safety standards - not true..'

'Okay..'

'Those rumours about that factory in India making figurines of me burning down and killing all the workers because the doors were locked to prevent thieving - not true..'

'*Chuck*, I've been there - okay?' She looked down. '...I was doing good at high school; good grades; winning medals in running; I was popular; had this hunk of a boyfriend and this group of girls started spreading rumours. They said I was a whore and saw me *being* a whore in the town's red-light district. They researched it all and made it sound believable. After a while, people started believing it. I tried to stop the rumours, but it was no good. Anything I said made it seem true. And what was worse; these girls weren't just telling lies; they were trying to make them come true. They prepared cards with an image of a naked woman offering an *array* of services and stuck them by public phones with my cell phone number on them...'

'...I had old pervs waiting in their cars outside the school trying to pick me up. Some of them would practically follow me home. I'd complain to the police, but they laughed. They also thought I was a whore...'

'...It didn't take long for my boyfriend to think I was a whore and dump me. Then my mother decided to believe what everyone else was saying and chucked me out... That's why I don't see my dog no more... I stayed over at some friends - the few friends who were still my friends - until their parents chucked me out. My ex-boyfriend started going with one of the bitches. Must have been what she was after... A few other things happened because of the rumours... but luckily it didn't affect me... So... spreading rumours... is bad.'

Chuck went silent for a while. '...Bastards... Fucking bastards... Give me their names and I'll get someone kneecap them or I could pay someone to anally rape them..'

'Chuck, I don't want any of that...'

'Are you sure 'cause I could get someone to sort them out..'

'No, no...'

'Okay..'

***

Mimi woke up to find Chuck had already left for the recording session. She held her chest as she started to cough. She needed a cigarette. She coughed some more. She needed a cigarette desperately. She picked up her packet. It was empty. There was no point looking for any cigarettes lying about the place. Chuck didn't smoke.

She tossed some clothes on and took the elevator. There was a kiosk a kilometre away. She opened the front door and found five of Chuck's bodyguards.

They smiled courteously. 'Good morning, Ma'm.'

'Hi. I'm out of cigarettes. I won't be long.' The bodyguards blocked her way.

'We'll get them for you, Ma'm.'

'It's okay, I felt like going out.'

'Don't worry; we'll come with you.'

'That's kind of you, but I felt like going out *alone*.'

'I wouldn't do that if I were you. It's dangerous out there...'

FIFTY

Disguised again as Peter, Opus entered the ambulance and gave the 'real Peter' his meal. The 'real Peter' did not say anything. Giving the others the silent treatment was a new tactic he had adopted. It had gone on for days. He grabbed the burger and bit into it.

'Peter, could you do me a favour and think back?' said Opus, 'Do you remember having a dream where you could plainly see a Harlem product?'

Peter carried on chewing.

'Did you have a nightmare where using that brand saved your life?'

Peter sighed and looked at his shoes again. '...Maybe once.'

'How many times?'

'Two - possibly three. Three dreams are not going to brainwash me!'

'Peter, they made sure you couldn't remember your dreams. They can manipulate you more if you don't remember your dreams! They can manipulate your subconscious! Have you remembered any of your dreams for the past year?'

'What the fuck has the Harlem Corporation got against me?'

'Absolutely nothing and that's why they can get away with it. We need to track down the Message Facilitator. You're our only hope. Will you let me hypnotise you, Peter?'

'Yeah?! Why not?! You kidnap me, tie me up - why not hypnotise me while you're about it?!'

'I can only hypnotise you if you want to be hypnotised.'

'Yeah, and I don't want to be hypnotised!'

Opus sighed. 'You weren't always a cunt, you know.'

'Thanks. Glad to hear it.'

'I mean it. A year - a year and a half ago you were a nice guy. The sort who helps mothers carry pushchairs up staircases.'

'Actually, that makes it easier to rob them, 'cause if you snatch their handbag, they can't run after you.'

'Peter, over the past six months you must have done some atrocious things and I don't want to hear about them, but one thing you've got to remember when you recover: don't be too hard on yourself. You weren't responsible for your actions.'

'Wow, that's, that's a load off my mind, 'cause I was feeling *really* guilty. No *really*, I've been losing sleep over it all..'

'Shut up!' Opus grabbed Peter's tray of food and threw it at the wall. 'Shut up! Your sarcastic cynicisms bore the shit out of me!'

Peter was startled. Opus grabbed his collar. 'Look at me! Look! Look at your reflection from a year and a half ago. You wanted to be an artist and you were an artist. Your lack of material success didn't deter you - you didn't care about that! But since you've worn that neck chain your life has turned to shit! When did you last paint? When? Can't you see? *Your* dream was stolen from you! *They* stole it! You used to have beliefs, now inside you there is only a hungry void crying out for Harlem products... You used to have friends - *good* friends who were always there for you and now you're totally alone... Look at your reflection from a year ago and tell me you wouldn't prefer to be him.'

Try as he might, he could not stop the tears. Oh God! He wanted to scoop up the tears and force them back into his eyes and pretend that nothing had happened. But he couldn't.

'Have a good cry and blow your nose.' said Opus, 'I'll get you some tissues...'

FIFTY-ONE

The ambulance reached a more scenic part of the motorway - Angel driving with Peter sat next to her. He watched the passing scenery: rolling hills, fields, sheep and cows. But gradually these idyllic sights became more and more obscured. All the wallets he had ever stolen and all the houses he had broken into started to whiz by. The faces of all his victims whizzed by also - crying faces, traumatized faces, afraid to go out at night faces. Too miserable to appreciate the scenery at all faces.

He turned to Angel. 'I don't know how I'm going to live with myself.'

'You couldn't help it.'

'I should have resisted more..'

'No one can resist the Message Facilitator.'

'If it happened to anyone else, I bet they would have been stronger..'

'I doubt it.'

'I should, I should have suspected what was happening.'

'It's *done*. No point getting depressed about it. At least you've got something you can blame. You can blame the brainwave machine...'

'I stole my parents' DVD player - I'm scum!'

'We all do things we regret... Sometimes it's years 'til we realise we should be ashamed... But if there's one thing I've learned; it's that there are always opportunities to redeem yourself - doesn't matter what you've done - except maybe rape or murder... You didn't rape or murder anyone - did you?'

'No.'

'Good.'

They continued down the motorway and started to talk - proper talk, not the usual bullshit that passed for conversation these days. And as they passed more sheep and cows, he had a revelation: Angel was the loveliest woman that he had ever met.

As they reached the junction, he felt that he was on the brink of something momentous - something was going to happen in his life. His waiting was over. The air was sweet with expectation. He felt a freshness that he had never felt before. As if he had had a shower that would keep him fresh forever and had put on some delicious aftershave that would never fade.

He could see it. He could see a reflection of he and Angel together in the future in the window. He could see him and her as a couple. Some good would come from all the shit he had gone through. It would make up for it. The ordeal would make sense. He would come out of it a better person - definitely a happier one.

***

It was dusk when they had reached the hotel.

While Angel parked the ambulance, Peter watched an elderly couple - sitting on a bench. The old man was white and probably in his eighties. His wife was black and looked younger. Their clothes were threadbare. They didn't talk to each other, but sat there - hand in hand - gazing at the setting of the sun.

Times must have been hard for them. They looked as if all they had was each other. But that was enough. Then, without a word, they got up and walked into the sunset.

***

Peter lay on the bed. There was a knock on the door. 'Come in.'

Opus entered. He didn't say anything, but paced up and down.

'Anything wrong?'

Opus turned to him. 'It's a shame it took so long to get through to you, because we're left with only two weeks to locate the Message Facilitator.'

'I'll do what I can.'

Opus paced again and turned back to him. 'I'll need you to be a receptive student. I need to train you in the art of 'lucid dreaming'. Have you heard of 'lucid dreaming'?'

'Sort of: you realise you are dreaming while you are dreaming.'

'Basically... It's very difficult. It normally takes months to master if not years, but with you; it's going to take six days...'

'How come you're such an expert?' asked Peter as Opus wound up an alarm clock.

'There was a time when I had no control over my life. I took up lucid dreaming so at least I had control over something... Right, I'm going to hypnotise you to fall asleep for an hour. The induction will condition you to remember your dreams. In that hour I want you to look out for any indications that you are dreaming. Before that I want you to constantly question your reality... So... How do you know this isn't a dream?'

Now there was a question. 'Well...' said Peter. This week - this whole year had been surreal. Could a dream be perceived to last a year when you were only asleep for a few hours? Could you experience a dream that broke the laws of time?

'...How many heads are on my shoulders?' asked Opus.

'One.'

'Are you sure there aren't five?'

'Yes.'

'That's a good sign that you're not dreaming - isn't it?'

'Suppose so...'

Grabbing Peter's arm, Opus pulled him out of the chair and got him to stand on it. 'Try to fly...'

'What?!'

'Jump off the chair and try to fly!'

'You're mad.'

'I'm only asking you to *try*.'

Reluctantly, Peter jumped into the air with his arms outstretched and landed on the floor.

'Get in the habit of doing this and when you do take off you'll realise you're in a dream.' Opus handed a book to Peter. 'Read and learn.'

***

The alarm clock went off. '...And now you're awake.' said Opus, 'How did it go?'

'I don't remember.'

'Please try. Write down anything in the note pad. It may come back to you.'

'I'm sorry I don't remember.'

'Okay, I'll hypnotise you again..'

'Again?! I've already been asleep ten times today!'

'We have only three days left...'

Peter stood on the chair again; tried to lift off and jumped to the ground. 'Try it for twenty minutes and then we'll start again.'

FIFTY-TWO

Angel put her bags of shopping on the hallway floor; rummaged for her key and opened the door.

'Surprise!'

Opus, Rex and Peter stood before her in top hats and tails - holding a giant Birthday cake. Her room had been transformed: Art Deco frescoes beamed onto the ceiling by a stolen slide projector; a feast was laid on a large candle-lit table and Irving Berlin cassettes playing in the corner.

Happy Birthday to you!
Happy Birthday to you!

Happy Birthday dear Angel!
Happy Birthday to you!

'Thanks,' said Angel, 'but we're looking for the Message Facilitator tomorrow. We should be going to bed..'

'No, fuck it - it's your *birthday*! We're going to celebrate.' said Opus.

'I don't want the mission to be ruined on my account.'

'Angel!' said Rex, 'Don't you ever feel like letting your hair down?'

'I have short hair. What are you talking about?'

'Don't you even want to look at your presents?' asked Peter.

'Presents?'

Rex handed her a novel. 'This is by your favourite author..'

'Thanks, but I have all of his books.'

'Not this one.'

She looked at the title. He was right.

'But how? I thought this wasn't coming out until next June.'

'Oh it comes out sooner if you break into the author's pad and print out a copy.'

Peter gave her his present. She unwrapped it to find a framed portrait of herself. 'It's my first painting... for a long time...' said Peter.

'Wow... When did, when did I pose for you?'

'I drew it from memory.'

'It's not much.' said Opus as he placed his gift in her hand. It was a bootleg cassette of a live concert by one of her favourite singers. He had stuck a photo of the singer and drawn funky lettering on the cassette cover with a felt tip to make it look more official.

'Nina Simone! Thank you Opus. Thank you everyone.'

***

Intoxicated with alcohol and joy, new ideas buzzed round Peter's head. Each can of beer brought him to a new level of contentment. Never had conversation flowed so freely. Never had he felt so connected - especially with Angel.

He felt so lucky to be caught up in such a group - so fortunate to be in the centre of the universe. He felt fresh - revived again as he had done when he was sitting next to Angel in the ambulance - in the ambulance that had saved him from his miserable life.

Everything had been leading up to this evening: his premature birth, his every mistake. Except his mistakes hadn't been mistakes after all because they had lead him to this evening. Yes, his long, long winter was finally coming to an end.

***

'Should only be about quarter of an hour.' said Opus as he went out with Rex to get more booze.

Peter and Angel sat cross-legged on the floor. Now was the time, he thought. Now was time to reveal his love for her. He slid nearer to her, determinedly. There she was... So near... And there was a beer... Even nearer...

He took a swig. What if she didn't feel the same for him? But why should that be the case? They got on well - didn't they? So why shouldn't she love him? *Yes*! *Why* not? She always seemed happy when he saw her. He was certain he could detect a distinctive glint in her eye. Was it not possible that the glint was present because *he* had entered her life?

He finished the drink. He had to tell her now. There was no time for prevarication.

He grabbed another beer.

He had to tell her that she was the meaning of his existence; that all his dreams of success in the contemporary art world wouldn't mean anything if they could not be together and that her smile jolted his still, still heart back to life. He had to tell her this very second, that to merely see her mouth with its perfect lips would resuscitate him if he were to fall into the deep side of a swimming pool.

He had to tell her this very nanosecond that if he were to suffer some weird selective blindness where he could see nothing except her; it would not matter - she would be all the visual stimulation he would require. If he were to never see another tree or another bird, it wouldn't matter. If he were to never see another sculpture or another painting or another sub-titled Art house film - it wouldn't matter - as long as his eyes could see her form shine out from the darkness. She would be all the art he would need.

He picked up another beer, but resolutely put it down. No... If he drank any more he would become incoherent and would probably make a fool of himself. He coughed politely.

'Yes?' said Angel.

'Y-y-you, you are gorgeous - you are. Even, even if you w-were blind and dead, you'd still be gorgeous to me - and, and - even, even if you had drowned in the deep side of the swimming pool - you'd still be a work of art...'

'Peter, what're you talking about?'

Peter's feeling of freshness and vitality was swiftly replaced by a feeling of queasiness as he edged nearer. That was love, all right. It always gave you a nauseous feeling. He drew his lips to kiss her, but blacked out briefly. He woke up to find her face and body covered with vomit. She trembled with the trauma.

'W-who did this to you?' cried Peter, 'I'll, I'll kill who ever did this to you!'

'You did! You puked on me!'

As she grew understandably hysterical, Peter tenderly removed the sweet corn from her hair and gently wiped away the semi-digested tomato skin from her eyebrows with the end of his shirt.

No! thought Peter, no! He couldn't have done this! It was such a *juvenile* thing to do! Only *immature* berks did that sort of thing. How could he redeem himself in her eyes? How was he going to impress her?

This had to be the most stupid thing he had ever done in his life! And if he had been reincarnated, it was the most stupid thing he had done in all his lives! It made all his other previous errors shrink to the point of insignificance.

If only... If only he could go back in time and make sure this never happened. Yes, go back in time. He wound his watch back half an hour. Maybe if he visualized time going backwards this would do the trick. If he visualized the vomit going back in his mouth, it would do it.

He scooped a handful of sick from Angel's shoulder and stuck it in his mouth. 'C-come on!' said Peter, 'L-let's go back in t-time!' But the sick was so disgusting that he started throwing up again.

To avoid subjecting Angel to another gastric-juiced onslaught, he turned his head, only to find himself vomiting on her Birthday presents.

No! thought Peter, no! It would ruin his chances with her *even more*! In all probability, he had only a dog's life chance with her, but this had to totally scupper them all now. Even if he donated his bone marrow or a kidney to her, she would never forgive him. This was such a nightmare, he thought.

Wait a minute, he thought. Maybe this *was* a dream. He pinched himself to check that he wasn't dreaming. Then he pinched Angel to make sure he wasn't dreaming.

It hurt each time, first when he pinched himself and secondly when Angel slapped his face. But pain could be emulated in dreams, he remembered.

Wait a minute! He ran to the lights and switched them on and off, on and off and on and off.

The lights went on and off, but maybe it was an extremely vivid dream. There was only one more thing for it. He staggered on top of the sofa and tried to fly.

Angel watched impassively as Peter flapped his arms, fell onto the floor and passed out.

***

'Poor boy...' said Opus as Rex and he picked Peter off the floor and seated him on the armchair.

Opus changed the cassette in the player and then pulled Angel up from the floor. Irving Berlin's 'Cheek to Cheek' blared. 'Would you care for this dance?'

'But I'm covered in puke!'

'At some point in our lives we will all be disgusting. All of us will create a stench and become repugnant.' He held out his hand.

'Maybe after a shower.'

'No, this song's special. It's 'Cheek to Cheek' - the best song ever. Let's dance while it still plays.'

'We could play it later.'

'The tape could break. This could be our last chance to dance to it.'

He put his arms around her and they moved in time to the music. At the end of the song, Opus drew his lips to kiss her.

Peter opened his eyes and confronted the full horror of the situation. 'No!!!!' he cried and tried to prise them apart. 'You can't go with him! You don't even know what he looks like! He could be hideously scarred!'

'Shouldn't you be going to bed?' said Opus.

Rex grabbed hold of Peter and pulled him out of the room.

'Angel! You can't do this! It's me who loves you!' Peter cried, but Angel didn't appear to hear him. It looked like Opus was distracting her with his tongue.

Rex dragged Peter out of the room.

'You saw me eat vomit! Doesn't that mean anything to you?'

***

Rex laid Peter down on the bed. 'Didn't you know that Angel and Opus have been engaged to be married for the past six months?'

'No!!'

'Well they are.'

'Why didn't anyone tell me?'

'Couldn't you tell?'

'No!!!'

'Couldn't you see the glint in their eyes when they spoke together?'

'No!!!!!'

'I don't know... Thought it was pretty obvious.'

'It would have been obvious if they wore engagement rings, held hands, slept in the same room - it would have been obvious if they did any of that!!!!'

'No, they're... they're not like that - not lovey-dovey and joined to the hip... Look, don't worry, Angel will be fine about the way you made a tit of yourself.'

'I'm not *worried* - I'm disappointed.'

'Don't let it get you down, Peter. At least she's rejected you because she has someone. I've known women with no husbands, no boyfriends, no friends and were homeless but still didn't want to go out with me. I'd ask them: 'Are you sure you won't go to a restaurant with me?' and they'd stay on their park bench and say 'No, no, this crust of bread will do me.' They'd be like *starving* and they still wouldn't go to dinner with me.'

Rex was going to continue with his comforting tales of woe, but noticed an alteration in Peter's complexion. A second wave was approaching. He barged out of the room and slammed the door behind him a split second before a crescendo of vomit splattered it.

FIFTY-THREE

'Come on baby! I know you can do it!' pleaded Rex to his backpack. It was bulging and would not shut.

Noticing his plight, Opus said: 'Let's see if I can lighten your load...' and opened out the pack and pulled out a stack of pornographic magazines.

'A man has needs.' said Rex.

'Take one.'

Rex grabbed the mags and flicked through the pages with an air short of urgency. 'It's so hard to choose... I like page thirty-two of issue one hundred and twenty-five, but I also like page sixty of issue seven..'

Opus pulled out a gigantic volume of the collected works of Gabriel Garcia Marquez. 'I don't think you'll be needing this...'

'But he's really good.'

Opus pulled out an ornately carved depiction of the crucifixion. 'Didn't know you were religious.'

'I'm not. That's worth a lot of money. I stole that from a church.'

Opus pulled out a pile of hotel bath towels. 'Won't need these...' Took out a hotel hairdryer. 'Won't need those...' Removed several bottles of hotel shampoo and shower gel. 'What's wrong with you, Rex?'

After removing six bars of hotel soap, and a hotel radio alarm clock, he zipped up the bag. 'I'll better get Peter up. You two wait in the lobby.'

***

Peter woke up alone, but not *totally* alone. A pile of sick lay beside him. He wished that vomit was Angel and not vomit. But after what he did last night there probably wasn't much difference between them.

He turned to find Opus sitting in the chair next to his bed - holding a glass of water and a capsule.

'Take it.' he said.

'What is it?' said Peter.

'I promise you it's not poison - take it.'

Peter swallowed the capsule. 'How's Angel?'

'She's okay. She's had a shower. She's almost the same person she was before you threw up on her...'

'...So I guess this is zero hour...'

'You need more training, but we're out of time. So I've decided to alter the induction.'

'How?'

'It's a technique I created myself. You won't find it in any textbook. You'll have to trust me on this... I think it will do the trick.' Opus took an identical capsule from his pocket and swallowed it. '...Ready?'

'Suppose so..'

Opus guided Peter's arm slightly above his own head. Opus sat down in a chair opposite him. '...Stare at your index finger...'

Peter complied.

'...Continue to look at it... As you fix your gaze on it you will notice that the other fingers tend to fade out of focus...'

This was in fact true.

'...and that your entire arm begins to feel heavier and heavier...'

This was in fact the case.

'...The longer you concentrate on that finger the heavier and heavier your arm will become...'

Peter's fatigue increased and he found it even harder to keep his arm up.

'...But you will not go into a deep state of relaxation until the arm has come all the way down. Keep concentrating on that finger while the arm gets heavier and heavier and heavier...'

His arm started to gradually lower as his eyes flickered.

'...Notice that as your arm gets heavier, it is slowly coming down, down, down. But you will not relax into a deep and profound state of relaxation until the arm is all the way down...'

Peter's arm slowly lowered more as his eyelids flickered, lowered and remained shut for longer.

'...Going down, down, down, deeper, deeper, deeper, deeper...'

Peter's arm slowly reached his side and his flickering eyes stopped opening.

'...You are now in a deep state of relaxation... Soon you will be asleep but you will still hear my voice. My orders will appear in your dreams... You are slowly diving into the sea of sleep... slowly as I deepen the induction...'

***

Peter found himself standing in a busy high street - teeming with people: mothers ferrying their children from school in their four by fours to stop them from being run over by other mothers driving their children in four by fours; people laden with shopping bags - watching with dread as street fundraisers came into view.

All was normal apart from the fact he didn't have any trousers or boxer shorts on.

He wondered why this was the case. There had to be a good reason for the amount of exposure he was giving to his nether parts.

Was he the victim of some *hilarious* stag night prank? He couldn't remember.

On the other side of the street, he spotted a hill with a pair of jeans hanging on a tree on the summit, so he turned away from the shops; and started his ascent. From no discernible direction, came a ghostly but booming voice. 'Don't go up the hill!'

'But I need trousers!' said Peter.

'They are Harlem trousers!'

'But..'

'Go without trousers and suffer the social consequences.'

With understandable apprehension, Peter returned to the street. But he needn't have worried. They ignored him and faded away.

Peter found himself walking in the Sahara desert and couldn't for the life of him remember why he was there. Was it something he was doing for charity? The weather was much hotter than he preferred -

even though it was a dry heat, which tends to be more bearable than a humid one... Why didn't he take any water with him? And a map might have been a useful. It didn't look like he had prepared at all.

For many hours, he trekked on - getting sand in his shoes; taking his shoes off; emptying the sand; putting the shoes on and getting more sand in his shoes.

By then he was thoroughly annoyed with himself. What sort of fool would do such a thing?! What sort of idiot?! What sort of plonker would embark upon such folly? What tosser would put himself in such a position?! What prat, dickhead and wanker would go by himself with no means of communication into the hottest place in the world?!!! Aaaaaaaaaaaaargh!!!! He felt like head butting himself.

As if drunk with thirst, he staggered for several more hours with the sun beating down on him. And then for several more hours he crawled on the sand, but at least by that time he had forgiven himself.

At the moment he thought he was about to collapse and let himself turn into a particle of sand and join all his billions of brothers and sisters, he saw before him a soft drinks machine.

It shone brilliantly on the sand amid the sound of angels singing. On his knees, he searched his person for a one-pound coin. Tears of relief fell upon his cheeks when he pulled a sovereign out of his pocket. But just as he was about to deposit the cash, a voice from nowhere came out again: 'Do not put the coin in the slot!'

'Why?' croaked Peter.

'Can't you read? It's a Harlem vending machine!'

'But I'm... *thirsty*.'

'Do not put the coin in the slot!'

'I think... I think I'm going to faint..'

'Endure the fainting! Endure the dying!'

Peter collapsed. A sand storm commenced. Everything went grainy and the scene disintegrated.

Peter opened his eyes to find himself standing in the yard of a Latin American prison in front of a Latin American firing squad desperately in need of emergency dental work.

They positioned their rifles and slowly drew aim. Again, Peter wondered why he was where he was. If this was some stag night prank, he was going to be furious. If only he had taken up dentistry, he thought to himself. He could have traded his life for giving them bridgework.

Something tapped him on the shoulder. He turned and found the end of a rope ladder lowered from a helicopter hovering from over head. As he grabbed the ladder, the ghostly voice boomed out again. 'Do not climb up the ladder!'

'Why?'

'Look at the logo! The ladder has been lowered from a helicopter made by Harlem enterprises..'

'For fuck's sake! They're going to kill me!'

'Endure the bullets! Endure the bloodshed!'

'You know what? I don't think I will..'

But it was too late, because of his prolonged heated discussion with the voice; the firing squad had already started firing.

The bullets went through him. His torso slightly disintegrated, but then solidified back to normality. 'That's funny,' said Peter, 'I'm not dead!'

'That's because it's a *dream*.' said the voice.

The firing squad continued to fire at Peter to no avail. Frustrated, they got out their knives and started running towards him. 'They're coming after me!' said Peter, 'What am I going to do?'

'Whatever you like! This is your dream now!'

'Yeah?'

'They're fascist bastards - beat them up!'

As the firing squad started ineffectually stabbing him, Peter started punching them. 'Er, take that - you fascist bastard...' It all seemed a bit half-hearted.

'You can do better than that!'

'Can I?'

'Haven't you noticed? They look like your housemates!'

The voice was right. They did look like those bastards.

'Why don't you fly and punch them?'

Peter soared into the sky; zoomed down upon them and then karate kicked them. Then he grabbed two of the squad; knocked their heads together and flung them against the wall.

It was the best violence ever. He felt no pain and he was smashing the shit out of all these gits. At last, all his pent-up frustration had found something to channel it self through. But all good things had to come to an end.

The squad disintegrated and turned into a green gas that went transparent and all the scenery followed suit. Everything faded into a totally blank canvas - devoid of any visual stimulation.

Peter rubbed his eyes. 'I can't see anything...'

'Good!' said the voice.

'What's good about that?'

Apart from the voice, all Peter could sense was a curious smell. 'Tsk, someone's burnt some toast..'

'You can smell *burnt* toast?' said the voice - moderately excited.

'Yes.'

'You're sure? Not burnt sausages?'

'No, burnt toast.'

'That's brilliant!'

'Why?'

'That's the smell you need to smell. It was probably present all the time, but you were too distracted to notice. Now the journey *truly* begins.'

'But I'm tired..'

'Now I believe that smell is caused by the brainwaves being pumped into your subconscious. You must motivate your body to sleepwalk and follow the trail of the smell.'

'Couldn't I have a rest first?'

'Of course this is a challenge since you will need to sleepwalk until you reach the source of the smell - the Message Facilitator. The average length of a dream is an hour. Assuming that the machine is more than an hour away that means that you will probably have to stay in that dream much longer than usual. So when you start to feel that the dream is fading you will have to spin your body. Spinning your body will keep you in the dream. Remember you cannot afford to lose that dream. You must not wake up until you are *there*.'

In the visual void, a pair of ruby-encrusted trainers appeared.

'That reminds me,' said the voice, 'you must put on those on..'

'You're joking. They're cack! They don't go with the rest of my clothes..'

'When people experience rapid eye movement dreams their physical bodies are paralysed. You have to wear those shoes. It's the only way you'll be able to release your physical body from the paralysis - the only way that your physical body will be able to enact what you do in your dreams...'

Peter shuddered at the thought of wearing those repellent trainers.

'Please, Peter... wear those trainers for the sake of the *world*.'

Peter gritted his teeth and slid his feet into the shoes.

'Thanks, Peter; I know how hard that was for you. Now I suppose you better start walking...'

FIFTY-FOUR

Opus woke up - sat in the hotel chair. Peter remained next to him - snoring. He checked his watch. He had been asleep for an hour. Good. That was as long as he had aimed to sleep when he had hypnotised himself.

He took a pen and pad from the bedside table, to jot down what had happened. No... Nothing... He couldn't recall a single thing... Mmmm... he hoped that it had worked... Hopefully he had managed to accompany Peter in his dreams or at least managed to make Peter dream that he was reminding him that he was in a dream.

It was good that Peter still had his eyes shut. It was good. But it wasn't good that he wasn't walking. 'Walk Peter, walk.' urged Opus. 'If you don't stand on your own two feet and start walking, everyone in the world will be brought to their knees.' He hoped that the psychotic drug, he had given him hadn't done any harm. God knows what the stuff does.

One of Peter's nostrils flared out. This was promising. Opus held his breath. 'Come on, Peter, flare both your nostrils out...' The other nostril flared out. 'You can do better than that! Use that huge, value-added conk of yours...' Then the other nostril flared out. 'Both nostrils... Both nostrils...'

Both nostrils flared in and out. 'That's more like it!' In and out. In and out. He proceeded to smell his surroundings - sniffing with a canine intensity. 'That's the stuff!' Engines were revved... 'Yes!!' Ignition... 'Yes!!!' Rockets were launched... 'Yes!!!!'

With his eyes still firmly shut, Peter got up from the chair and started to walk.

Hooray! thought Opus. This had made his day, his week, why, his whole fortnight!

Outwards they strayed - one man with his eyes shut and his nostrils flared and one man with his eyes open and his nostrils contracted - bumping into the maid with her trolley of disinfectants.

'Good day to you!' Opus cried. 'My manners! I mean: Jo napot kivanok!' They passed the Philippine maid and the Iraqi maid and Opus wished them a 'Maayong adlow!' and an 'As salaam alaykoum!'

***

Coffee and bacon smells drifted into the lobby as they did every morning. Sometimes coffee overpowered the bacon smell. Sometimes bacon was victorious. And as with every morning, a mob rushed into the dining room one minute before breakfast officially stopped being served. The floor polisher hummed by. The TV was inaudible, but contributed to the ambience.

Keys were handed in and taken out. 'Hope you will enjoy your stay... Hope you have enjoyed your stay... Hope you will enjoy your stay... Hope you have enjoyed your stay...' And so continued the revolving door of life. 'Hope you will enjoy your stay...' Many a time the receptionist had told a customer that she hoped they *had* enjoyed their stay when in fact she should have said that she hoped that they *will* enjoy their stay, but no one had ever bothered to correct her.

Rex and Angel were stationed on a leatherette sofa - newspapers open. Rex preferred the article Angel was reading so he read over her shoulder.

'Read your own paper.' said Angel.

'I'm not reading your paper... Could you turn the page please?'

'I haven't finished it yet.'

'Tsk, you're such a *slow* reader...'

Peter appeared - closely followed by Opus. Angel shut her paper, rolled it into a ball and stuffed it in a bin. 'Hey!' said Rex.

Opus smiled and put a finger to his lips. 'Shhh...'

***

Drudging through the car park, the group saw an old-fashioned ambulance shoot by - its siren singing its anxious song.

'Isn't that ours?' said Angel.

'Yes, I'd arranged for another member of the agency to look after it.' said Opus mysteriously.

'I thought the news agency was just us.' said Rex.

Opus slowly turned to him. 'Well... you... thought... *wrong...*'

***

Footsteps. Footsteps. Disciplined, following footsteps. Footsteps following Peter's footsteps. Footsteps with purpose. Footsteps with pride. Footsteps full of energy and optimism - despite not knowing their destination or the duration of their journey.

Footsteps. Footsteps. Footsteps over roads. Footsteps over concrete. Footsteps that took them through the grass verges of the M25 - past drivers stuck in tailbacks - their faces drained and listless.

By then, Rex's footsteps faltered. Only ten minutes had gone by. He turned to Opus. 'Are you sure you need me?' Can't I stay somewhere, then hire a car and catch up with you later?'

'The amount of people I need assisting me is *two.*'

'Come on! How many people do you need to open a door for him?'

Opus stopped and pulled from behind Rex's ear, the Ace of Spades. 'Peter will have more than doors to worry about...'

***

Footsteps... Footsteps... Beyond the traffic cones, they continued - beyond the lay bys and women crouching behind car doors - trying to pee in privacy - beyond comfortably lit signs and service stations - following their sleepwalking leader.

Footsteps... Footsteps... Roads shrivelled and shrank. Belisha beacons came into view. A sign welcomed them to Watford. It was dark, but they weren't missing anything.

They passed the Head office of Camelot. Its windows seemed to leer at them and say: 'You'll never win! You'll never win anything!! You'll have to work for the rest of your lives!!! Har!! Har!! Har!! Har!! Har!!'

Footsteps... Footsteps... Peter took it upon himself to suddenly jolt across the road.

Opus joined him and authoritatively held up his hand to stop the traffic. The chorus of beeping drivers got so loud - it almost woke Peter up and he had only gone halfway. This necessitated in him spinning his body to remain in the dream - further delaying his progress in crossing the road, which made the drivers even more impatient and noisier with their beeping.

Walking up and down the road with his finger by his mouth, Opus told the drivers to shush. Interestingly and paradoxically, this did not make the drivers any quieter. So left with no other options, Opus began to sing:

Amazing Grace, how sweet the sound...

His was a fine, resonate voice. The song began to calm down the drivers. Opus gestured to Rex and Angel to join in. Rex sang:

That saved a wretch like me...

His was a fine voice also - verging on the operatic. The beeping had practically ceased and Peter had stopped spinning.

Opus coaxed Angel. 'You too!'

'I'm not that good.'

'I'm sure you are.'

After psyching herself up, she sang her heart out. The beeping started again. Her singing was atrocious. 'Not all Black people can sing, you know!'

Footsteps... Footsteps... All too often, Opus and his group had to intervene when Peter bumped into hoards of drunken revellers and had the physical mementoes to prove it.

Footsteps... Footsteps... By Sudbury, their noses had ceased bleeding and on they strode towards Harrow - their sore feet eager for long-term retirement or short-term amputation.

'...After all this sleepwalking, Peter's going to need some rest.' said Angel wearily.

Opus wasn't so disconsolate. He had gone through odysseys like these in previous lives and had therefore built up greater spiritual stamina. The worst epic journey he had made was when he was a leper. He only had his top torso left when got to the end of it. Though the fallen bits of his limbs did help him find his way back.

Angel sustained herself with a vision. Once they had found the laboratory with the Message Facilitator, they would notice a cell next to it. They would force open the door and out would come her father and all the other disappeared smokers.

There would be a golden glow to him. He would have given up the booze and the cigarettes.. Oh, who was she kidding?! she thought. He'd probably ask her if she had a few dollars spare and then piss off to the races.

Rex sustained himself with a vision too: a torn-out page from his porn collection. Whenever he felt that he was truly flagging, he would take it out of his pocket, unfold it and look at it a while and find he had more energy.

***

Footsteps... Footsteps... And yet more footsteps... It grew blustery as they trudged up Harrow on the Hill - past vintage cars, tea-rooms, an over-priced school uniform shop, and a procession of boys from the private school - holding on firmly to their straw hats.

It was as if the hill clung onto the past with its fingernails and barricaded itself against the present.

St Mary's church chimed in the distance as Peter resisted the force of the wind. It wanted to blow him in the opposite direction of the smell, but he overcame this malevolent force and sleepwalked into 'The Castle' pub.

'Good on you!' said Opus as he and the group ventured in.

Everything and everyone was in Technicolor. The snooker balls and snooker table had never looked so colourful. Everything *smelled* in Technicolor too. The cheery, welcoming smells of cider and cheese and onion crisps were most intense. Separately, these aromas wouldn't be much to write home about, but together... well, it was the sort of smell that made Great Britain great.

These smells could no longer be savoured as Peter walked into the flight path of a passing dart. 'Watch out!' Opus leapt into the air and caught it in his teeth. Regulars applauded and bought them drinks.

***

By St Mary's Church, the group sipped their pints of cider and gazed at the horizon. From here, you could see the West End - real London - London undiluted - in all its frothy, intoxicating glory.

'Maybe the Message Facilitator is in the BT tower.' said Rex.

'Maybe it's in Big Ben...' said Angel.

'Maybe...' said Opus - smiling enigmatically.

Footsteps... Footsteps... Downhill footsteps - past the cemetery, through the bushes and trees. Past the bench where sixth form college students snog. Past dogs returning to their exhausted masters with sticks without showing the slightest sign of tiredness. Past couples pushing prams - wondering if they will ever have time to see any of their friends again. Past an old man in a skipper cap and nautical clothing - struggling up the path.

The old skipper stopped halfway - catching his breath. What a beautiful place... He had explored many countries but he had never seen such a green as he had seen in Harrow. He wondered why he felt so tired. Normally, he could have walked up all the way up the hill.

Lower down, a woman drove by on a mobility scooter.

Maybe that would be him someday he thought. He lit himself a Woodbine to console himself. Several years ago, unbeknownst to him, an artist had painted the skipper walking up the hill on the verge of evening - a lone figure on the green with a silhouette of the church in the horizon. The painting was given as a wedding present. To this day, it hangs in the couple's living room wall. It was a shame the skipper had never seen the painting or knew of its existence. Seeing himself on that wall would have been comforting to him.

***

Footsteps... Footsteps... Hendon footsteps... Barnet footsteps... Footsteps - traipsing through Highgate cemetery. The cramped, crowded gravestones said it all. So many people *exhausted* themselves, *killed* themselves trying to achieve something during their short existence - smearing *oceans* of forehead blood from one wall to another - going *round* and *round* trying to find their parking space in life and even when they were *dead* there was *still* nowhere for them.

They paused at Marx's monument. 'That's funny,' said Opus, 'I had a book with a photo of this sculpture... He didn't look this miserable... Suppose it could be a trick of the light.'

***

Footsteps... Footsteps... Footsteps accompanied by different smells. Fried food from the fast food restaurants. Drains and the chalky scent of wet pavement after it had rained. Rotting vegetables of market stalls. Cakes being baked. Smells that would make you hungry and sick. Coffee and vanilla. And the unique mustiness of the Underground. But those smells petered out as they approached a residential area...

The feet situation had deteriorated and several more injuries had been accrued due to Peter's unhealthy habit of bumping into strangers. Deviating from the pavement, he began to walk down the footpath of a resident's front garden.

This sight almost brought tears to Rex's eyes. Peter stopped at the front door with his face pressed against it. 'We're here then! Halleluiah!' said Rex. 'Thank God! *Thank God*! For a minute I thought I was going to totally *lose* it..'

'Not necessarily...' said Opus.

'Not necessarily - what?' said Angel.

'We're not necessarily there.' said Opus.

'What do you mean?' said Rex.

'Maybe Peter wants to walk through this house's hallway, kitchen and back garden and continue on his trail.'

'You mean: the machine might *not* be here?' said Rex.

'Yes, that's what I said.' said Opus.

Going up to Peter, Rex grabbed his arm and said: 'Okay, buddy, we'll have to use a different route - okay?'

'What are you doing?' said Opus.

'We can't walk through the building, so we'll have to walk round the corner and he'll catch the smell again.'

'He might *not* catch the smell again.' said Opus and rang the doorbell.

'What're you going to tell the owners?' said Angel.

'An edited version of the truth..'

They waited a while... Opus used the doorknocker.

An elderly, dishevelled woman opened the door. 'Hello?' she said.

'Oh hello...' said Opus, 'I was wondering if it would be too much of an imposition if we entered your house so that we could walk through it and go out through your back garden. It would save so much time..'

Angel nudged Opus, 'Though if we found something interesting here, we may possibly want to stay.'

'Okay.' said the old lady and unchained the door and let them in. The first thing noticeable in the house was the preponderance of cats - white disdainful moggies - totally and obviously resentful of their intrusion. Angel counted at least ten roaming in the hallway - sneering at the group with their nasty insolent eyes. It was almost as if the cats were telling them: 'Miaow! Fuck off! Miaow! Go on - fuck right out of here!! Miaow!!'

It had been years since this property had received guests. Complex cobweb metropolises covered the ceiling. Bright wallpaper had browned to sepia tones. Patches of the carpet were bleached by the rays of the sun through the stained glass of the front door and had been peed and pooed upon by generations of thoughtless pussycats.

It was so squalid there that even Jehovah Witnesses didn't want to come in. 'No, it's okay, we'll come some other day...'

'Carol' was as oblivious to the place's blemishes as she was to her neighbours' hostility and proudly led the group to the mantelpiece.

There stood a framed photo of a young ravishing woman sat by a grand piano. 'Such great days...' said Carol. In the corner was the piano - the piano that featured in the photo - still pristine. 'Don't play it anymore, because of my arthritis...'

No hi-fi speakers could be seen but the group swore they could hear some music - 1930's piano music - something like Gershwin - a distant echo of the music the piano used to play.

They went to the kitchen. Several cats lay on the kitchen table - casually nibbling Carol's dinner. She unbolted the kitchen door and Peter and the others continued into the garden - which was covered in the same make of cat.

'Why only white cats?' said Rex, 'Is she racist?'

'Shhh!!' said Angel.

Through the weeds and brambles they battled to find the fence covered in weeds and brambles. Peter pressed himself hard against it. His hands and face were bleeding, but he pressed himself against the thorns all the more - as if he was embracing the pain in his life - as if he was hugging it.

'I wonder,' said Opus, 'Would it be possible to borrow some shears?'

'I might have a pair in the shed.' said Carol.

'Where?!' said Rex. Angel kicked him.

It may not have been obvious to some, but a shed lay nearby. Despite the apparent wilderness, Carol found it instantly. She returned to the group a little cut up and with brambles and weeds in her hair and handed the shears to Opus.

***

Ready to depart, Opus poked his head over the fence and thanked Carol. 'You have been most kind. Is there anything we can do to repay you?' Carol hunched her shoulders and looked conspiratorially left and right... Then she whispered: 'Could you get rid of the cats? They're getting on my fucking nerves...'

***

Having shooed, cajoled and tossed two-dozen cats over the fence, Opus joined the others with only a few scratches to show for it. He got out a tube of disinfectant cream and smeared it on Peter's wounds.

***

Footsteps... Footsteps... Most people didn't let Opus and his esteemed colleagues into their abodes. Something about not knowing them got in the way. Doors were slammed in their faces. Faster and faster they were slammed before they could even say: 'Hello, would you mind most awfully if we came in?' And then even faster before they could say: 'Hello, would you mind most awfully..' And even faster before they could say: 'Hello..' and then 'He..'

Undaunted, Opus would ring the doorbell or the intercom buzzer for a second or a third time and if that drew no response, he would say to Rex: 'The crowbar, please...'

The group didn't like breaking into people's houses and tried to put the occupants' mind at ease. 'Don't mind us. We're only passing...'

***

Footsteps... Footsteps... Opus, Rex, Angel and a rat crouched in the moonlit undergrowth of another back garden as police sirens droned backwards and forwards.

Opus looked at Rex's ginger hair and offered him a wig.

'That's not a good enough disguise!' said Angel, 'They're going to catch us!'

'No...' said Opus stroking a hedgehog, 'They'll probably arrest the *wrong* people by mistake. In fact we'd probably be more likely to be arrested if we *hadn't* broken into those houses... Ahhhh... these animals are so adorable and *prehistoric*...'

Angel wasn't so certain of Opus's theory. 'How many groups go around with a guy with his eyes shut - asking strangers if they can walk through their living room? Don't you see? They'll get us!'

Opus recognised the fear in Angel's eyes and sang:

Amazing grace how sweet the sound..

'Shut up!' said Angel.
The police siren became more distant.
'They're going... We're okay...' said Rex.
'Good...' said Angel - getting up.
An eerie mad lament tore through the trees. Rex's hair stood on end. 'What was that?'
'Fox.' said Opus.
'That's a fox? It sounds so human..' said Rex.
'Sounds like a fox who needs therapy.' said Angel.
Opus held his hand up for quiet, listened to the cry again and said: 'No... She needs a shag...'

Up ahead, the group could make out Peter's form - his face pressed against the glass of a conservatory - his drool drip, dripping down the pane.

After some persistent knocking, a bespectacled, fifteen year-old boy opened the door - pointing a rifle at them. 'What're you doing in my garden - and it is my garden - I own it. I've owned it since I was fourteen.'

The group regarded 'Christopher' - an online venture capitalist who had apparently not invested in personal cleanliness or shower gel. He had attempted to compensate for this failing with copious sprayings of Linx deodorant until his armpit hair was frosted with the stuff and looked quite Christmassy.

'Yes...' said Opus, 'We're sorry for intruding. It is rather a long story..'

'I'm in the middle of a meeting! Get out!'

'We will indeed leave your charming backyard if you let us enter your house..'

Christopher snorted in disbelief. 'I'm not letting you enter my house - and it is my house. I bought it when I was fourteen.'

Angel put in her penny's worth: 'You must let us enter. It could mean the end of civilization if we don't..'

Christopher hadn't noticed Angel before. He studied her intensely. His nostrils flared with attraction. '*You* can come in.' He pointed his gun at the others. 'But not the rest of you!' He turned to Angel, 'We'll have some drinks and I'll show you my new PlayStation. You'd like to see my new PlayStation - wouldn't you?'

'Why sure!' said Angel, 'I find PlayStations fascinating and so do my friends. I'll come if my friends come..'

They watched Christopher's eyes rotate with conflicting emotions: Lust... Distrust... Lust... Distrust... A sensible part of him told him that if he let them in they could rob him. They could steal his whole comic book collection. And that was worth thousands. But another part of him (lower down) told him that she was so attractive and that she was... phoar!! Lust... Distrust... Lust... Distrust... Lust... Lust... Lust.'

'All right!! All right!!' spluttered Christopher, 'You can come in, but remember I have a gun and it is my gun - I bought it when I was...'

With rifle aimed, they entered the building. The walls were covered in action film posters; the shelves filled with Superhero figurines.

They went into the study. A twelve-foot PC monitor was fixed to the wall. Through a web cam attached to his PC, Christopher spoke to six teenaged entrepreneurs from six other countries - appearing split screen. One was picking his nose; one was squeezing his spots and another was scrapping the wax from his ears.

The videoconference continued. This was all well and good but the room smelt. It didn't take long to detect the source.

'Could we open a window?' said Opus, 'It's awfully stuffy..'

'I don't want to be cruel,' said Angel to Christopher, 'but do you know that you smell?'

'Smell?' said Christopher.

'How often do you have a bath?'

'Well, I'm a busy man...'

'You'd have more luck with the ladies if you bathed or showered regularly.'

'No one else says I smell.'

'That's because they're inside a monitor!'

'Oh...' said Christopher, 'I'll have a shower and then I'll show you my new PlayStation - okay?'

Noting that Peter was now rubbing his face against the bay window, Angel said: 'Look, we're running a little late, Christopher. Could we have a rain check on the PlayStation?'

The boy pointed his rifle at the group. 'You lot aren't going anywhere! I'm going to have you done for trespassing. I'm going to tell mother and father - they're upstairs - *working* for me..'

Rex took off his backpack and opened it.

'Hold it! What're you doing?' said Christopher.

Rex handed him a porn magazine. 'Look, this is precious to me... Would you let us go if I gave you this?'

The boy stuck the rifle under his armpit and flicked through the pages. He doubted that he was going to be interested in the magazine with all the online porn he had access to, but he was pleasantly surprised.

All the models were far better looking than the ones he had come across on the net and the pages seemed to come from several eras with different hairstyles and different clothing before they undressed which provided an interesting *historical* insight. 'Mmmm... Not bad... It looks like some of the pages are from other mags..'

'It's a compilation of the best bits of my porn collection - and it is a *vast* collection. I've been collecting for years.'

'Wow...'

'So will you let us go - without calling the police?'

'...Okay.'

Chris saw them to the door. He turned to Angel. 'I know I'm too young for you, but I will get older.'

Angel kissed Chris on the forehead and said: 'Remember to bathe...'

***

Footsteps... Footsteps... From Highbury to Finsbury Park... Along a disused railway track... The platform remained - overgrown with weeds and covered in spray paint. A water pump chugged continuously. And as the wind blew, they swore they could hear an announcement of a train cancellation.

'I wonder if this station gradually died.' said Opus, 'Maybe people stopped coming here because there were too many trains being cancelled and in the end everyone abandoned the place since they lost faith that any trains would arrive here anymore... Or maybe this station stopped operating because Dr Beeching closed it down in the 1960's?'

By now, Opus had honed his spiel for getting let inside stranger's houses: They were doing a survey... They would like to talk about recycling... Their bladders were bursting, could they use the loo, please? No dice... They still had to force their way in.

***

Footsteps... Footsteps... The rubbish had got deeper. They had to be in Haringey. Their travels took them into a Turkish restaurant where they had a wonderful meal and then a Greek barber's shop where Rex had a very good and very quick haircut and then another front door in a residential area.

What a wonderful ring the doorbell had - pitch perfect. Its resonance evoking the happy doorbell rings of youth. That ding dong ring from a sunny day when one visited one's best friend and slaughtered him at table-football.

The door slowly opened to reveal a ginger haired woman with an Alsatian and a bright orange hallway. The walls almost appeared to radiate sunlight and so did the woman. 'Hi, what can I do for you?' she said - beaming.

Rex stood agog. Was he dreaming? Her eyes were... captivating... and so was her nose... Her dog was nice too... He would have placed her in her mid-thirties - so ripe for harvesting... No need for cultivation...

'Hi...' said Opus - taking out his web cam. 'We're scouting for film locations, could we come in?'

'Sure, come in. Would you like a cup of coffee?' said the woman - smiling serenely.

No! Such a smile could not exist! thought Rex. He watched her body sway as she led them into the living room. Her hips were hypnotic. So was her ponytail - bobbing down her back - far more effective than a watch on a chain.

'So what's the film about?' said the woman.

'Well...' said Rex, 'It's about a boy who gets product placements in his dreams and learns to do lucid dreaming so that he can sleepwalk and find the corporate machine that put them there. A group of undercover journalists follow the boy and pretend that they are making a film about a boy who gets product placements in their dreams so that they can enter people's houses and go out the back of their gardens so that he doesn't deviate from his route.'

'Sci-fi, is it?'

'Well... we're aiming more at a *cross genre* piece...' He shook her hand. 'I'm Rex, I'll be directing it.'

'I'm Emily.'

The living room was messy. However, as we all know, there are three kinds of mess: good mess, bad mess and mediocre mess. Good mess shows that you have a life and puts visitors at ease. Bad mess pisses people off and stops them from visiting. And mediocre mess isn't worth writing home about. Suffice it to say, this was good mess. Postcards from around the world adorned her walls - bright orange walls. A few pieces were missing from the parquet flooring. Rex found a dislodged bit and put it in the gap.

'It's like a gigantic jigsaw puzzle really...' said Emily.

Books were piled up on the shelves - stacked horizontally, vertically and forty-five-degree angles - books on top of books - precariously balanced.

Emily handed Rex a mug - a brightly coloured mug nearly as vibrant as herself. Shit! thought Rex. Even her mugs were wonderful! Wasn't there something *unattractive* about this woman?

He browsed through her shelves and said: 'What did you think of 'The Good Soldier Svejk'?'

'Loved it.' said Emily.

'What about 'Catch 22'?'

'It would be hard to come up a novel that's as funny as that.'

Shit! thought Rex. A woman who loved 'The Good Soldier Svejk' and 'Catch 22'! So many women he encountered weren't interested in those books because the main characters were men and in fact were only interested in reading books with female protagonists. He knew guys who only wanted to read about guys and they annoyed him almost as much.

Shit, thought Rex. She was perfect. More than perfect! Pleasantly grounded, not all uptight and full of insecurities like some women he knew. And she was friendly - friendly to *him*! Shit, he bet that if he laid his head upon her breast he would only ever have pleasant dreams. Shit, by the looks she was giving him, he could tell that his girth wasn't an issue with her. Possibly the haircut had helped. Fuck, thought Rex... fuck... What a time to fall in love!

Emily watched Peter press his face against the kitchen door. 'Why has he got his eyes shut?'

'Yeah, I've always wondered about that...' said Rex.

Opus handed a mug back to Emily. 'I'll let you know about the film... Actually, could we have a look at the garden? We'll need to do a few exterior shots.'

'Sure...'

Rex helped Peter over the garden fence and said: 'Opus, would it be all right if I caught up with you later? I need some time to talk to Emily *alone..*'

Already on the other side of the fence, Angel grabbed Rex's collar. 'No you don't! You're coming with us!'

'Love is an important thing...' said Opus, 'I suppose we could cope without you.' He shook Rex's hand. 'Best of luck.'

'Thanks.' said Rex and made his way back to the house and his destiny.

'I can't believe you let him leave us!'

Opus shook his head. 'This may have been his only chance of happiness. Do you think I would stand in the way of that?'

'You sentimental old fool.'

The depleted group continued in the back streets of Haringey. Tacky, creepy Christmas lights twinkled from a window one floor up. Christmas had been several months ago, but it still persisted in this household.

Maybe the occupants had kept them on because the winters were too long. Maybe they needed to cling to something cheerful - even though the bulbs were too dark blue to be classy. Or maybe they had died and no one had noticed so that the lights continued to pulsate in perpetuity or at least until the bulbs burnt out.

Opus's cell phone rang. It was Rex. 'Where are you guys?'

'Rutland Gardens. What went wrong?'

'It was like this...'

***

The sun had set. Emily and Rex were sitting together on the sofa in the living room. It was all getting intimate. Neither of them had clicked with another person so well before. Rex's journey had come to an end. Of that he had no doubt. He had found his golden parking space.

The front door opened and thud shut.

'Oh, that must be Nick.' said Emily.

'Nick?' said Rex - ready to spring to his heels.

'Don't worry...' said Emily, 'Nick's my son.'

'Ahhhh...' said Rex relieved.

Heavy, clumping footsteps could be heard going up the stairs.

'How was school?' shouted Emily.

'All right!' shouted her son.

Emily turned to Rex. 'Sometimes it's difficult *meeting* people when you've got children.'

'No, no, children are great. I used to be one myself..'

Emily smiled. 'He should be joining us soon. He's getting changed...' She popped out of the room and called up the stairs. 'Nick! Where are you? There's someone I want you to meet!'

'Coming!' Thump! Thump! Thump!

Emily returned with a large and muscular sixteen year-old youth by her side. 'Nick, this is Rex.'

Rex got up and offered his hand. 'Hi Nick.'

At first, Nick did not say a word. He stared at the hand with incredulity. His face went red and his eyes bulged with rage.

'What's wrong, Nick?' said Emily.

'What's wrong?! I'll tell you what's wrong?!' yelled Nick as he lunged towards Rex - forcing him and the armchair onto the floor - and pounding him with his fists. 'This was the git who swiped my wallet when we were on holiday in Florida two years ago!'

He pulled Rex by the hair and smacked him in the jaw. Emily tried to prize Nick off him. 'Nick! There has to be some mistake! Don't hurt him!'

Rex tried to dodge the blows - knowing that if he retaliated, he would probably alienate Emily. 'Ow! Maybe I should be leaving...'

'This was the guy at the cash point!' snarled Nick and whacked him again. 'There's no mistake mum! This guy's a piece of shit!'

'Is it true?' said Emily, 'Are you a piece of shit?'

Rex sadly nodded as Nick kicked him again. Emily looked so disappointed; it broke his heart. 'That's enough, Nick.. You've hurt him enough.'

'I haven't even started!'

'Look! I'll make it up to you!' said Rex.

Nick stopped. 'Empty out your pockets!'

Rex took out a ten pence piece and a torn, folded up page from his porn collection. He unfolded the page and showed it to him. 'I don't suppose that you'd be interested in this..'

Nick grabbed Rex and shoved him out of the room. 'Right! Get out!'

***

Rex finished his sorry tale. '...Then he kicked me out of the house. Emily was *crying*... The whole thing was *horrible*.'

'Well,' said Opus, 'let that be a lesson to you: never rob anyone, because you might fall in love with their mother.'

***

Footsteps... Footsteps... Tired, weary following footsteps... Footsteps following Peter's footsteps through the turnstiles of London Zoo.

'No! No! No!' said Angel.

'Yes! Yes! Yes!' said Opus.

'This is ridiculous! Ridiculous! Ridiculous!'

'This is necessary! Necessary! Necessary!'

'We'll get killed and torn to pieces!'

'Not *all* of us...' said Opus.

***

'That'll be fifteen pounds each.' said the woman at the ticket counter.

'Can't my friend enter at a concessionary rate?' said Opus, 'He's going to go in with his eyes shut.'

'Is he registered blind?'

'No...'

'Then fifteen pounds each please...'

'But he's only going to listen to the animals. He's not going to see them.'

'Fifteen pounds.'

Opus handed the woman the money. 'Here... What about me then? I'm colour blind - how much do I pay?'

'Fifteen pounds...'

'That's ridiculous! I'm only going to see the animals in black and white - surely I should pay less.'

'I'd recommend looking at the zebras then. Fifteen pounds.'

'But people pay less for black and white TV licences than for colour...'

'Fifteen pounds...'

***

It was cheering to see all that shit with straw in it. It seemed to smell less depressing than other shit.

As you get older, the child in you gets filed under C. But when you go to a zoo - you pull out the contents of that drawer and gaze in awe at the animals. From your first teddy bear (assuming you had teddy bears) those wonderfully mysterious non-humans seemed to be there for you - to comfort and entertain.

'Where did all those teddy bears go?' murmured Opus to himself. Most got dismembered. Ended up in charity shops and then with other masters. But you hope that some had managed to escape into the woods and have a picnic.

Peter pressed himself against the tiger cage.

'This is what I thought would happen.' said Angel.

'Well predicted!' said Opus.

'Please tell me where're not going to go into that cage.'

'We're not going to go into that cage.'

'Thank God...'

'We are really, I just said that to cheer you up.'

'For once,' said Rex, 'Could we walk round the cage until Peter catches the scent again?'

'Too much of a risk.'

'It's not as if the Message Facilitator is in the cage.'

'We don't know that yet. We can't make those assumptions. It would a stroke of genius if it was. Okay, we'll better get some help...'

He sauntered off towards the gorilla cage and gestured to the dominant gorilla to come nearer. The gorilla shrugged and approached.

For a while they conferred in sign language and then Opus returned to the group. 'He said that getting into the tiger cage is going to be difficult. There are cameras everywhere, but he will cause a distraction for us. It was about time someone taught that tiger a lesson, he says. He's a right arrogant little sod.'

'He said all that?!' said Angel.

'Yes, and he asked if I had any bananas.'

'Have you got any bananas?' said Rex - licking his lips.

'No, not today. Anyway, what I propose is for Peter and I to disguise ourselves as zookeepers and enter the cage..'

'Do you want me to use the old 'spiders and worms' trick to get the zookeeper's uniforms?' said Rex.

'What's the old 'spiders and worms' trick?' said Angel.

'I dig up some worms and find some spiders - put them in a plastic bag and then I drop them into the zookeeper's shirt while you distract him. He'll feel all those things wriggling under his vest; take off his uniform and then I'll take it and rush off. So...' said Rex turning to Opus, 'should I use the old 'spiders and worms' trick?'

'No.' said Opus.

***

Angel returned from her shopping expedition with a bag of zookeeper uniforms and rendezvoused with Rex by the cockatoos. 'Got the entry cards?'

Rex shook his head. A zookeeper came into sight. He patted Angel on the shoulder and said: 'Watch and learn...'

Rex sidled up to the keeper and then held his chest. 'Aaaargh! It's my heart!!!' And then fell to the ground.

The keeper rushed to him. 'Are you okay?'

'Aaaarrrgh! My heart! Aaarrrrgh!! It's not fair! I've - I've been trying to lose weight as well!'

'Don't worry!' said the keeper, 'You're going to be all right!'

While he loosened Rex's clothing, Rex pinched his swipe card from his jacket pocket and substituted it for a similar looking card. As the keeper started dialling for an ambulance, Rex got up and said: 'It's okay, I feel better now... Thanks for helping. You've increased my faith in human nature...'

By the kangaroos, Rex handed the entry card to Opus. 'Thanks. The keepers don't start feeding the animals for another hour, so they shouldn't be alerted about what we're going to do...'

'I am curious to know how are you going to enter the cage without being eaten.' said Rex.

'Wait and see...'

***

Decked out as zookeepers, Peter and Opus returned to the tiger cage. The head gorilla did his stuff. He pounded his chest until a riot ensued. The keepers ran into their enclosure. This could be a PR disaster for the zoo - especially after spending all that money to make their habitat appear more humane.

While the keepers tried to calm the gorillas down, Opus took out a small torch and pointed it at the tiger's eyes and twirled and rotated it. The tiger's eyes grew heavy and shut. Purring with sleep, the pair entered.

Peter sleepwalked until other bars obstructed his journey. After marking the spot where Peter had been forced to stop, they retraced the track of the smell from outside the cage and moved onwards.

It was when the group was about the leave the zoo, that Opus saw him - behind the bars: the teddy bear of his youth. Those same, innocent, endearing eyes - but on a body of a larger scale. He so much wanted to hug him. It was a shame that he didn't have any limbs to spare. Peter went on ahead as Opus tried to tear himself away from the cage. 'Are you okay?' said Rex.

'I'm fine,' said Opus and walked on sadly.

***

'Don't be a sinner! Be a winner!' droned a Northern evangelist with a mic - his amplified voice so loud; his offer of eternal salvation not falling upon deaf ears but deafened ones. The entrance to Oxford Street station used to be his lair, but he was given an ASBO and now the traffic around Piccadilly Circus was his congregation.

Down Charing Cross Road, the group continued past the nightclub queue - merging with the queue for the cash point.

Bouncers stood by the entrance of the club - inscrutable and rigid as if made of breezeblock. Not a hair was visible on their shiny domes. It was Samson in reverse. Their strength would be sapped if they allowed even an eighth of an inch growth of hair on their heads.

As much as they might have liked, they couldn't just let the punters in. Their job was more complicated than that. The queue was the club's advertising. It always had to remain at a certain length to attract other clubbers. Clubbers only want to go to crowded nightclubs because it would have 'great atmosphere'. Places where all the seats are taken and the dance floor is cluttered and is so noisy you can't hear what your friends are saying always have great atmosphere. Places that don't just let 'anyone' in always have great atmosphere.

Due to exhaustion and a general lowering of morale, the distance between Peter and the group had lengthened. He walked past the queue and approached the entrance - alienating the punters greatly.

Gazing at the list of DJs performing that night, Angel said: 'Could he have chosen a *crappier* club to go to?'

'I'm not so worried about that.' said Opus, 'It's the music. Isn't it going to be too loud?'

The largest bouncer looked at Peter and said: 'You're late. The guvnor wants a word with you.' And with that, Peter walked in.

'What's happening?' said Rex.

'The bouncers think Peter is a bouncer because of his short hair.' said Angel.

'Right,' said Opus - taking his giant Afro wig off to reveal his shaven scalp, 'I'm joining him.'

But this time, the bouncers weren't having it. 'Who are you?!'

'The new bouncer.' said Opus, 'The agency sent me.'

'The new bouncer's already come. Who the *fuck* are you?!'

There was no time for clever plans such as pretending he was a detective inspector - investigating a murder, so he did the only thing that sprang to mind: he shut his eyes, head butted the smallest bouncer, karate kicked two other bouncers in the balls, sprang over the barriers and legged it down the street.

The three bouncers ran out after him, leaving only one bouncer to handle the impatient crowd.

'Now, look, you've got to be patient... You can't all come in at once - can you?' said the bouncer, 'Haven't you heard of the expression: good things come to those who wait?'

But the queue was not having it. They surged into the club - pulling Rex and Angel in with them - past the ticket office - past the cages with people having their nether regions pierced and tattooed and whisked off to Casualty after it had gone wrong and onto the dance floor where Peter was wildly spinning his body.

'The music's too loud!' said Angel.

'What?! What's that you're saying?' said Rex.

'I'm saying the music's too loud! We've got to turn it off!'

Behind an enclosure, stood the DJ, DJ Tinnitus. Right, she thought, it was time for her to be sexier than she had ever been in her life. She checked her lipstick, hitched up her skirt to belt dimensions, thrust out her chest and jutted out her jaw. She took off her backpack and handed it to Rex. 'Look after Peter.'

'What's that?' said Rex.

Edging towards Tinnitus, she gyrated her already alluring body and transformed herself into a sex goddess. The DJ could not help but notice Angel as she danced around his enclosure and told security to let her in. After attaining an even higher level of sexiness, she entered.

'Hi, would you like a drink?' said Tinnitus.

Angel nodded seductively.

He handed her a can of Stella. She shook and shook the can in her hands, pulled the ring pull and sprayed the foam onto her chest. Her top was now quite translucent.

To encourage the translucency, Tinnitus handed her another beer and she shook it again and let the foam go on her thighs and on the deck while shaking her booty for all she was worth. Dancing faster and faster, she pulled out all the leads from the music equipment in such an entrancing way, the DJ didn't seem to mind. The music ended.

With the racket gone, Peter stopped spinning and continued on his sleepwalk with Rex close by his side. Angel jumped onto the mixing desk and carried on dancing - ready to be grabbed by the bouncers. Waving to Tinnitus as she was carried away, silence had never sounded so beautiful.

Without much ceremony, the bouncers dumped Angel outside. She took out her cell phone. 'You guys alright?'

'Sure.' said Rex, 'We're in Covent Garden. Opus is with us. He wants to know if you'd like a crepe...'

***

Footsteps... Footsteps... Embankment Bridge. Big Ben chimed and the Tate Modern, the Oxo Tower and the Gherkin glistened in the distance. Amid these vibrant works of architecture, Peter suddenly halted.

'The machine must be here, then..' said Rex.

Opus peered closely into Peter's nose. 'Have you got a handkerchief?'

Both Rex and Angel shook their heads.

Opus pulled out his shirtsleeve and wiped Peter's nose and Peter started walking again. Evidently Peter had stopped because his nose was congested.

Rex handed Opus a tissue. 'I've got this, though...'

Opus wiped the snot from his sleeve. 'Thanks.'

***

There was a steep decline in the number of four by fours driven by glamorous forty year-old women as they continued on their journey.

By the time they had reached Barking, they had all but disappeared. Young men in hoods and bobble hats without the bobbles on stared at the group. Like the white pussycats, they resented the intrusion into their territory.

But what a territory it was. It was such a horrible place Opus wondered why the hoodies wanted to protect it from outsiders. He shook his head. Could happiness inhabit such an area? Could it share its postal code? Could happiness reside behind the damp cold breezeblocks; the abandoned shopping trolleys full of rubbish; the boarded up windows; the burnt out windows and the fast food wrappers? And what about love? Could love flourish in those Tower blocks? Could love drown out the heated arguments about money? Would it be the heated arguments or the love that would keep them warm? Would the heart become as cold as the building? Would the heart breakdown like the lift?

What force compelled him to look upwards, Opus knew not, but when he did, he noticed a man - standing on top of a ten-storey flat.

He wondered what the man's intentions were. Was he off his face? What was going through his mind? What goes through the mind of anyone standing where he was?

Ten storeys were probably enough to do it. You wouldn't merely end up in a wheel chair. In the blink of an eye, all the boarded up and burnt out windows and all the abandoned shopping trolleys full of rubbish and all the fast food wrappers would disappear.

Opus turned to Rex and Angel. 'I'll catch up with you…'

***

The lift only catered for people who lived on the ground floor so Opus panted up the staircase. Gasping for breath, on the top of the building, Opus finally saw the features of the silhouetted man.

Arthur was older than Opus had imagined - late sixties - early seventies. He was aware of Opus's presence but continued to stare at the horizon.

'Hi…' said Opus, 'Are you alright?'

'I ain't got nothing, so you can forget it…'

'I don't *want* anything from you. I want to..'

'Help? Pull the other one...' As far as Arthur was concerned Opus was just another drug pusher trying to 'befriend' him. 'Yeah, you'll 'help' me all right. You'll do my shopping for me... Give me cigarettes and have cosy little chats with me... Then you'll offer to stay with me to keep me company... And then you'll ask me if it's all right if a few 'friends' join us - they won't stay for long... And then *more* 'friends' come to stay. And then 'visitors' come by at all hours... And the day I say it's not all right if your friends stay, you'll chuck me out. You'll chuck me out of my own home...'

Arthur pointed towards the housing estate. 'Look at it. That used to be my gaff. Now it's a drugs den. Took years for the Council to get me a place of my own... God knows how long it'll take for them to do it again... I've been a bloody idiot...'

Opus grabbed Arthur and held him tightly.

'What're you doing? Get off me!'

'You were going to jump!'

'So what if I was? Who gives a toss?'

'Have you called your social worker?'

'I have... Line's engaged... Run out of money...'

'Use my phone.'

Arthur dialled. 'Still busy...'

'Where is your place?' said Opus.

'See where those junkies are standing? Over there...'

Although in the distance the people were silhouettes, there was no mistaking the distinctive gigantic form of Rex - accompanied by the other two.

Opus handed Arthur a tenner. 'Here you better get yourself something to eat... I'm not promising anything, but I'll see what I can do...'

***

Opus's countenance completely changed as he approached the flat. He slouched and sneered and spat everywhere and swore excessively. 'Fuck this! Fuck that! FUCK!! FUCK!! FUCK!! FUCK!! FUCK!!' Never had he looked so tough. He rang the doorbell. No one answered. He rang again and then head butted the door.

It opened slightly. A thin, young, shaven headed man with a tattooed neck poked his head out. 'Yeah?' he said. Two front teeth were missing from his mouth. Evidently, someone had taken upon himself to guarantee that the blowjobs the youth was forced to administer in prison did not end in pain for the 'blowjobee'.

'Can we come in or what?' said Opus with a harsh East End accent.

Phil eyed the group. Having gone without sleep for three nights and being so sweaty and unshaven and dishevelled - they didn't look that dissimilar from their usual customers - especially Peter. However, Phil had his reservations. 'Don't know you...'

'John said it would be okay.' said Angel in a terrible Mockney accent.

'John?' said Phil - opening the door, 'Should've said.'

After a thorough frisking, the group was led into the living room. It was a hive of activity. George was hoovering. Dan was emptying the ashtrays and wiping the surfaces. Like Phil, they were in their early twenties and appeared to have the same problem with their teeth. Sat by the dining table was a short man in his mid-forties.

Phil picked up the teapot and filled the man's cup and then carefully poured the milk. 'Can I go for a break, Tony?'

'No, you can shoot up later. I've got other things for you to do.' said the man - revealing a perfect set of gnashers and turned to the group. 'Want a tea?'

'Ta...' said Opus.

He sat down with his friends and coaxed Peter down with him.

'Milk?' said Tony.

'No thanks...' said Opus.

'Sugar?'

'Sweet enough already...'

Phil prepared their drinks.

'Ta...'

'So what can we do for you?' said Tony.

'What you got?' said Opus.

'What do you want?' said Tony.

'Well, I was thinking I'd like some rocks and some tabs and pills and some brown for the boy and some speed and some rocky...'

Phil took out a notebook and started jotting down the order.

'And some grass and some shrooms and some uppers and some downers and some GHB and some methyl nitrate. Actually, better cross off the methyl nitrate - don't want to go overboard...'

'Have we got all this?' asked Phil.'

'Take a look in the back.' said Tony.

Peter sprang up - suddenly and with every element of surprise in the Periodic Table, spun his body round - knocking down the table and sending the drinks onto the floor and Tony's lap. 'Arrrrrrgh!!!!'

Phil, George and Dan picked up their baseball bats. Tony grabbed Peter and took out his gun. 'You did that on purpose!'

'I can assure you it was unintentional, mate..' said Opus.

'*Don't* call me *mate.*' said Tony and gave Peter a shaking. 'I give you tea and this is how you repay me? Oi! Look at me when I'm talking to you - look at me!'

'Don't wake him!' said Opus.

'*Don't* wake him?!' said Tony, '*Don't* wake him?! If I *want* to wake him - I'll *wake* him!' He shook Peter even more. 'Look at me! Look at me! You can't get away with knocking tea on me by pretending that you're sleepwalking. I tried that when I was caught knee-capping a Paki. I still had to do two years!' He slapped Peter's face.

Peter started spinning again.

'Leave him alone - you bastard!' said Opus - suddenly reverting to Received Pronunciation.

Tony turned. 'Your accent's changed. What the fuck's going on here? What the *fuck's* going on?'

The situation was both untenable and intolerable. Opus knew what he had to do. He shut his eyes; jumped into the air; karate kicked the weapons out of the villains' hands and then karate kicked them in the stomach.

Angel went on her knees in search of the gun.

Tony, Phil, George and Dan piled upon Opus - dragging him down. He had his work cut out defending himself.

'Opus!' yelled Rex - giving Tony a kick, 'You might have a better chance if you open your eyes!'

'No, no,' said Opus, 'I'll stick with what I know...'

While Angel continued to search for weapons, Rex prised off the thugs piled on top of Opus. 'Get off him - you bastards!' The criminals piled on top of Rex.

Opus prised the thugs off Rex. 'Get off him - you bastards!' They piled back on top of Opus.

Rex prised the thugs off Opus. 'Get off him - you bastards!' They piled back on top of Rex.

Opus prised the thugs off Rex. 'Get off him - you bastards!' They piled back on top of Opus.

Rex decided it would be better if he helped Angel find the gun.

Tony left his henchmen to it and also decided to search for the weapon. They didn't really have that much to do since Opus appeared to have passed out, so they only prodded him.

Three pairs of eyes roved around the broken crockery. The gun barrel poked out from under a broken teacup. A split second faster than Rex and Angel; Tony pounced upon the weapon and pointed it at them - forcing them back against the wall.

'You must be well gutted that I've the gun!' He turned to Peter. 'Now what should I do with you? If I shot your hooter off I'd be doing you a favour. Now, what I could do..'

Angel gave Tony a high kick in the mouth. 'Arrrrrrgh!!!!' Two teeth ricocheted off the ceiling. Tony fell to the ground and dropped the gun. Rex seized the weapon.

The gang stood transfixed by the unreality of it all. They watched Tony get up, wipe away the blood and open his mouth to reveal a gap where his two front teeth used to be. 'What you staring at?'

'He's been beaten by a *girl*...' said Dan. This was more surreal than a Guinness ad.

George, the largest of the group, pushed him back on the floor.

'Oi! Whatcha do that for?!'

It was as if Angel had broken a spell. The gang looked at Tony in a whole new light.

'I didn't want to sell drugs at all.' said George, 'I only went along with it because I was scared of him..'

'I didn't want anything to do with all this neither.' said Dan, 'When I got out of the nick I wanted to go straight, but Tony wouldn't take no for an answer...'

Phil picked up the teeth and clenched them in his palm. 'I don't know why he had this 'hold' on us, but now he's lost his front two teeth, he's nothing.'

Enraged, Tony got up but Phil pushed him back to the floor. 'He's so short... I never noticed before...'

'Yeah! He's like a dwarf!'

'Yeah! Like a leprechaun!'

Tony got up and George pushed him down again and kicked him. 'Where's your pot of gold, Tony? Where's your pot of gold?'

Phil shook his head with bitterness. 'To think we let this little squirt rule our lives... It makes me laugh...'

The entire group started kicking Tony. After a while, they saw something they had never seen before: tears running down Tony's cheeks. 'Aaaaah... Look... He's crying! Like a baby! Dan, give us your phone!'

Having filmed the moment on the handset, Phil dragged Tony to his feet. 'Get up! You're getting the fuck out of here!' He handed him his teeth. 'Here, take them! And I wouldn't come back if I was you 'cause if you do we'll post this footage of you crying on every website we can find and send it to all your mates!'

Tony stared back with vengeance in his eyes. It had no effect. For a change he decided to keep his mouth shut and limped away.

Phil picked up his cell phone. 'Is that Arthur? Look... Look... I know... You can have your place back... No... I'm being serious... You don't have to worry about Tony anymore... Naaa, I can't... I'm going to try to track down my old boyfriend...' He turned to his mates. 'Any of you going to stay?'

George shook his head. 'I'm going to rehab...'

Dan also shook his head. 'Haven't seen my mum for ages... No one makes a Yorkshire pudding like she does... But I'll visit.'

'I will too...'

'Arthur, we'll stay in touch.... How long you going to be? Yeah, we should still be here when you come back. Got the washing-up to finish... Okay, see you soon.'

Opus came to and groaned.

'I'll get some bandages.' said George.

***

Opus put his arm over Angel as the group followed Peter into the backyard.

'Opus,' said Rex, 'why do you shut your eyes when you fight?'

'It's simply because I can't stand the sight of violence.'

***

Footsteps... Footsteps... Deeper into the estate footsteps... Footsteps... Footsteps... Even deeper... By now, Rex was finding that even his torn out porn page was losing the ability to revive him.

Sleep deprived seconds became sleep deprived minutes. Sleep deprived minutes became sleep deprived hours. Sleep deprived hours became sleep deprived days...

It would take a thousand Big Bens to keep Rex fully alert - a million ringing alarm clocks - a billion air raid sirens - a zillion naked nymphs.

The pavement looked so comfortable to him... 'That brick would make a lovely pillow.' he thought. As the rest of the group continued ahead, he brushed away the used needles and fragments of broken glass and lay his body down.

Opus's suspicions were aroused when a minute went by without hearing Rex moaning about his feet. He retraced his steps and found Rex on the ground - snoring away. He pulled him up and shook him. 'Are you all right?'

'Yeah! Yeah! Gonna get some shuteye...' said Rex.

'You can't sleep *now*..'

'After walking non-stop all this time?! I think I could!'

'It's not *safe* to sleep here..'

'They could rob me or fuck me up the arse. I couldn't give a shit!'

'But you can't sleep now, Peter's still walking..'

'Then wake him up so we can get some sleep.'

'We can't risk Peter losing the scent..'

'Okay! I will then!' said Rex and ran up to the sleepwalker - yelling: 'Wake up Peter! WAKE UP!'

Opus sprang on Rex - covering his mouth with his hand. 'I'm going to release my hand and you'll be quiet - won't you?' Rex nodded. Opus removed his hand.

'WAKE UP PETER!!! WAKE UP!!!'

Opus put his hand over Rex's mouth again. 'Shut up... Please.'

Rex's eyes expressed remorse and Opus removed his hand again.

Peter had his face pressed against another door of another low-rise block of flats.

Opus rang the doorbell. A man in overalls answered the door. 'Yeah?'

What should he say to him? wondered Opus. The film making spiel had only worked once. What should he say in here of all places? 'Er... can we come inside? We've just robbed a bank.'

'A bank?' said 'Giles', 'You better come in...'

The group entered. The hall and the living room were covered in the most amazing murals. Every animal in the world seemed to be depicted and every type of lush green vegetation.

'Can't stand banks myself. They deserve what's coming to them...' said Giles as he put the kettle on.

'These murals are marvellous!' said Opus, 'Did you paint them all yourself?'

'Yeah... Milk and sugar?'

He didn't live in paradise, so he painted paradise - a gigantic Rousseau-like world of animal enchantment. Peter would have loved it had he been awake. As the group drank their teas, the man resumed his painting. 'If you don't mind...' He dipped a brush into a bucket of paint and finished a leaf.

'So... are you an artist?' said Angel.

Giles gazed at the murals. 'Who knows? It's not how I make a living.'

'What do you do?' said Angel.

'I'm a traffic warden.'

'But you're so nice!' said Opus.

'Some of those other wardens are complete gits, getting disabled people's cars towed away an' all, but I try to be fair. If a person seems genuine I let them get away with it if they've parked somewhere they shouldn't. If they haven't stayed that long they haven't caused much harm... Though I have to be careful, if I'm too lenient I could lose my job... Doesn't make me too popular with my colleagues, my approach... I don't care... I don't see them much socially anyway... I tend to give them a wide berth...'

'How long has the mural taken you?' said Opus.

'Two years. Still got the ceiling to do. Going to paint a sky full of birds... Gulls, woodpeckers, albatrosses, maybe a few species gone extinct...' He pointed. 'On the right... There were still some Caribbean Monk seals left when I started painting those... All gone now...'

Opus turned to find that Peter had also disappeared. 'Excuse me, did you happen to see where my friend went?'

'I think I saw him go to the bathroom...'

Giles and the group found Peter standing with his feet in the toilet bowl with his face pressed against the cistern. Opus handed Giles his cup. 'Would it be all right if we got out through the bathroom window?'

'Be my guest.'

Poking his head through the window, Opus said: 'Thanks for the tea...'

'That's fine... Well, good luck with your criminal career.' said Giles.

'Cheers.'

***

Footsteps... Footsteps... Very wet footsteps... They were walking through a river - their eyes completely bloodshot and sore.

It was getting to Rex and Angel. They had had it up to here with being exhausted. The water went up to their necks - precisely matching the level with which they had had it up to.

'Opus, has it crossed your mind that Peter isn't on the trail to the Message Facilitator and that he's having a dream that is taking us nowhere?' said Angel.

'That's a worrying thought...' said Opus, 'But I've been looking at his nose and it still looks quite irritated by the smell of burnt toast, so I'm pretty sure he hasn't lost the trail.'

'What about the last place we went in?' said Rex, 'Their toaster wasn't working properly and their bread was getting burnt. How can you be sure *that* wasn't what Peter was smelling?'

'He's smelling every bit of burnt toast in the land?! That's highly unlikely!'

'Then how come we haven't been travelling in a straight line?' said Angel, 'How come we've gone up and down, backwards and forwards and up and down again? How does a smell work like that?'

'Er... the world's a mysterious place...'

'No it isn't.' said Angel.

'No it isn't,' said Rex, 'Angel's *right*.'

'Well, the world *could* be a mysterious place, if we put our minds to it...'

Angel pointed frantically. 'What's that between those trees? Isn't that a laboratory?'

Opus squinted into the distance. 'I'm sorry, but I think that's a hallucination.'

'Opus! What have you done to us?'

'I'm sorry. I didn't anticipate such a long journey. Rex, do you see anything over there?'

Rex peered into the distance. 'No... But I see something over there!' he shouted jubilantly as he pointed at some other trees.

'...I'm sorry, Rex, but that's a hallucination too.'

'*No*!!! It looks so real!'

'We have to focus on Peter, okay? Ignore everything else.'

'So that isn't a door on that oak?'

'Hallucination.'

'*Damn...*'

***

The old skipper sailed by Canary Wharf in a third-hand yacht that he had recently purchased. If his health got worse, he decided that he wouldn't live out the last of his years using a mobility bike. No, a mobility boat would be what he would use. He would die as he had lived: on the water.

***

Footsteps... Footsteps... Sigh... Yet more footsteps... Very slow footsteps... Crawling past Silver Town with the Tate & Lyle factory with the resplendent gigantic Lyle Golden Syrup can attached to it. Footsteps... Footsteps... Even slower, even more pathetic, practically inaudible footsteps... Through a maze of cranes, scaffolding, mixers and vans. Greenwich was going through a transformation - new offices, new homes. They dragged their feet through wet cement and felt at one with the substance. Soon their bodies would dry up, freeze and turn into concrete.

'If we don't find this machine, this instant, I'm going to join a religious cult!' gasped Rex who was practically crawling.

'Shave my head! I've converted!' cried Angel, 'I've seen God, Buddha, Krishna and Spiderman! It's all true!'

Opus slapped his own face again - his consciousness flickering like an old silent movie.

The walking stopped. The group watched Peter stand by a condemned tower block. It didn't look promising. Opus examined Peter's nose again. No - no snot. Could he have briefly blacked out? Had they even been following the right Peter? Or had they been following a hallucination?

'Is this it?' said Angel, 'I don't see a transmitter.'

All that could be seen on the blot on the landscape was an old Sky Satellite dish.

'It's the satellite dish!' said Opus, 'It's the satellite dish!'

'Yes, I know it's a satellite dish.' said Angel, 'What's the big deal?'

'That's the transmitter for the Message Facilitator!'

'But dishes receive signals - they don't give them out.' said Angel.

'It doesn't take a genius to construct it so it goes the other way round!'

Peter opened his eyes. 'This is it.'

A vehicle could be heard getting nearer. 'Quick!' said Opus. 'Hide behind the crane.'

Two security guards came out of the tower block as a limo parked outside. A well-dressed man - smoking a cigarette stepped out and followed the men into the building.

'Well, well, well...' whispered Opus, 'Mr Fahrenheit, if I'm not mistaken...'

FIFTY-FIVE

Mimi was jogging and was outside. But in a sense she wasn't outside because Chuck's bodyguards surrounded her. She wanted to be outside because she felt she couldn't breath when she was inside and when Chuck was away, she found that she was inside a lot. But though she was outside - jogging in Central Park, she still felt that she couldn't breath. It was almost as if the bodyguards were insulating her from the outside air.

'Do I need to have eight of you with me?' said Mimi.

'Mr Harlem's orders.'

Being surrounded pissed her off, but what she really detested was being followed or more precisely the sensation of being watched from behind. One of the bodyguards gave her bad vibes. She didn't like the way he looked at her.

He was jogging behind her and she could sense he was trying to will her jogging bottoms away. Maybe, she thought, she should pull them down and say: 'Here! Have a good look! This is my ass! Finished now? Can we move on?'

They passed a group of campaigners standing behind a fold-up table. Their stall was concerned with Chuck Harlem's business activities and how he should change his ways. Few were drawn to them despite their pithy chant: 'Harlem makes you want to chuck! Chuck your Harlem trainers out! Harlem makes you want to chuck! Chuck your Harlem trainers out!'

Mimi turned towards the protestors. 'They've got some nerve!'

A bodyguard placed his hand on her shoulder. 'It's best to ignore them, Ma'm.'

'Get out of my face!'

'It wouldn't be advisable.'

She tore through the bodyguards, ran to the stall and screamed: 'How dare you! How dare you!' and pushed their table onto the ground.

A female protestor tried to grab her. 'Hey, fuck off!'

'No you fuck off! I don't have a go at the man you love!'

A mellow-seeming member of the group with a panama hat and no eyebrows, raised his hand benevolently. 'Let's hear the poor *deluded* wretch out...'

He only appeared mellow because he had no eyebrows to express his emotions with.

Raising her chin defiantly, Mimi gasped. '...You don't know him like I know him! He's so kind!'

'Kind?!' said Mr Panama Hat, 'Kind?!!! Kind?!!!!!!!' - snorting in derision.

'Frigging right! He buys me things and takes me places..'

'You really don't know *anything* about him..'

'Sure I do!'

Panama Hat bent down and gathered some of the leaflets and handed one to Mimi. 'No, after you read this leaflet then you'll know *something* about him.'

From a distance, Mimi regarded the leaflet. Was this the 'Pandora's Box' of protest leaflets?

'Go on... What're you scared of? You know he's so kind... Read it.'

Mimi snatched the leaflet. 'I will! I'm going to check them with the lawyers to see if Chuck can sue you!'

As she was about to look, one of her bodyguards snatched it and screwed it up in his hand. 'It's better if we go, Ma'm...'

'Hey! I was going to read that!'

'It's propaganda, M'am. You won't want to read it.'

'Let me be the judge of that!'

'Yeah! Leave her alone!'

'You stay out of it!'

'Look,' continued Mr Panama Hat, 'I haven't begun to tell you about the harm he does..'

A jeep came up and stopped two metres away from the stall. From it a platoon of park security officers stepped out. One of them spoke into his cell phone and put it away. Another spoke through a loud hailer. 'Break it up! Break it up! You have no right to express your views here!'

'But it's a public area!' said the activist.

The security officer put his hailer down and approached the protestor. 'A public area managed by the Harlem Corporation. Permission should have been sought from the Harlem Corporation.'

'Where can I protest?'

'That is not my problem. You have five minutes to move your stall away..'

'No, what public area don't you bastards control? I want you to tell me!'

'You have five minutes to vacate this area before the police come...'

The bodyguard placed his hand on Mimi's shoulder. 'Let's go, Ma'm...'

'I want to read the leaflet!'

'Best not to, Ma'm.'

'Why won't you let me read it?'

'You won't like it.'

'So?'

'You're happy aren't you, Ma'm? Why make life more complicated?'

The world appeared to be rotating too fast for her to stay on it. The leaflets were only inches away from her feet. She was afraid she was going to fall. She was afraid that.. She needed something to eat and drink. That was what it was. 'Okay... let's get out of here.'

'Right, Ma'm.'

***

Mimi found Chuck in the gym, on the bench - lifting and lowering barbells. 'Hi Chuck, you got a minute?'

'Soon, baby, soon...' He grunted as he forced the barbell above him.

'It's that I heard...'

He lowered it to his chest and breathed out. 'Look over by the exercise bike... I've got something for you...'

All she could see was a towel on the saddle. 'Under the towel...' There was a comb bound document. 'It's the screenplay for my new movie... You're the female lead.'

She flicked through the pages. 'Oh... Thanks... I have lines... I actually have things to say...' Her eyes bulged with amazement. 'I get to keep most of my clothes on. Oh my Gawd... That's some... that's some departure for me...'

Would she be able to do the role? she wondered. Would she be good enough? Before she had depended upon the pert characteristics of her body, but now could she depend on her acting ability? But what a role... She pecked him on the cheek. 'Thank you...'

'What did you want to talk to me about?'

'Oh, it's... it's nothing...'

FIFTY-SIX

Carrying Angel in his arms, Bryan Fahrenheit staggered into the motel room. She was dressed in red leather micro skirt and wore a peroxide wig. He deposited her on the mattress and dropped himself next to her.

She got up, took off his clothes and said: 'Shall I tie you up?'

'Yeah! Yeah!'

She obliged with the chains.

'Tighter! Tighter! I want my wrists to bleed!'

'Okay.'

'Piss on me! Piss on me!'

'I'll come to that.' She took out a bottle of water from her red handbag and sipped from it.

'Yeah! Drink loads of water so you can piss on me lots!'

At that auspicious moment, Opus, Peter and Rex got out from under the bed and emptied his pockets.

'What's going on?'

'Well, Bryan,' said Angel, 'I've got a confession to make: I'm not really a prostitute. My friend over here is going to take your entry card; enter your laboratory and make a live broadcast exposing your company while the rest of us keep you captive.'

'Wow! How did you know? That's my *ultimate* sexual fantasy!'

'This isn't a fantasy; Bryan, this is real.'

'Yeah! Yeah! That's real enough! Now get on and piss on me! I'm paying a hundred bucks for this!'

'Tell you what; Bryan, I don't feel like peeing on you at the moment, but I'm sure Rex will oblige you.'

With that, Rex unzipped his flies.

'No! No! That's okay! There's nothing sexy about being peed upon by a guy!'

***

Bryan remained tied to the bed. Peter, Rex and Angel watched TV.

'You better release me you know.' said the captive, 'Me and Chuck are like this...' He crossed the first two fingers on his left hand. 'He is going to be... *angry* when he finds out you've kidnapped me... *Real* angry... You are going to know trouble like you've never known trouble before... Think he's going to let you get away with it? Think again... He'll send his private army here... He'll track you down... He'll *hunt* you down... He wouldn't leave a single stone unturned... You'll need more than masks to disguise yourselves... I hope you know a good plastic surgeon... Because that would be what it would take and he'd still *find* you... And when he finds you - you'll wish you died of pancreatic cancer years ago... You'll wish you died in the core of the mushroom of a nuclear apocalypse... You'll wish you'd were Jewish and died in the Holocaust! You'll wish you had dissolved slowly in an acid bath without even a rubber ducky to keep you company, because when Chuck does revenge; he does it big time...'

FIFTY-SEVEN

Opus stepped into the lift and pressed top floor. Floor 1... Floor 2... Floor 3... Floor 20... Floor 13... Floor 7... Floor 26... He opened his briefcase and studied the plan of the building. Floor 4... Floor 15... Floor 2... Mmmm... *Interesting*... Floor 8... Floor 22... Mmmm... He supposed he would get there *eventually*...

He had toyed with the idea of disguising himself as Bryan, but it was too much of a risk. It was one thing to pose as Peter in front of security cameras, but trying to fool people in person was a different thing entirely. He only got away with impersonating Gavin's lawyer because he had a beard and sunglasses. No, he had decided upon posing as Bryan's 'new' assistant, Colin Gravity.

Communications had been made that due to ill health; Colin would take Bryan's place - overseeing the activation of the brainwave machine. Opus had borrowed Bryan's cell phone and emulated his voice perfectly.

Top floor. 'Oh...' said Opus as he stepped out of the lift. He had entered a rather plush reception with water features, state of the art sofas and a Damian Hirst. The receptionist was on the phone. He walked over to her.

She put the phone down. 'Can I help you?'

'Professor Chong. I've got an appointment at 6.30.'

'I'll let him know you're here. If you could sign yourself in...'

For a second, Opus started to write his real name. He couldn't believe that he could have been so foolish. He changed the first letter to a 'c'.

'Please take a seat. The professor will be over in a few minutes.'

Opus sat down on the black leather sofa and picked up a magazine.

***

'Sorry to keep you waiting.' said Professor Chong - shaking Opus's hand.

'That's fine..'

The professor led him to the laboratory. 'Here it is... The Message Facilitator... What do you think?'

Opus surveyed the place. Where was it? He couldn't see any gigantic, menacing monstrosities of technology. 'Er... yeah... Sorry... I... Er... Could you point it out?'

'Of course! Here...' and the professor handed him a device no larger than a calculator.

'Oh... It's very compact...'

'We were hoping for it to be smaller, but you can't have everything. Certainly the next generation of Message Facilitators are going to be no larger than a thumbnail...'

'Very impressive.'

'We'll know that after we use it. A few last minute checks and then zero hour... Very exciting - isn't it?'

'Yes... yes it is...'

'We're going to grab some dinner - coming?'

'No, it's okay; I already ate. I'd like to er... *look* at the machine more - if you don't mind.'

'Be my guest. See you later.'

Opus took out his web cam; parked it on the work unit and started his commentary: 'Tomorrow morning, you may find yourself with the uncontrollable urge to buy a Harlem product - a product that you had never wanted before. This is why: the Message Facilitator...'

FIFTY-EIGHT

Bryan continued to warn Rex and Angel of the dire consequences of their actions. '...You'd better go far... Runaway and jump on a plane... Go to the other side of the universe... Because when Chuck finds you - you'll wish you were never born... When he finds you, you'd wish that your parents and your parents' parents were never born and their parents too... Yeah... when he finds you, you'll wish evolution had never happened... and the apes had remained apes... Yeah... when he finds you, you'll wish the world hadn't been created and there was no big bang. Yep, don't expect any mercy... Because *mercy* is one thing you *won't* get... What you'll get is the *opposite* of mercy... Yep, I'd be really, really scared if I was you, because once he's found you..'

Angel pulled out a bandage and gagged him. 'He was starting to bore me...'

***

'...And that's it. That's Mr Harlem's plan...' continued Opus, 'It sounds unbelievable that anyone would go to such lengths to attain certainty in the profitability of their businesses, but this is the case... There are many things in life we're not certain of: the existence of a spiritual entity or aliens or a decent plumber, but one thing we can be certain of is this: there are people on this planet. There are people and there are animals and there are plants and trees and if Mr Harlem thinks these things are worth sacrificing for his ends, if he thinks it's okay to throw our lives into chaos then that's his lookout. This has been Opus Merriman, XTC News, goodnight.'

Security guards burst into the room. Opus switched off his web cam and handed it to them. 'Here, you can have it now. I've finished with it. Everyone knows. This was all broadcast live on Channel XTR News. Your logo is dirt. Millions of people watched this.'

A guard shook his head and handcuffed Opus. 'No one saw it.'

'What?!' exclaimed Opus.

'Chuck bought the channel five hours ago. Guess which item got spiked?'

'Our..'

'You'll find that your website hasn't broadcast it either. Seems to have got a bad virus – what a shame...'

'Er...' said Opus, 'We're holding Bryan Fahrenheit captive.'

'So?'

***

Morale was low. Rex, Angel and Peter had sat in the motel room - expecting the broadcast to happen at 8'o clock. When 8'o clock came and went; the group began to feel nervous. 'Maybe after the commercial break, the item would come' they deluded themselves. 'Maybe after *that* break...' But the news item didn't feature after any of them and failed to materialize on their website.

Because they had company and captive company at that, the group concealed their emotions. 9 o'clock reared its ugly head and then 10 o'clock reared it's hideous head and 11 o'clock reared its obscenely horrific head, then Angel screamed: 'Fuck! What went wrong?'

She tore the gag out of Bryan's mouth. 'You know - don't you?'

Sweat poured off Bryan's forehead as he murmured: 'Pills... give me... my pills...'

'Cut the crap! Why didn't the broadcast happen?'

'Pills... give me... my pills...'

'Where are they?' asked Peter.

'My... inside... jacket... pocket...'

Peter searched the jacket. '...Can't find them... I think Opus emptied out the pockets and took everything with him...'

Angel grabbed Bryan's collar, 'Look, I'm going to give you one last chance..'

'I think he's sick.' said Rex.

'Sick?!' said Angel, 'Of course he's sick - anyone who invents the Message Facilitator is sick!'

'No,' said Rex, I think he's *really* sick.'

'He's faking it!' said Angel.

'Look at him. You can't fake sweat like that!'

Rex stuck a thermometer into Bryan's mouth and showed it to Angel. 'And you can't fake a temperature like that!'

'What do you propose that we do about it?' said Angel.

'Take him to hospital.'

'If Opus has been captured, he's our only bargaining chip! He stays here!'

'What do you say, Peter?'

'I'm with her.'

Rex sneered as if to say: you're only going along with Angel because you want to fuck her. 'Okay...'

He took out his cell phone and dialled. 'Hello... I'd like to speak to Mr Harlem... You better make him available to take my call! Look, we've got something he wants and he has something we want... I am not playing funny games! Listen! We have kidnapped one of his highly prized staff. Now do you think he will want to speak to me?'

He turned to the others. 'They've put me on hold! For several minutes he held the receiver away while a recorded voice told him that they valued his call.

Eventually there was a human voice. 'Hello? Who is this? Who?!'

Rex shrugged his shoulders and turned to his friends, 'How do you like that? I only get to talk to the monkey and not the organ grinder... Hello? Hi... Yes, I have a message for Mr Harlem, Mr C. Harlem... We've got Bryan and he's got Opus, we'd be prepared to make a swap. Bryan's pretty unwell, so... Yes, you do know who I'm talking about! You don't remember a Bryan Fahrenheit?! That's ridiculous! I didn't even tell you we had kidnapped Bryan Fahrenheit, I only said Bryan!'

Rex turned to his colleagues. 'They put the phone down on me... They denied everything... Unbelievable...'

'So what now?' said Angel,

'We take him to hospital.'

Bryan shook his head. 'Don't... don't need to go to hospital... Give me... my... pills...'

'Wait a minute, did anybody check his neck chain?' said Peter.

Angel broke open the amulet on the chain. 'It was bugged!' she said, 'That's why Chuck knew about our plan and stopped the broadcast!'

Rex put Bryan's arm over his shoulder and lifted him off the bed.

'What're you doing?' said Angel.

'He's still sick. Help me carry him out...'

FIFTY-NINE

Slap! 'Who helped you?' said a male voice.

Opus awoke to find himself completely naked apart from a blindfold tightly wrapped around his face.

In the plane, he had been hooded - his chained up body rolling left and right as he lay on the cockpit floor. Despite the stress of recent events, the whirr of the engines had lulled him to sleep.

Slap! 'Give us the names!' said a different male voice.

Was that an Afrikaner accent? wondered Opus. Possibly... Though that would give no indication of his actual location.

Sweat poured off him. It was certainly a hotter climate. He had better start screaming. Acting brave only encouraged torturers. 'Arrrrrrrrrrrrgh!!' he went.

'What're you going 'Arrrrrrrrrrrgh!!' for? I hardly touched you.' said the Afrikaner voice. 'Give us the names.'

'I want to talk to Chuck.' said Opus. If he could reason with Chuck that would be only way disaster could be averted. Get him to turn off the Message Facilitator. It was worth a try.

People aren't *that* bad. You'd be surprised what vestiges of humanity could still reside in such a person. People are never total arseholes - never total, he tried to reassure himself. Hey, Hitler and Stalin may have helped an old lady across the road once and not killed her.

'Chuck's not here. You talk to us.'

There was a click and Opus heard a crackling sound. He hoped that it wasn't what he thought it was... The soles of his feet were met with searing pain. 'AARRRRRRRGH!' It was what he thought it was: electrodes.

'Give us the names!'

'I want to see a lawyer!'

Now it was his testicles' turn. 'ARRRRRRGH!' It was naive of him to think that he would have a final confrontation face-to-face with his nemesis. Naive to think that Chuck could be bothered with the likes of him or even intrigued. He was probably thousands of miles away. Business as usual. He hadn't even caused a ripple in his life.

'What you're doing is totally illegal!' said Opus.

'Not where we are.'

'Not if you own the island.'

'Give us the names.'

More pain. 'AAAAARGH!! I take exception to this!'

'Yeah? Do you take exception to this?'

'AAAAARGH!!!!! Look, AAAAARGH!! I understand you two are obeying orders. AAAAAARGH!! I appreciate that.. Ow! The pressures' on you! AAAAAARGH!! I understand that! AAAAAARGH!! Just let me go. AAAAAARGH!! And.. AAAAAARGH!! I'll - I'll make sure the International Criminal Court go easy on you..'

'People from Head Office must have co-operated with you for you make that documentary.' said the first voice. 'Give us their names!'

'ARRRRRRGH!!!!!!!!! Let me get this right... You'll stop hurting me if I tell you who helped me?'

'Yes!!!'

'ARRRRRRGH!!!!!!!!! Okay... It was you. You were both incredibly helpful.'

Opus was socked in the jaw and he and his chair was sent flying onto the floor. Then he was kicked and kicked. Ribs were broken.

'ARRRRRRGH!!!!!!'

'The names!'

'ARRRRRRRRRRRRRRRRGH!!!!!!!!!! Okay, it wasn't you really..'

'The names!'

'ARRRRRRRRRRRRRRRRRRRGH!!!!!!!!!!! You know, you both got extremely distinctive voices.' said Opus.

'What's that supposed to mean?' said the first voice.

'Nothing. Nothing. I was thinking once this was over and done with I'll pay you a visit you sometime. Obviously I'll try not to hold a grudge against you.'

Opus was kicked and kicked and kicked. 'Shut up and tell us the names!'

'How?'

'Shut up and tell us the names!'

'A journalist keeps his sources secret...'

'Okay, if that's how're you're going to play it.' said the second voice. 'Get the pliers...'

***

Opus spat out a tooth as his hands were released. A pen was put in his right hand and it was guided to a piece of paper on a clipboard. 'Sign this.' said the first voice.

Blood dribbled out as Opus tried to talk. 'What's this about?'

'Sign it.'

'What's it say?'

'Chuck's been wanting us to clear this up for over a year. Sign it... Look, we've had a long day. You're not the only one that we've had to question, you know...'

'Can I see what it says?'

'In the form you admit to sabotaging Chuck's February concert of the previous year..'

'I don't know what you're talking about..'

'Sign it!'

'What went wrong in that concert?'

'The wrong lyrics appeared on the monitor! Sign it!'

'It's going to be a bit hard. You removed the fingernails on my left hand. I write with my left hand, you see...'

'Sign it!'

'There's no way I could have sabotaged his show..'

'Sign it! If you sign it we'll leave you alone - promise.'

Opus shrugged his blood soaked shoulders and signed the confession. He was handcuffed again. Then he heard the crackling sound again.

'Okay,' said the first voice, 'there's one more thing to clear up. We relayed your story about you disguising yourself as Gavin Priestly's lawyer and getting information through subterfuge and Head Office reckons it's a pile of crap. Tell us the real story.'

'AAAAAAAAAAAAAAAAAARRGH!!! That is the real story.'

'No it isn't.' said the first voice.

'Give us the real story!' said the second voice.

'AAAAAAAAAAAAAAAAAAARRGH!!! I've done that!'

'Give us the names - all the names!' said the first voice.

'AAAAAAAAAAAAAAAAAAAAAAARRGH!!! I've done that! AAAAAAAAAAARRGH!!! There's no more I can give!'

'You had to be helped by more people than that!'

'AAAAAAAAAAAAAARRGH!!! I wasn't!'

'We're not dumb you know!'

'AAAAAAAAAAAAAAAAAAAAAAAAAAARRGH!!!! Do you believe in reincarnation?' asked Opus.

'Give us the names!'

'Because I reckon I saw you both in previous lives by a lamppost. And you both came out of a dog's arsehole!'

Opus felt a knock on his head. It was probably a baton. 'Give us the real story!' He felt his whole body being pummelled again and again. Despite wearing a blindfold, he shut his eyes.

Through space Opus drifted in his specially converted ambulance. From planet to planet, he rescued people occasionally hearing some muffled voices in the background. The more people he collected the bigger and stronger the ambulance got...

'Tell us the story!' He put his tape in the player as he glided through the Milky Way. It was a wondrous music accompanied by a drilling sound and a buzzing sound...

'Give us the names!' The ambulance started to skid. He switched to auxiliary engines, but it was no good. The ambulance was being sucked into a black hole.

Opus fell on the floor. The floor shook.

'Fuck! Not again!' said the first voice.

'You'd think we'd get danger money for working in an earthquake zone.' said the second voice as they ran out.

'Release me!' screamed Opus. 'Release me! Release me you bastards - release me!!!'

SIXTY

Peter was impressed by the staircase. It was covered in red carpet and stretched out to infinity. Opus stood on the first step with a gigantic suitcase by his side.

'I'll carry it for you...' said Peter.

'That's most kind of you, but I'll be fine.' said Opus, 'I can manage on my own.'

'No, no, let me do it.' Peter grabbed the case, but could barely drag it off the ground. 'It's even heavier than it looks. What've you got in there - the kitchen sink?'

'Just everything that's important to me...'

Opus shook Peter's hand and patted his shoulder. 'Thanks for all your help... I enjoyed knowing you... Well... better be going...'

He effortlessly lifted up the case and went up the stairs - becoming more and more of a diminutive figure as he ascended until he disappeared from sight.

At that moment, Peter woke up and knew that he would never see Opus again.

SIXTY-ONE

Pitter-patter. Pitter-patter. Rain pelted the rickety windows of Mrs Connolly's guesthouse. In the dining room, Rex, Peter and Angel sat round the table - trying to coax their subdued appetites. Pitter-patter. Pitter-patter. All the other lodgers had finished and left half an hour ago. Pitter-patter. Pitter-patter. No conversation - only pitter-patter.

By the table opposite, Mrs Connolly collected the crockery and the debris of the previous incumbent's breakfast. She was eighty years old and had no plans to retire. Her husband had died half a lifetime ago - her son, a few years later.

Everyone she loved had died, but still she carried on - if not heroically then stoically. 'Are you finished with your breakfasts?'

'Er... yes.' said Peter.

She scooped up their plates. 'Don't know why you ordered it if you didn't wannae eat it...'

The rain intensified and noisily spattered the window. Pitter-patter. Pitter-patter. Pitter-patter... 'It's not knowing, that's the worst..' said Angel.

'It's been weeks. He must be dead by now.' said Rex.

'*Thanks*.' said Angel. She stared at the window.

They had reported Opus's disappearance to the police to no avail. They couldn't find the Message Facilitator. No doubt it had been relocated. 'When's it going to stop raining? It's always raining over here.' said Angel.

'That's not true.' said Peter, 'It was sunny two months ago.'

The newspapers weren't interested in the story. Opus lived under so many aliases it was impossible for them to prove his existence. Human rights organisations needed more evidence. Their letters to Harlem Enterprises were ignored. Setting up websites demanding the release of Opus Merriman hadn't helped either.

'Rain. Rain. Rain. Your country stinks.'

'I agree, but I think your's is worse.' said Peter.

'How can you say that? You've never been there. Every state is different - like a different country...'

When Opus's report failed to appear on the TV or on their website, they had stretched their optimism to breaking point - hoping that he would somehow manage to contact them.

'It's a shame we don't have his body,' said Rex, 'then we'd know for certain.'

'Can't even give him a proper send off.' said Peter.

Angel sprang out of her seat and ran out of the room. Rex and Peter bolted after her.

'Can't give him a proper send off?! Did you have to remind her?' snapped Rex.

'What about *you*?! It's been weeks. He's must be dead by now! Now that's sensitive!'

They followed her up to the bedroom and found her frantically emptying out Opus's backpack onto the bed.

'What're you doing?' said Rex.

'There has to be something! There has to be something!' said Angel.

Peter put his hand on her shoulder, but she ignored it and carried on rummaging through Opus's luggage.

She pulled out a comb and held it up victoriously. 'Opus's comb - it's still has some hairs of his. We'll bury the comb... and the wigs and masks. We'll bury them also.'

***

The ambulance sped down the motorway - the pitter-patter getting heavier - as if the rain had been given steroids.

Hour after hour, Angel drove - passing lay-by after lay-by and carried on driving until she stopped.

She parked by a lay-by that was identical to all the other lay-bys they had passed. 'This will be perfect... because Opus isn't really dead... He's just parking himself for a while until his next incarnation... Yeah... this is the *perfect* parking space...'

Rex glanced out of the window. 'Doesn't look that different from all the other lay-bys that we..'

Peter interrupted. 'No Angel, you're right. This is the place! The grass here is much greener than all the others we passed!'

A frown of doubt appeared on Angel's face. 'You think so? Maybe there's a lay-by out there with even greener grass... Harrow on the Hill seemed pretty green... Maybe we should..'

'No! No!' said Peter, 'This is fine!'

'Okay...' said Angel - getting out of the ambulance as the rain really got into its stride.

'For fuck's sake!' said Rex, 'I'm not going out in that! Have we got any umbrellas?'

'I can only find one.' said Peter.

'We'll have to share...'

***

'Could you lower the umbrella a bit?' said Peter, 'I'm getting drenched here! Look, let me have it back..'

'No way! You had it down so low I was getting neck ache!'

Angel had now found the perfect plot. She went down on her knees and scraped up some soil with her hands. She looked up at the others. 'Aren't you going to help?'

Rex and Peter kneeled and dug next to her.

Wigs and masks were stuck into the hole. After it was covered in soil, Angel found a stick and planted it into the grave.

The group bowed their heads and silently stood in silence as the rain pelted down. As a mark of respect, they had closed the umbrella.

When they reached the point of saturation, Rex put his hand on Angel's arm and opened the umbrella. 'We've got to go...'

'I know...'

SIXTY-TWO

In the most sparsely populated recesses of The Green Man sat a forlorn Ken. His patience had been exhausted. 'A *fine* turnout for my Birthday this turned out to be: Chris, me and a packet of crisps... Where is everyone? Have they all written me off? I've still got the spirit and passion I had when I was in my early twenties! I blame Facebook! What on earth is Chris twittering on about now?'

'Do you know who would have made a great Willy Loman in Death of a Salesman?' said Chris.

Ken shrugged.

'...James Stewart... You couldn't get anyone better because he symbolised the American dream... Don't suppose there's much we can do about that now...'

The doors banged open. Joseph barged in - catching his breath. 'I've had an email from Peter..'

'You said you'd come here on *time*.'

'I'm sorry, but anyway..'

'I said meet here at seven o'clock. What time is it? *Nine* o'clock..'

'Yeah sorry, but anyway..'

'Can't you tell the difference between seven and nine o'clock? Maybe I should draw you a diagram..'

'Oi!! I'm trying to tell you something! For once in your lives shut up and listen to me!!!!'

Ken and Chris turned to him with startled expressions. After all those years, his anger had finally burrowed out.

'Yes, it speaks! I'm not some appendage - some bozo from rent-a-crowd hired to make you look popular! I've got something to tell you!'

Ken turned to Guy. 'Do you feel like listening to Joseph? I don't feel like listening to Joseph..'

'Fucking listen to me! It's important! Peter says that tonight Harlem Enterprises is going to activate a brainwave machine that will put product placements into our dreams!'

'God, I didn't know that Peter was *that* bad.' said Ken, 'Does he claim that's why he been such a bastard?'

'He doesn't go into it. He warns us that we could wake up addicted to Harlem products.'

'Really?' said Chris, 'What does he suggest we do about it - wear saucepans on our heads?'

'It's more complex than that. We'll be fine if we go without sleeping. He says that at least knowing about it will help you fight the addiction..'

'I've never heard such rubbish in all my life.'

'I believe it.' said Joseph.

'That doesn't mean much - you believe in Father Christmas.' said Ken.

'No I don't!'

'You're so gullible. You believe anything that anyone tells you...' said Chris.

'That's not true!'

'If I told you that blindness causes masturbation you'd believe me.' said Ken.

Joseph turned away. 'It's not worth talking to you when you're like this...'

SIXTY-THREE

The shops were packed with people clamouring for Harlem clothes, Ken snorted at them. What a bunch of sheep. They had all got worse. Spending with wild abandon. Why couldn't they be more sensible with their money like him?

He felt the urge himself, but he resisted. When the urge felt unbearable, he found that a long cross-country run did the trick.

Despite the considerable sway Ken held over his friends; they all found themselves squandering their money in the same way. He pitied them for their lack of self-discipline, but tried not to make too much of an issue of their folly.

One night, Ken entered the pub to find them talking about a series of murders in the news. Apparently all the victims had been killed and mutilated in the same way - left fully clothed with the letter 'H' etched into their forehead. This was the worrying bit: all the victims happened not to be wearing any Harlem clothes.

First of all, Ken didn't believe it: a serial killer who only killed people who didn't wear Harlem clothes. It was ridiculous. But then he saw more news reports.

'Ticket inspector, Morris Blakely, was found dead outside Totteridge and Whetstone station in Barnet at 3.30 this morning. It looks likely to be the work of the 'H' killer. As with the other murders, an 'H' was etched onto his forehead. This was the third incident in this area for the past fortnight. The victim was thirty-nine years old...' said the reporter.

The reports made Ken think, but he had his principles to consider.

'Another youth has been found murdered outside the Three Johns Pub in Islington. Again he appears to be the victim of the 'H' killer... This is the fifth incident...'

'This morning, fundraiser and fitness fanatic, Terence Charles, was been found dead outside the Camden Odeon. He is believed to be the seventh victim in the area of the 'H' killer...'

The murders were occurring closer to home. It made Ken think some more. When a victim was found in Finsbury Park, Chris and Joseph insisted that he wear something with the Harlem logo on it.

The next time they all met in the pub, Chris offered him his baseball cap. 'Wear it for your protection.' Ken resisted: 'I wouldn't dream of it! I'm not prepared to acquiesce just because of a mad man!'

'It wouldn't be like that! It's not as if you paid for it!'

'Thanks for the offer, but no.'

'You don't have to wear it all the time! Just wear it when you're going out at night.'

Ken was secretly tempted, but he wouldn't capitulate. 'I refuse to wear such a garment. I haven't worn a baseball cap since I was seven.'

'For fuck's sake we're trying to save your life!' said Chris.

'Spare us the melodrama. I'm going to have an early night. See you tomorrow.'

Outside, it was dark and deserted. Ken whistled to himself.

There would have been crowds of people making their way home from the pubs, if he had waited half an hour.

He stopped whistling. He could hear someone breathing in a weird way. Loud pronounced breaths. The breathing got louder.

He started to run, but it was too late. As the blade tore at his flesh he screamed, but the pubs were too loud for anyone inside to hear him. 'I'll change my clothes tomorrow! Arrrgh! I promise! Arrrrrgh! Please! Please! Arrrrrrgh! Haven't you done enough?' cried Ken, but the fashion conscious serial killer showed no mercy.

***

Ken woke up wondering why he had never bought a Harlem baseball cap before.

***

Joseph wasn't waiting for a bus, but sat by the bus stop all the same and watched the parked car opposite on the double yellow line. With a newspaper in his hands, the driver had been sitting there for over twenty minutes. Frowning, Joseph got out his notebook and jotted something down. He walked towards the car and handed it to the driver.

'What's this?' snarled the driver.

'You know how people can give out citizen's arrests, well this is a citizen's parking ticket.'

'You strike me as the nosey type.' said the driver.

'You strike me as a person with no curiosity about the world.' said Joseph.

The driver said: 'This is what I think of your parking ticket.' and ripped the sheet of paper into two. Joseph chose not to dwell on the remark and wrote him out another one.

Two masked men carrying a sack brimming with cash ran into the car. The vehicle pulled out and zoomed off before Joseph had fully explained which council department to send the fine payment.

This was terrible, thought Joseph, parking on a double yellow line and committing a bank robbery at the same time! If only there was something he could do to bring them to justice, he thought, then it came back to him that he was in fact a superhero.

He was always forgetting this and had in fact watched several buildings burn to the ground while regretting his powerlessness to help.

To activate his special powers, he bit into a Harlem chocolate bar. Transformed, he burrowed into the pavement and pursued the robbers underground - tunnelling faster than a speeding bullet. The chocolate bar also gave him the power of omniscience so that he knew exactly where the robbers were driving.

When he had caught up with them, he tunnelled upwards and created a crater in their car. The police caught up, arrested the robbers and thanked Joseph kindly.

After that, the sky went yellow and the Sentinels came down. While a warped trombone sound penetrated the air, Twitawoo - the Supreme, the most masterful of Sentinels, descended on his floating throne and said unto Joseph: 'We have witnessed your deed... We witness *everything*... Due to a dislocation in the time-space continuum and quantum physics, if those robbers had been allowed to get away with robbing that bank, it would have meant the end of the universe. We are eternally grateful and as a reward shall grant you one wish. Anything that you so desire.'

Joseph stroked his nose and thought for a while. There were so many things he wanted. He would have liked a date with Deborah Harry when she was only fifty, but no, that wasn't his ultimate desire... He said: 'I wish for a moustache of my own.'

While the angels sung, a mirror materialized in the sky and he could see emblazoned on his upper lip; a moustache of wonderment - bushy beyond his wildest dreams.

'Remember,' said the Time Lord, 'use your moustache wisely.'

'I wonder if this is a dream?' said Joseph as he fell into a deeper sleep.

***

In the high street, Chris was on his way to the hairstylists - wondering what he was going to have done when a young bespectacled woman in a lab coat ran by - chasing a man with a crew cut and a handbag. 'Stop him!' She cried, 'He's stolen the cure for cancer!'

'Mmmm...' thought Chris, 'Maybe a crew-cut would look good on me...'

'Please!' pleaded the scientist, 'I've twisted my ankle, because I stopped wearing Harlem shoes! Please go after him!'

'I'm sorry, but I've got a hair appointment.' said Chris.

'Please! I am the famous scientist, Phyllis McCauley, and he has the cure in that handbag that he swiped from me!'

Chris looked at Phyllis. She had her hair in a bun. He certainly wasn't going to have his hair like that. He weighed up his priorities: haircut, cure for cancer.

'Please!' said Phyllis.

The pros and cons, well and truly weighed; Chris decided to pursue the thief. With his Harlem trainers, he soon caught up. 'Hand it over!'

The thief grunted something incoherently, stabbed him with a flick knife and ran off.

Groaning to himself, Chris and took some Harlem bandages and Harlem anti-septic cream from his Harlem manbag. Maybe he wouldn't have a crew cut, after-all. He took out a pair of Harlem binoculars. The thief was heading towards the tube and the hourly train was about to arrive. Chris had to put his skates on. From his Harlem manbag, he took out his Harlem roller blades and soared towards the tube barriers.

'This is your last chance!' said Chris.

What the criminal said was still unintelligible and he drew out a pistol.

Right, thought Chris, he had no alternative. He took out a vial of Hepatitis B and threw it at the thief.

The crew cut man dropped his gun. 'I... I... I don't feel well...'

'That's because you've got Hepatitis B.' said Chris, 'Harlem Enterprises have come up with a cure. Once you've served your time in prison, you have it administered to you.'

As the police and the ambulance arrived, Chris changed his mind again about what he was going to have done to his hair.

Phyllis limped over and thanked him for all he had done. He said that it was nothing and then noticed that if Phyllis loosened her hair, took off her milk bottle glasses, took off her white lab coat and the rest of her clothes that she would be naked and gorgeous. 'Your laboratory or mine?'

Phyllis unlocked the door and pulled Chris onto the table. They knocked over Bunsen burners and test tubes as their limbs joyously entwined.

Such was their ecstasy, that they ignored the sulphuric acid burns they were subjecting themselves to as they worked down the table - knocking over cures for the Common Cold and countless other ailments.

They fell to the floor - lab notes stuck to buttocks and breasts. As they rolled over Phyllis's handbag, the test tube with the cure for cancer was crushed.

'Oh well,' said Phyllis, 'I better start looking for the cure for cancer again.'

***

Chris woke up and picked up his cell phone. 'Fancy going to the shops?'

SIXTY-FOUR

Through out the night, the product placements continued - seeping in and out of people's subconscious. In. Out. In. Out. In. Out. Cars will save your life. They will prevent you from dying from using public transport. Cigarettes will save your life. Your last lit cigarette will light the bonfire, which will attract the ship that will rescue you from the desert island that you were shipwrecked on.

As the months went by a change was discernible. You realised something was up when your own flat was being broken into twice a month. You definitely knew something was up when police officers started mugging you. It turned out that not every policeman or military man wanted to wear the neck chain that supposedly immunised people from the brainwaves.

The Chief of the Metropolitan police rounded up his staff. 'I've heard substantiated stories of officers robbing banks. It has to stop. It's unprofessional.' He suddenly felt his jacket pocket. 'Wait a minute, who's stolen my wallet? No one leaves this room until my wallet is returned...'

SIXTY-FIVE

'Can't we just go to a Registry Office and get married now and forget the rest?' said Mimi - finding all the preparations and rehearsals a chore.

'Are you kidding?' said Chuck, 'It's not everyone who can get married in St Paul's Cathedral. Even if you reek of wealth, they can still turn you away. No, you have to be members of the Order of St Michael and St George, or the Order of the British Empire or holders of the Imperial Society of Knights Bachelor or their offspring. I didn't lobby for an OBE and get that FaceBook petition organised so that we can get married at some stinking registry office.'

'But this isn't fun!'

'Mimi, we can't be selfish. We can't just think of ourselves. My fans would felt let down if I didn't have a fairy tale wedding. They've got to see *someone* living the dream. It gives their lives *meaning*.'

***

Chuck stood by the mirror in the hotel suite and fastened a carnation to his lapel. This was the day. The day he thought would never come. This wasn't going to be his first marriage but this would be his last - of that he was certain. He gave his hair another comb and then had a thought.

He took out his cell phone. 'Hi... Zack... How you doing? Fine... Yeah... Just checking, you're not going to say anything at the wedding to stop the marriage - are you?'

He listened for a while. '...I know... I know... You're a happily married man and you wouldn't do anything to sabotage my wedding to have a chance to get your greasy paws on Mimi... Yeah... I thought as much... Yeah... That was exactly what I was thinking... Yeah... See you there... bye.'

...No, he didn't need to worry, thought Chuck. He only had to get through this day and then that would be it. Then he would be able to relax. His days of restlessness and searching would be over. He would have finally found his golden parking space.

SIXTY-SIX

Rex, Peter and Angel ascended the steps of St Paul's. The boys were dressed in black morning suits and top hats, Angel in an elegant white silk number. With a full two hours to go before it kicked off, they approached the guards - manning the entrance.

'Name?' said the guard holding the guest list.

Rex answered in his most refined voice: 'Smith, Smith and Smith.'

The guard went through the list. 'There ain't no Smiths invited.'

Rex acted quickly. 'I didn't say Smith, you old cloth ears! I said Smyth, Smyth, and Smyth.'

The guard went through the list. 'Oh... Right... Can I see your invitations?'

The group had decided to overcome not receiving any invites by playing the 'I'm too important to bother with the likes of you' card and walk past the guards with their noses in the air.

For a second there, they thought they had got away with it, but then they heard the guards shóut: 'Hey!!! Can I see your invites?!' They overtook and blocked any further progress.

'Why, of *course*, my good man!' said Rex and slid his hand into his tuxedo pocket. He raised an eyebrow in dismay and searched his other pockets. Then he raised his other eyebrow, slapped his own forehead and snapped his fingers in frustration. 'Oh bother! I left them all on the grand piano.' Rex turned to Angel and Peter. '*Do* forgive me!'

His friends feigned annoyance. He turned to one of the guards. 'What time do you make it? I left the gold watch on the chaiselongue. Is there enough time for me to go back and get them?'

'It's starting in two hours.'

'Oh, then it's simply *out* of the question; you'll just *have* to let us in. There is simply no way that we could return in time. We wouldn't want to be late.'

The three attempted to proceed.

'No invite, no entry.' said the guards and ungraciously escorted them out.

'Chuck will be *devastated* that we weren't able to attend.'

'Yeah, yeah..'

***

The group stood in Ludgate Hill and surveyed the situation.

'You didn't really think that was going to work?' said Angel.

'It was worth a try,' said Rex.

'Let's face it,' said Angel, 'without Opus, we're nothing...'

'Wait a minute... I think I've got it...' said Peter - pointing at a manhole. 'What about if we go down there, walk through the sewers and get into St Paul's that way?'

'Mmmm...' said Angel, 'Has anyone got any *sensible* ideas?'

'Thanks!!'

'Not yet...' said Rex, 'but I'm working on it...'

'...Well...' said Angel, 'I'd love to stay and chat, but I'm inappropriately dressed... See you around...'

'Don't go! We might..' said Peter.

'Bye...'

'But..'

'Forget it.' said Rex, 'She does what she wants to do...'

***

The commentary began even though there was nothing to say. '...We see assembled before us the great and the good... Film stars... Pop stars... And captains of industry... I think I mentioned before that this wedding recreates in many ways the wedding between Prince Charles and the late Lady Diana Spencer apart from having the Archbishop officiating since he can only marry royalty...'

'Yes,' said the other commentator, 'I think you said that before...'

***

Rex leant upon a lamppost. 'I feel so inadequate...'

Peter kicked a can. 'Bet you don't feel as inadequate as me...'

Several yards away a cab screeched and halted. A latecomer in top hat and tails (with only an hour to go) jumped out of the vehicle - tossing some money at the driver.

For some mysterious reason, Rex took it upon himself to suddenly run. And run he did - smack into the latecomer. Both fell to the ground.

'I do apologize!' said Rex as he helped him to his feet and dusted him off.

'Hmph!' said the latecomer as he didn't talk to strangers as a matter of principle and rushed to the cathedral.

'What a strange thing to do...' thought Peter. But before he could ask Rex for an explanation, Rex hailed a taxi; jumped into it and was whisked away.

Several minutes later, the latecomer returned - looking down at the pavement and the road.

The latecomer having overcome his aversion to talking to strangers turned to Peter and said: 'You haven't seen an invitation - have you?'

'No...' said Peter.

'Where's that person who was with you?'

'Don't know...'

'Why don't you know?'

'We're not that close.'

The latecomer cursed and hailed a taxi.

A few minutes later, the other taxi returned. Rex strode out - brandishing an invite.

'You can't go in on your own!' said Peter.

'There's no time to wait for anyone else to pickpocket.'

'Look, *I'll* go in. *I'll* expose Chuck.'

'No, Peter, it's okay, I'll do it.'
'No, Rex, it's okay, I'll do it.'
'No... Don't worry...'
'Why?'
'I don't think it's such a good idea. You're too emotionally affected by all you've gone through. You might not make the right decisions if you were in there alone..'
'You think I'm going to fuck up?'
'Yes.'
'Thanks a bunch! Thanks for that vote of confidence!'
'I can't lie! I don't have any confidence in you!'
'How am I ever going to have any confidence if you keep on telling me you have no confidence in me?'
'I see what you're saying but..'
'Give me this chance to win your confidence.'
'It's a bit of risk..'
'Please! I think I'm owed this opportunity at the very least..'
'Really?'
'Look, I'll buy you some hardcore porn!'
'Oooh... okay!'

Peter made his way to the entrance. Was he looking forward to disrupting Chuck's wedding. That bastard, *fucking* up his life... He didn't deserve matrimonial *bliss*. He deserved matrimonial *piss*.

And he didn't deserve to marry such a beautiful woman. He didn't even deserve to marry a human. He deserved to marry a dog.

Though not a Collie. He didn't deserve to marry a creature with such a nice glossy coat. And if he really thought about it, he didn't even deserve to marry a dog - far too *loyal* a creature for the likes of him.

What Chuck deserved was to marry a cat - a cat specially bred to be a sociopath... Though cats do have quite attractive eyes... Okay: an ugly, old, one-eyed moggie with a cataract and an abscess - that was all Chuck was fit to marry.

Fortunately, a different group of security guards was manning the entrance this time. Peter took a deep breath. 'Adams...' he said - flashing his invite and walking on.

'Hold it there.' said the guards.

Fuck! thought Peter. 'Anything wrong with the invite?'

'No, nothing's wrong with the invite. The usher there will show you to your seat...'

Peter was shown the vacant space at the very back with two thousand guests sitting in front of him. 'Here you are, Sir...'

'But no one will be able to see me back here!' said Peter, 'Would anyone like to swap seats?'

'No one is swapping seats, Sir.' said the Usher, 'Please sit down. Filming has commenced...'

***

Mimi and her recently 'un-estranged' biological father disembarked from the glass coach. Like Diana at her wedding, Mimi wore a puffball meringue wedding dress.

It could be said that St Paul's had been reincarnated five times. Each time it had been destroyed by ill fortune, it had been rebuilt.

The current incarnation had survived the Second World War and with it's recent restoration appeared formidable - a resilient building. Mimi on the other hand, seemed a far more fragile construction as she made that long walk down the aisle - shuffling awkwardly - unsteady on her feet.

Chuck waited by the altar nervously with his Best Man, Zack Contemporary and turned to Mimi.

'Dearly beloved,' began the Dean, 'we are gathered together here in the sight of God, and in the face of this congregation...'

***

And on the ceremony continued: '...If anyone knows any reason or impediment why this couple should not be legally wed, let them speak now or forever hold their peace...'

Chuck gazed at his friends. This was it...

***

At that precise moment, Peter (having eluded security) puffed as he stepped into the Whispering Gallery situated above the altar.

He had managed to run up the 259 steps during the ceremony and was just in time. This place was famous for it's strange acoustics. No one would be able to ignore what he had to say.

That would prove to Jez and Angel that he could think on his feet - that he had *good* ideas and that he wasn't going to fuck up. That would make them shut up and perhaps compliment him once in a while...

Inevitably, he found a guard waiting in the gallery. He had one split second to think of something to say before he was going to be chased away. Was he going to mention the Facilitator or all his other industrial atrocities? There was so much to say and so little time...

***

Just as the Dean was about to continue, a loud but ghostly, disembodied voice said: 'THEY CAN'T GET MARRIED BECAUSE CHUCK HARLEM'S A CUNT!!!'

The congregation gasped.

'Did someone just call me a cunt?' screamed Chuck. 'Who said that? He turned to the Dean. 'Was it you?'

'For Heaven's sake! Would I use such language?'

'Sorry..'

'It came from above - the Whispering Gallery. It has very strange acoustics.'

'You can say that again..'

'I'm sure security will deal with this presently. Anyway I won't take such statements seriously. It was obviously a prank, so let's proceed shall we?'

'Aaah... good...' said Chuck.

Chuck couldn't believe it... The voices had stopped and he had reached home base. The thirty-second broadcasting delay would have bleeped the obscenities. Now he could get on with the rest of the ceremony and not worry any more...

He turned to Mimi and found that she was crying. 'Baby! What's wrong?'

'I... I can't do it!' she slurred.

There were murmurs in the assembled crowds.

'Course you can, honey! We'll talk afterwards... Let's carry on...'

'Do you Charles Harlem take this woman to be your wedded Wife, to live together after God's ordinance in the holy estate of Matrimony? Will you love her, comfort her, honour and keep her in sickness and in health; and, forsaking all others, keep only unto her, so long as you both shall live?'

'I do.' said Chuck.

'Do you Mimi Johnson take this man to be your wedded Husband, to live together after God's ordinance in the holy estate of Matrimony?'

The tears continued. Unbecomingly, her nose began to run and go an unflattering shade of red.

'...Will you obey him, and serve him, love, honour and keep him in sickness and in health; and, forsaking all others, keep only unto him, so long as you both shall live?'

She turned to Chuck. 'I don't love you anymore!'

The congregation gasped.

'Course she does! She's crazy about me! Isn't that right; honey?'

'I'm, I'm (choke) ashamed of you!'

'Please answer the question' said the Dean, 'and do wipe your nose...'

Chuck turned to him. 'She's nervous, let's carry on...'

'But she hasn't said 'I do'.' said the Dean.

'Let me remind you that a pretty hefty percentage of the broadcasting revenue is going to your church. The wedding continues.'

'...Er... This is most irregular... Look, would you like to meet in sacristy (the vestment room) to reflect upon your vows?'

'Does it look like I want to meet in sacristy to reflect upon my vows?' said Chuck. 'What's wrong with you? Why don't you want us to get married?'

Mimi stumbled and Chuck caught her. 'Mimi! You're drunk!'

'Get your hands off me!'

'Please say those words!' begged Chuck.

'No! I know too much about you!'

'Mimi, I love you'

'It's no good!'

'Mr Harlem, I do insist we abort the ceremony.' said the Dean, 'Nothing can be gained from..'

'You stay out of it!' snapped Chuck.

'Fine...' said the Dean. 'I shall leave you to your own devices...'

The guests murmured in dismay as he made his exit.

'I can't love someone like you.' said Mimi.

'Mimi, *please*...'

'Haven't been in love with you for weeks. I've been acting all that time and people say I'm a bad actress.'

'I don't believe you!'

'You offered me a film part, and I accepted... Can't keep the performance up any longer - not after what I found out..'

'Baby, what're you talking about?'

'I looked at those websites. I know how you make your money.'

'Come on! You can't believe what they say about me! It's not true!'

'Don't lie, I checked. I looked at your company's records.'

'Look, Mimi..'

'I could stomach you having all those trade union leaders assassinated - they're Commies so they had it coming to them... I could stomach you having all those political prisoners in dictatorships around the world forced to make your stuff for nothing - they're criminals, so what do they expect. I could stomach you causing wars so that you can sell your military equipment and take their oil - it's good for the economy, but I couldn't stomach all the *other* stuff..'

'You don't know what you're saying..'

'I know what I'm saying... You don't have to patronise me just 'cause I'm forty years younger than you..'

'Please! This is being broadcast live!'

'...Now putting product placements into people's dreams - that - that really sucks! Can't you leave their dreams *alone*? I don't want anyone fucking with my mind!'

Chuck went on his knees and held her hands. 'I can still make you happy...'

'I thought you were the one!' said Mimi, 'Thought you were the one for me! Thought you were the one after all those sons of bitches, after all those scumbags. All those bastards who *used* me..'

'Mimi, *please*!'

'...Why do you care? I'm as dispensable as everyone else. Plenty of girls will do what you get me to do - for the right price...'

Chuck grabbed the ring from his Best Man and forced it onto Mimi's finger.

'Ow!' yelled Mimi.

'Now listen! You will marry me! No one refuses Chuck Harlem! No one disobeys me!'

'Let go! I'll call the police!'

'They ain't going to touch me! *I'm* Chuck Harlem! You're not leaving here until you marry me!'

'Yes I am!'

'If you don't marry me you'll never work again! Do you hear me? I'll have you blacklisted! From everything! You hear me? Your life will be worth nothing! You won't even be able to work as a hooker! Do you understand who you're fucking with? Without me your life won't be worth living!'

Mimi smiled bitterly. 'You're soooo clever. Looks like you've thought of everything. But guess what? I thought of something too.'

She pulled out a revolver from her bridal dress, poked it in her mouth and pulled the trigger.

'No!' Chuck cried, but it was too late. The bullet and the blood spewed out of the back of her skull.

The guests screamed in terror and scrambled out of the cathedral.

Chuck grabbed his dead fiancee and gently rocked her in his arms. Sobbing, he looked upwards towards the Heavens.

She was indispensable. Of all the billions of people in the world, all the hundreds of thousands of people who worked for him in those sweatshops and all those thousands that he had met; she was indispensable. Everyone else meant nothing. She was indispensable. And now she was dead.

She was the sort of girl he would have liked to take to the high school prom. At high school, he had *no one* to take to the prom.

She was the type of girl he would have liked to take to a drive-in. He could imagine his arm over her shoulder in the red warm darkness of the late summer night - comforting her as they watched a teenaged werewolf slay another victim.

She was the type of girl he would have liked to take to a ten-pin bowling alley, the sort of girl he would have liked to share a soda with - two straws in the same soda glass.

She wasn't there when he was young - really young. She wasn't even born. And now she wasn't there again. As he held her in that increasing pool of blood, he loved her even more than he ever had. As the pool grew larger, he loved her even more. As her temperature decreased, he loved her even more. As her complexion grew paler, he adored her even more intensively.

Couldn't she appreciate that everything he did was for her? And before, when she wasn't on the scene, he was doing it for the concept of her - the hypothetical version of her - the woman that he would meet one day... The world is a wicked place. He was going to protect her. Now she was dead. Her eyelids were still open. The world is cruel. She was indispensable and now she was dead. The sweetest thing in his life: gone forever.

What was left? Only fragments. They couldn't provide the foundations for any kind of life. Friends... he had plenty of friends, but they meant fuck all. It was her voice that he listened to - her face he watched. She was the only one who existed in his world. What a world... Chuck picked up the revolver and held it to his forehead.

Peter sprinted towards Chuck and grabbed the gun. 'Don't do it!'

'Go to hell!' said Chuck - tugging the gun back.

'I know you can't stand yourself! But this isn't the answer!'

'Let go!'

'Just stop being such a cunt! Do something good! Do something good to make up for it all! Turn off the brainwave machine!'

'Get off me!'

In the struggle, the gun went off.

Peter held his chest and fell to the floor. It seemed to him that he had fallen from a long distance. And on that long journey to the floor, the blood gushed out of him - copiously.

As Peter lay bleeding, Chuck crawled on his knees to him; grabbed his collar and said: 'Why me?! That's what I'd like to know - why *me*?!'

'Arrrgh...' groaned Peter.

'...Why does this have to happen to *me* all the time?' said Chuck, 'I'd like someone to tell me! Is it some kind of curse? Why? Why?'

Peter wished he could answer his question, but he had other pressing concerns. His head flopped as he floated on a shallow pool of blood.

SIXTY-SEVEN

Too depressing. The atmosphere in the hospital ward was too depressing thought Angel and Rex - too depressing to even make you feel gleeful that you were at least less sick than the person you were visiting. Row upon row of people in different states of disrepair: bandaged up, plastered, and hooked up to drips and machines - each trying to vie for the nurse's attention. 'Nurse... Nurse!! NURSE!!!!'

Bedpans were duly administered - sometimes in time - sometimes not quite so much in time. 'NURSE!!!!!!!!!!!' When Angel and Rex had arrived, they instantly wanted to leave.

They traipsed and sweated through the excessively heated ward and found Peter lying in bed - without the usual exuberance common in people with near death experiences. One reason for Peter's despondent mood was that he felt like shit; another was that Angel and Rex were holding hands. He asked the nurse for another painkiller. 'Nurse!!'

Of all the mysteries in the world: the Yeti; the Bermuda Triangle and the assassination of JFK, the most mysterious of them all to Peter had got to be what Angel saw in Rex. Okay, Peter may have blotted his copybook by vomiting on her face, but why did it have to be Rex? Angel placed a bunch of flowers on his bedside table and sat down next to her new partner.

It was also too boring in the hospital. One could never think of anything to say in these places and neither could Rex and Angel. For want of something to do, Rex studied the chart on the front of Peter's bed and pretended to understand what it said. 'Mmmmm... Yes... Mmmmmmm...'

Peter thought he would break the ice, so he said: 'So... how are *you*?'

'Did you have to save his life?' snapped Angel.

'I - I felt sorry for him.' said Peter.

'You felt *sorry* for *him*?! The guy who fucked up your life - you felt sorry for Chuck Harlem?!'

'His fiancee had just blown her brains out. He was upset.' Surely after losing a loved one, Chuck would have an altered perspective on life, thought Peter. Surely he would value life more and change his ways.

'If you thought that after losing a loved one, Chuck would have an altered perspective on life and would value life more and change his ways, then you thought wrong. He's got worse and he's kept the machine on.' said Angel.

'Oh.' said Peter.

'Peter, promise me this: if you ever see Chuck trying to kill himself again you won't try to save his life.'

'Oh go on, let me do it one more time?!'

'No, we're *serious*.' said Rex, 'Don't save his life. Okay? Do *not* save his life!'

***

'How dare you ask me such a question!' said Chuck to the interviewer. 'How dare you ask me if I use a brainwave machine!'

'There've been numerous accusations. I have to ask..'

'Do you know who I am? Do you? You have the audacity to ask *me* that question when my fiancee is barely cold - when she hasn't even been buried yet? How insensitive is that?!'

'I did express my condolences earlier in the interview..'

'What sort of a guy do you think I am? Huh? What sort? What sort of guy do you think I am to do such a mad and crazy thing! Your question stinks!'

'Your fiancee claimed that you did at the wedding cere..'

'Mimi was obviously out of her mind when she said that! She did kill herself if you hadn't noticed!'

'Then what about the AI report concerning the poor safety standards in your factories around the world?'

'I haven't read the report, so I couldn't possibly comment.'

'I've got the report here, would you like to read it?'

'Naah, haven't got my reading glasses with me...'

***

'...But there must be a lot of protests about Chuck now!' said Peter.

'There are but there were loads of protests around the world anyway before this,' said Rex, 'only thing was they weren't getting reported. All that's happened is that even more people are getting arrested and beaten without media coverage. As well as that, half the world still loves Chuck. Even if he blow torched an elderly married couple to death as they celebrated their Golden Wedding Anniversary live on TV, they would still think the couple had it coming to them! Now if Chuck was dead you wouldn't have all this bullshit!'

'Oh, I thought you'd console me...' said Peter - remembering the puke night.

'Console you?! Why, I want to throttle you!'

There was an uncomfortable silence. The silence was more uncomfortable for Peter since he was still recovering from his operation. There were stitches on his chest but also lower down. 'Why've I got these stitches down here? I was shot in the chest.'

'Oh that's because you've had your kidney removed.' said Rex.

'What?! But there's nothing wrong with my kidney!'

'I know; that's how I was able to sell it.'

'You sold my kidney?'

'Er... traded it to be precise. They were keeping you waiting for so long in the corridor, I had to bribe them with something to see you sooner.'

Peter gazed at his torso. 'I've only got one kidney now?'

'They wanted two, but I haggled.'

'I thought Chuck's people put me here.'

'Naaa, they left you bleeding on the floor. Me and Angel got you here.'

'Oh... thanks.'

'Anyway, we better make tracks, got a movie to catch.'

'Right... Seeing anything good?'

Rex looked at Angel and winked. 'I don't think we're going to be giving the film that much attention.' He graciously patted Peter's shoulder.

'Anyway, we'll collect you when you're discharged tomorrow.'

'I'm in no condition to be discharged tomorrow!'

'How far do you think a kidney goes?'

SIXTY-EIGHT

The leaves had fallen by Manor House station, but hadn't rotted yet. Peter carried on lugging his suitcase. He had decided to stay on the pavement and not walk in the park. It would be a quicker journey.

A minute later, he put down his luggage, and gave his hands a rest. He had walked from Finsbury Park station since there still weren't any barriers. Travelling with a travel card for only one stop was becoming a harder feat to accomplish these days.

He put out his sixteenth last ever cigarette and searched his pockets. A half pack of Bensons. He threw them in the bin and continued - gazing over the park fence.

So far what a failure, he thought. Still single, still undiscovered and still bald. And the Message Facilitator was still on. Guess he would have to fight it with his mind. All those urges - all those desires. Everyone else had to. He wasn't special. No one was.

His hands felt sore again, so he put the suitcase down and swapped hands.

He wondered how his mates were going to be tonight. It had been over a year. They weren't going to be 'funny' with him - were they? Joseph sounded enthusiastic about meeting over the phone. Even said he could kip on his sofa.

Shit, he still owed them money. He returned to the bin and retrieved his pack of cigarettes. He lit up and took a deep drag. They could compare notes.

Did they become as big a bastard as him after those brainwaves? He tried not to think about all the people who had suffered because of him. If only he had been caught the first time he tried to mug somebody. So unlucky...

He took another drag of his cigarette. Why did he think he would end up with Angel? Why had he been so optimistic? Why did he think that something good would come out of something bad? Why did he think he was going to snatch happiness out of the jaws of misery? It wasn't like he was some supernatural, time-travelling dentist. *Why*? Maybe it was the Greek blood in him.

He didn't even think the experience had made him a better person. He was nicer before. It was just a bad experience and he went through it. He had gained nothing from the past two years and that was that. Misery begot misery and nothing else. No consolation. No silver linings..

Squelch! He looked down. He had stepped on a freshly made dog turd. The culprit scampered across the road and had another crap by the traffic lights.

Great!! Great!!! That was just what he needed! Single, bald, undiscovered and now with added shit! His friends were really going to welcome him with open arms! Yes! Come in! Leave a trail of dog poo on the carpet!

It would have to happen when he had sold all his other shoes. He would never be able to get rid of the stench. Dog shit smell clung on - no matter how much you scrubbed - clung on like debt. He might as well throw the shoes away and meet his friends bare-footed. Though then again they might think he had gone religious and shut the door on him.

Someone called out: 'Jasper! Jasper!! Jasper!!!' Peter watched an old lady with milk bottle thick glasses squeeze through the gap in the fencing and catch up with her dog and put his lead back on. 'Naughty dog! You've made me really angry this time! Don't look at me like that! You won't get by me that way!'

Peter grinned to himself. How many years did she have left to not know the time and let her dog crap all over Haringey? He didn't have to worry about his mates. They probably had bad consciences too.

Everybody had shit on their shoes to a certain extent. God bless that old lady he thought, God bless everyone.

SIXTY-NINE

'Not bad,' thought Joseph, 'War and Peace' only 50p...' Having completed his Dalston charity shop run, he paused by a closed down video hire shop to recuperate.

A poster had remained on the window for an action movie nobody watched anymore. Even the Nintendo game version wasn't being played.

Bleached by the sun, only the blue and black colours of the poster had remained - the yellow and the red having faded long ago.

Joseph thought to himself: 'If they ever make a film about my life, I hope they get their facts straight...'

SEVENTY

It was too quiet. Without Mimi's laughter and her delightfully inane chitter chatter, it was too quiet in Chuck's bedroom.

Propped up in bed, Chuck increased the volume of the TV with the remote control. But it did not help. He hurled the remote across the room. His eyes - bloodshot and dry - had not seen sleep or dreams for weeks.

The smell was bad - the smell of the pyjamas he inhabited. Stank far worse than you would expect from garments worn non-stop for three weeks, two days, fourteen hours and sixteen minutes. Scientifically, it was hard to explain, but something happens to people who experience traumatic events. For months afterwards, their armpits emit an odour far worse than usual - a stench that perfume cannot disguise.

The TV was the only light in his life. In all that time the curtains had remained shut. When the images on the screen turned into hazy black and white hail, he switched to another channel.

A mountain of empty whisky bottles and empty beer cans covered the floor. From the peak, some of the bottles weren't completely empty and dripped onto the crushed cans below.

That's all that remains of my life now, thought Chuck, the dregs - the foul tasting, saliva-diluted dregs.

A beard was growing on his face - a white beard. If he let it grow a few more weeks, he could pass for Father Christmas. The last day he had shaved was on the day of the funeral. That day was also the last he had looked into a mirror and got dressed.

It was the anger that had kept him going until then. It was their fault she was dead! *Their* fault! If they hadn't put up those websites, she'd still be alive. If she hadn't found out about him, everything would have been all right! How would she have found out if those websites hadn't existed? *He* wasn't going to tell her!

Initially, he told his minions that it was 'Business as usual...' Sales were up. Protests were up also, but that did not concern him greatly especially since most of the protestors were wearing Harlem gear. His New Year's Day concert was still going to happen - the only thing was he wasn't planning on being there.

When he had returned from the funeral, the effects of the anger had worn off. Totally drained and exhausted, he went to bed and had been there ever since.

Hours were spent re-thinking the moment. The moment Mimi pulled out that revolver and blew her brains out. He tried positive visualization. He tried to imagine Mimi not killing herself and shooting his Best Man instead. He somehow thought he could rectify the moment if he visualized strong enough. But try as he might; as he played and rewound he kept on seeing the same thing: Mimi dying.

The phone rang, but he didn't pick up the receiver. He had ignored its ringing for weeks. The Butler entered, collected the untouched plate that was lunch and approached the door. He stopped. 'I may be speaking out of turn, Sir, but you really should eat something.'

'You *are* speaking out of turn.'

'Forgive me Sir, but you haven't eaten anything at all this week..'

'Does it look like I want to discuss it with you?'

'Be that as it may Sir, I think it is wise to tell you that not eating can only make you feel worse..'

Chuck stared at 'Jackson'. He was tall and thin - in his early fifties. He stood perfectly straight and held his head up high. No trace of fear visible - dignified and calm. Being examined or scrutinized didn't bother him.

His face was long and had obviously suffered acne in the past. His hair was strawberry blond, receding, thinning and going a little white. He kept it short and had it neatly combed back. His forehead was large and had the stern wrinkles of a practical man. His eyes looked like they had seen everything and that the last time he had seen anything that surprised him was when he was eight. Something about those eyes told you he knew poverty - in fact that he had intimate experience of it.

'...Where're you from?' said Chuck.

'Glasgow, Sir.'

'Scotland - isn't it? Thought you spoke weird... How long you've been working here, Jackson?'

'I've had the pleasure of serving you for the past two months, Sir.'

'Well, if you want that pleasure to continue I'd shut up if I was you.'

'Be that as it may, I would rather risk losing my job than let you make yourself worse.'

'Is that a fact?'

'Poor nutrition exacerbates bereavement..'

'What - what do you know about it - dude?'

Jackson looked down towards the floor. 'I had a wife once... A bonnier lass you couldn't find... She was... *murdered* fifteen years ago.'

'Oh... sorry..'

'I neglected myself... It was more than the grieving process I was going through... I was destroying myself... Eventually, after a few drunken escapades that went wrong I was diagnosed with... clinical depression... Good food and exercise helped me considerably. There're a few recipes I know that could... *help* you... make your brain as healthy as circumstance *allows*.'

'Yeah, well, er, maybe, maybe I'll try them out some time.'

'Very good...' Jackson raised his eyes. 'Now if you'd get up I could get the maid to change the sheets...'

Chuck shook his head. 'She can do it some other time.'

'I'm afraid not, Sir. We need you out of the room so we can clear up properly..'

'Some other time, dude!'

Jackson drew the curtains and opened the windows - flooding the room with light and fresh air.

'Did I tell you to do that?' said Chuck.

'Not in so many words, Sir, but I believed you wanted me to in your heart of hearts...'

'That's where you're wrong! Draw them back!'

Jackson didn't draw them back, walked to the bed and pulled the duvet off.

'What's the meaning of this?'

'Enough is enough Sir. You're getting out of bed.' He grabbed hold of Chuck and dragged him out.

'How dare you!'

'Grief is no reason to live like a pig, Sir...'

'That's it! You're history! And if you don't watch out you'll become archaeology!'

'I don't care. You're getting out of bed.'

'Do you know who I am?'

'I am well aware of your identity Sir and may I say: a great admirer of your work...'

'Get off me! I need to sleep! I haven't slept in days!'

'Of course you haven't slept Sir. You've been stuck in bed all that time. You need a good long walk.'

'No! I need to sleep!'

Chuck was pulled to his feet. 'If you'd be so kind to put your arms up, Sir...'

Too tired to resist any longer, Chuck complied.

Jackson took his pyjamas off, dragged him into a shower, shaved him, put freshly laundered clothes on him and put on a freshly polished pair of walking shoes. Then he grabbed Chuck's hand and walked him down the stairs, through the front door and around the grounds of the estate.

***

For five hours they walked. It was a vast area to explore. 'Man, I'm beat, let's go back..'

Jackson solemnly shook his head. 'No Sir, I think it would be advantageous if we did the circuit again.'

'Again?! That'll be another five hours.'

'Precisely Sir. Ten hours of walking should guarantee a healthy appetite and a good night's sleep.'

'Tomorrow, you're sacked - you're through - you hear me? You're... You're...'

'Breathe that air, Sir. Get it into your lungs...'

***

After a long sleep, Chuck woke up the next day and felt slightly better. 'What do you know?' he thought. Maybe he wasn't going to sack his butler after all. If he thought about it, it was refreshing to encounter a member of staff who wasn't timid.

This guy knew his stuff. This guy may well get him through it. May well help him break through the despair barrier. He may well sack Jackson tomorrow, but he wasn't going to sack him today.

There was a knock at the door. 'Come in.'

Jackson entered. 'I trust Sir had a good night's sleep.'

'Yeah...'

'Some friends have called. Do you want to see them?'

'Naaa, can't be fucked. Send them away.'

'Very good, Sir... Er... have you got anything planned for today?'

'Nothing. Don't want to see anyone...'

Jackson gave a polite little cough. 'If I may be so bold to make a suggestion...'

SEVENTY-ONE

Jackson and Chuck approached the riverbank. The bodyguards, at the express orders of their employer kept their distance.

'Doesn't the air smell fine here, Sir?'

Chuck took a drag from the atmosphere... 'Hey... You're right...'

No one could disagree. It smelt good in Llyn Gweryd. More than good. It smelt healthy. It smelt alive. And the more this air was inhaled the more alive people felt.

'Used to come here on my holidays, Sir... Couldn't afford to go to Brazil but I could afford North Wales...'

After unfolding their stools, Jackson and Chuck sat down. They cast their fishing lines into the water - causing brief ripples into the perfect calmness of the river and waited.

As the hours strolled by, the pair watched the clouds circulate. All at the same speed, all in the same direction, the clouds drifted - none of them competing and speeding off and overtaking the others. There were no Sebastian Coes in the cloud world - at least not that day. As the sun sank and reddened, the sky glowed and grew tinged with green.

As pleasant as this was, Chuck was dissatisfied. 'Damn, we haven't caught anything.'

'But we experienced this wonderful sunset!'

'I promised myself I'd catch at least one fish.'

'We don't always need to keep to our targets, Sir.'

'Yeah, but I don't want to go away empty handed.'

The moon was becoming visible. 'Shall we stay longer, Sir?' said Jackson.

'Yeah, pass the flask...'

***

'Shouldn't we be going now?' said Jackson, 'I think the bodyguards are getting tired.'

'Not until I've caught something.. Wait a minute..' Chuck reeled something in. He shone his torch on it. 'Damn, a shoe.'

'Let's go, Sir.'

'Not until I've got something to show for the day.'

Jackson took the hook off the boot and held it in the moonlight. 'Why don't we take the shoe, Sir?'

'The shoe? Why should we take the shoe?'

'It might have belonged to Elvis, Sir!'

'Did Elvis ever go to Wales? I think he might have gone to Scotland..'

'He may well have lost it in Hawaii. The shoe may have drifted through the seven seas to get here. It's amazing how far a shoe can travel without a foot in it.'

'Okay, let's pack up.' Chuck took the shoe. It was a size four. 'Let's keep it...'

SEVENTY-TWO

A thin layer of soil was scraped away with a trowel.

'What's this?' said Chuck.

Jackson put on his reading glasses and scrutinised the discovered remains. So far, the pair had found little at the Peruvian excavation site. 'If I'm right,' said Jackson, 'We've found part of an ancient ceramic..'

'Oh... a pot.' Chuck got up to go to find another area to excavate.

'No this is important Sir, we're talking about a work of art - an idol - something made to be worshipped from far back..'

'People worshipped *this*?'

'Yes... You'd be surprised at what people worship. I suppose people will always need something - something to channel their hopes through...'

SEVENTY-THREE

Space... Some would say that it's a place to look at to make you philosophical... Dark and eternal... Its infinity impossible to fully comprehend... A humbling experience indeed... Would you have it any other way?

On the top of the hill in Easter Island, at half past midnight, Jackson and Chuck sat in deck chairs - examining the fore-mentioned through an electron telescope.

Jackson adjusted the lens. 'Take a look.'

'Wow...'

It was something to behold: galaxies awash with stars - many long extinguished - just the light of something that used to be alive. Though the point of advertising a dead star proved to be elusive. And if you thought about it, light at the speed of light really wasn't fast enough. Though it could be worse, you could have had light at the speed of sound or the speed of the Northern Line.

Jackson turned to Chuck. 'Did you know Sir, that broadcast waves never disappear?'

'Is that a fact?'

'It is, Sir.'

To say that it was a fact actually was enough for Chuck, but Jackson carried on: 'After appearing on the television screen they go on in space never finding an end destination... Theoretically speaking, if you went in a rocket, you could possibly catch an old episode of 'Doctor Who' that the BBC wiped from their tapes..'

'What about phone calls?'

'I'm sorry Sir?'

'Could you get back phone calls that you never recorded? Phone calls from someone you.. Er... phone calls that you could talk to?'

'Of that I'm not sure..'

'If it looked like a feasible project I'd put a billion bucks into time travel research. I'd pay to have a time machine made..'

'Don't you think Sir, you've interfered with the laws of nature quite enough?'

'What d'ya mean by that?'

'The Message Facilitator, Sir, don't you think it's time you turned it off?'

'I don't know what you're talkin' about.'

Jackson looked at Chuck straight in the eye. 'I believe you do, Sir.'

Chuck shook his head. 'To turn it off would be like admitting I'd turned it on..'

'But you know this can't go on, Sir..'

'Dude, change the subject.'

Jackson ushered Chuck back to the lens. 'Look Sir, a meteorite shower!'

SEVENTY-FOUR

The digital film cameras were set on stand-by. From behind the bushes in the Congo Basin, Chuck and Jackson waited for the mountain gorillas to get into view.

'There he is...' said Jackson. The 'silverback' led his group into the clearing. They approached a large leaved plant; tore off the leaves and put them in their mouths.

'Man, this is better than 'Planet of the Apes'!' said Chuck.

Jackson whispered: 'If we keep really quiet they might get nearer to us..'

Another group of gorillas approached the clearing. Its leader expressed dissatisfaction with the presence of the other group on their territory.

The 'silverback' faced the leader of the other group. He beat his chest. The other beat his chest. Then the first silverback bashed some nearby bushes. Surprisingly, that was enough to deter the other leader and he retreated with his followers.

'Shit, the little one reminds me of a girl I used to go with.'

'Think I dated her as well, Sir.'

Chuck laughed and then looked at Jackson. 'You know for the past few months I've managed to go for hours without thinking about Mimi. It's all thanks to you.'

Chuck put his arms around the butler and hugged him. Awkwardly, Jackson reciprocated. 'I've been that close to ending it all - loads of times. But no, I know it's worth carrying on - worth carrying on with the fight - because of you.'

'It's nothing, Sir.'

'Don't be so modest.'

***

The bodyguards ushered the pair into the SUV. Jackson turned to Chuck. 'Sir, I think it's only fair for me to point out that the gorillas here are about to lose their habitat.'

'Why?'

'A subsidiary of yours is planning to use the land for logging.'

Chuck stared at his reflection in the car mirror. '...That can be sorted out.'

'Thank you, Sir... I was wondering while you were about it whether you gave any further thought to my suggestion that you switch off the Message Facilitator..'

'Man, d'ya want to ruin my day? I'm going to rescue the gorillas - okay?'

SEVENTY-FIVE

Chuck put the phone down and sat by the bed half dressed. A knock at the door. 'Come in.'

Jackson entered carrying two suitcases. 'Are we ready Sir? The plane leaves at three..'

Chuck avoided Jackson's eyes. 'There's been a change in plans, dude.'

'Yes Sir?'

'Some buddies called... They're going to Vegas.'

'Are they, Sir?'

'They've... persuaded me to come with them.'

'I suppose I better unpack our snorkelling gear then. What should we take with us?'

'I'll need my purple and my white suit... You - you won't need to pack anything for yourself... You'll be staying here.'

'Oh... Are you sure you won't be needing me, Sir?'

'Yeah, yeah, I'll be fine... I've been thinking... Maybe - maybe we shouldn't see so much of each other...'

Jackson took off his glasses. 'Really, Sir?'

Chuck looked down. 'Yeah... Don't get me wrong. It's been good - you know - what we've been doing together and... and... I'm sure we'll still do stuff, but er... only... not so often.'

'Very good, Sir.' said the butler and emptied out the suitcase.

SEVENTY-SIX

Jackson entered Chuck's bedroom without the customary knock.

Las Vegas was six months ago. No more hugs had been exchanged.

'What're you doing here?' said Chuck - lying on his bed with a book in his hands.

'Checking if you are all right, Sir... You've been up here for some time. Your guests have been waiting in the dining room for over an hour.'

'Send them home. I don't feel like seeing them.'

'I quite understand... Are you... are you *all right*?'

'No, I'm fine, fine. Don't worry about me. You've really helped me come through. I'll never forget that... No... I've reached an interesting bit in my book... Tell them to leave...'

'Shall I send dinner up?'

'Later... Later... I'll eat it cold.'

'I'll have it warmed up.'

'No, no, sometimes it tastes better cold.'

'Very good Sir.' The butler approached the door and then paused and gave Chuck a meaningful look.

'Anything else?' asked Chuck.

'I was wondering whether you'd prefer to have the Message Facilitator switched off.'

'What sort of question is that to ask me? You're the best butler I've ever had apart from this asking me about switching the machine off stuff all the time!'

'So you're quite sure you don't want the machine switched off?'

'Dude, the machine stays on! What's wrong with you?'

'So you wouldn't rather have it switched off.'

'That's right! How many times!'

'And that's your final decision?'

'Yes!'

'Very good, Sir.' said Jackson - grabbing an Oscar trophy on the shelf and striking Chuck's head with it.

Dazed, Chuck fell back onto the bed. He could barely respond as Jackson sat on him and held a pillow over his face. His pleas were smothered and so were his screams. He tried to resist, but got weaker and weaker... There was darkness and then even less...

Jackson sat on the bed, took out a handkerchief and mopped his forehead. He wiped what appeared to be a tear from his eye and blew his nose. After taking a deep breath, he picked up Chuck's cell phone and dialled.

When he spoke, he produced a perfect emulation of Chuck's voice. 'Hi dude, it's yours truly... Switch off the machine... Yeah... You heard me... I know what I said before... I've been having a rethink about how we should run this outfit... Switch it off... *Pull* the plug... Right... Yeah... That's fine... Got to shoot... Bye.'

He got up and sat by the dressing table mirror. It was worth another try. From his inner pocket, he took out a mask, a wig and sunglasses. He put them on and studied his reflection.

No, it wasn't good enough. He couldn't pass for Chuck. He couldn't fool anyone that he met in person. Perhaps if he dimmed the lights and held his head at a certain angle, he might getaway with a few short web conferences...

The phone rang. 'Hello? Yeah, I'm serious... Larry was speaking the truth. It's not someone impersonating me telling you this - it's *me*... Yeah... I want the machine off... I don't want to discuss it with you... Just do what I say... Good... Another thing, could you send the machine and the transmitter to my place with all the discs and laboratory notes? Good... Yeah, my place in Virginia... Yeah... Okay... I'll let you know about that by Monday... Yeah... Bye.'

Before he had a chance to put the phone in his pocket, it rang again. 'Hi... Yeah, sorry I didn't get back to you. Been busy. How're you doing? That's great... Look... Could I call you tomorrow? I know... I know... The project sounds interesting... The thing is; I'm not sure of my availability... Yeah... I'll call you tomorrow... Midday... I'm not shitting you... I will call, I swear... Okay, take it easy, dude... Bye.'

Jackson turned off the cell phone. For how long, he thought, for how long could he keep it up? In time to receive the machine and destroy it? In time to get the company to change its ways? For how long could his authority as Head Butler hold back the suspicions of the maids and servants? For how long would they believe that Chuck doesn't want to see anyone apart from his Head Butler? Shouldn't he make a run for it? Wasn't he mad to stay? No... he had to see it through and do his best - otherwise what had happened a moment ago would have been completely pointless.

He turned and gazed at the body. One thing was for certain: he couldn't be a journalist after this. Not after what he had done. He had completely lost his objectivity.

ABOUT THE AUTHOR

All you need to know about me is that I'm a human being with human needs. I thirst, I hunger and I sleep.

www.ingramcontent.com/pod-product-compliance
Ingram Content Group UK Ltd.
Pitfield, Milton Keynes, MK11 3LW, UK
UKHW041257180426
11947UKWH00008B/526